EMPIRE

EMPIRE

The Richmond Saga
1066 A.D.

Tim Richmond

iUniverse, Inc.
New York Lincoln Shanghai

Empire

The Richmond Saga 1066 A.D.

iUniverse, Inc.

For information address:
iUniverse, Inc.
2021 Pine Lake Road, Suite 100
Lincoln, NE 68512
www.iuniverse.com

ISBN: 0-595-27841-8

C O N T E N T S

▼

Preface

Empire, as a novel, is a work of historical fiction. While the characters contained within its pages are real, the interplay and events cannot be shown as they actually happen. Much of it is from accounts of myth and legend. I have tried to create a flow that is consistent with historical fact, but one must realize that legend and supposition are not fact.

Judith, the witch, was William and Alan's grandmother and there was a story circulated about her deal with the devil, hence her son Robert being called the Devil by many of his enemies. In reality, by all accounts, he was a very pious man who tried to live down the legend as much as possible. He never married but did sire the future conqueror, William. He died on a pilgrimage to the holy land.

William was considered a Bastard, since his mother and father never married and his enemies to belittle him used the term. William became one of the greatest statesmen and generals of his time. He was able to amass an Empire that spread from the Med. Sea to northern Scotland and into Ireland. Had he lived longer, perhaps the World would have looked very different today, though he was sixty years old at his death.

Alan Rufus de Richmond was William's cousin and also the grandson of Judith. He led an army of Brits into battle at Normandy on the side of his cousin, and for his help received many titles and lands within the British Isle. During the years in which William fought in Normandy, Alan and his brothers held the front in England and protected their empire. His relatives played a major part in the empire for over five hundred years. His ancestral line also remarried into the Royal line of England more than once through history.

No account exists of a relationship between Alan Rufus and Lady Godiva. However Alan did acquire title to the lands of Godiva after the defeat of the Saxons by William and his followers. One can assume that they at least met.

I hope the reader will enjoy this installment of the Richmond Saga and read the others, as I try to bring their historical story to life.

—Tim Richmond 2003 A.D.

CHAPTER I

▼

The Strength of Desire

Judith sat alone upon the hearthstone and pouted. For six months now she had been learning the arts of a dutiful wife, and for each day of that time it has been playing upon her mind. Suddenly she screamed and violently lashed out at her sewing basket, skewing its contents around the hearth room. She closed her eyes and bitterly wept, lost again in her self pity and loathing for her predicament. At fifteen years she had come to realize that hers was not to be a perfect life. Her status in Brittany society was due to change soon and she had no control over those or any other events in her life.

Judith was the daughter of Count Conan I of Rennes and his wife Emengarde of Anjou. Her mother's parents were Geoffrey I, Count of Rennes and Brittany; and Adelaide de Vermandois, Countess of Grisgonelle, a royal family with generations of truly regal bloodlines. But it now appeared that even royal lineages of the past would not save her from the future, which was quickly descending upon her.

She had grown through her pre-teen years in a home where she was the apple of her father's eye and the Princess of all she surveyed. She had been a child of blissful play, with dreams of slain dragons and hero's on white chargers. But, with the marriage of her older brother Geoffrey and the true knowledge of the ways of her world, she had begun to realize her true status.

Time is like a wheel, she had heard it said, never stopping, ever turning. Perhaps she was the hub of that wheel and around her all things were spinning, changing and moving at an ever faster and faster pace. It was spring now and all life was suppose to renew its self in the spring, a magical time. Oh if she could just renew her unfettered childhood and not have to think on this future that bore down on her so rapidly now.

She was a girl child, almost woman now, but a second class of souls and of little consequence. She was also second born, even if she were the child of the most important man in all Brittany. She knew that her status could only lead her to the unwelcomed prospect of marriage to one of her father's knights. She would be a lady of Royal blood with no title or lands, nor prospects of any. To her, the story book Princess of all she had surveyed, it was a most bleak prospect indeed.

As a child she had been pampered, but with the coming of age of her brother and the realization that she could not, nor would not inherit settled in; she had become rebellious, striking out against both her tutors and parents alike.

They would have her learn of menial things, the common trades of the common woman. Why need she learn to do that which she had no desire to learn; to sew and cook and tend babes?

She should be a Lady of the Land, pampered and painted, learning of books, poetry, art and Courtly manners. She should be admired and looked upon for advice—a Duchess, Princess, or even Queen; with handmaids to await her every whim.

Her father, Conan I "Le Tort", and mother Ermengarde D' Anjou were both of Royal birth. Her mother's lineages were traceable to the Great Charlemagne, Emperor of the Romans and beyond, and except for fate would now be Queen of these lands. Her father, true enough, was Earl of Brittany; but it was a title she could not inherit. Her brother Geoffrey would hold that fame, and she and her future heirs would have to learn to live in his shadow, as his minions and of lesser stations. *"By Lugh's Lungs"*, as her pagan wet nurse, Annis, was fond of saying *"'twas not fair."*

Judith knew that she was fair to the eye and had a lithe body, which was already catching the eye of the Knights of Brittany. Her waist length braided hair was so blond it was nearly white and her eyes were of the deepest blue, a trait attributed to her Viking ancestors through her father Conan I, a direct descendant of King Njord who had ruled Sweden in the 2nd Century.

She knew what affect the rounding edges of her figure had on the young men of her father's court. When she swished by, all heads turned, though none spoke openly. They feared the heathen temper of their Brit leader too greatly to speak of her in less than terms becoming of a lady, and lady she was fast becoming with all the wiles that it implied.

A few courageous young men had made timid forays in gesture or word designed to catch her attention, but she never returned nor even seem to notice them; for Judith did not desire their looks or touch. With her gifts, she felt that she would be able to draw the attention of a more prominent man, one that would become a force in the known world. These foolish boys were merely practice for her future quest.

Think as she might though, there were few of which she felt held the promise for which she searched. King Henry of France had no son of the right age. The other sons of the several Dukedoms were either to old, young or married. There was only one right now whom she judged to be remotely appropriate. He was the son and heir of Richard I "the Fearless", Duke of all Normandy. Richard was the only man in the world to whom Judith's father felt subservient, including the pompous French Capetian King Henry.

Richard I ruled more of France than the King did. His was an empire carved out of the center of France, and one day it would probably encompass the entire Continent. His eldest son, Richard II, potentially the fourth Duke of Normandy, would surely inherit this potential **Empire** and more importantly, he was only a few years Judith senior; a boy, nay a man of whom to dream.

They had first met at a gathering of the clans to celebrate one of the holidays of the New Religion. The Christians, with their Priest, Cardinals, and Popes were quickly replacing the Druid and Viking faiths of old. Though most of the people still clung to the faith of their ancient fathers, the present aristocracy of Europe were converting to the new faith of the Romans, for it's political ties would help with their access to new territories. Politics and power were the life's blood of the new Religion.

The boy Richard, had early on taken a liking to the pretty Brit girl-child of his cousin Conan, but he knew 'twas not to be; for he had been promised to marry upon his ascension, to the daughter of the Duke of Paris, and granddaughter of the King of France. His marriage was to be used as a tool to solidify control, not for some silly idea of love. Richard accepted this as a matter of course. It was a necessity for his lands. Margaret was after-all comely enough, even if she had no grace or poise. She would easily serve as a brooder for his future heirs, and after-all that was what it took to expand ones lands—marriage, heirs, and a loyal army for conquest.

Still the youthful Richard's eyes and loins were not controlled by the logic of a marriage of necessity. These eyes had betrayed his interest in his beautiful blond cousin and he had asked of her at their occasional meetings. Judith had also mentioned him hopefully to her mother Emengarde, but their union was not to be his. Duke Conan's interest in her marriage was to extend his own lands and power, if he could. He had seen the interest in the eyes of the young Richard, but Richard was promised, a promise that could not be easily broken. He was destined to marry into the family of the French King. Judith's only place at his court would have to be as a concubine, and no daughter of his would ever go to the Norman Court as a concubine. Not to anyone, and certainly not to the son of his cousin Duke Richard I. A concubine might live a pampered life, but one without future for either herself or her spawn.

An outright marriage between the two was another thing, it could have been a very good match and would have been welcomed by Conan, but he knew that Richard wanted his son to acquire an interest in the French Crown; therefore the idea of a marriage with a Brit was, at this point at least, unthinkable.

Technically the Duke of Normandy was a vassal of the King who had even the Norman Vikings their lands in 911 A.D. through the treaty of Claire-sur-Epte. Rollo (Rolf) had plundered the lands of the Seine valley while the Muslims and Magyars also threatened the French from its outer boundaries. Charles the Simple, the then King of France sought the treaty and a pledge of loyalty from Rollo to help fend off the others and in doing so, gave up a huge slice of his own territory as Rollo's fief. In time the Normans, through treaties and marriage added the areas between the valleys of Bresle, L'Epte and L'Avr. With the marriage of Richard's son to the Royal house of France through Princess Margaret, the fates could be arranged for the Normans to become heir to all France.

The French King was no fool either. He knew the Norman wanted access to his kingdom, but he foresaw through this arranged marriage a way to bring the troublesome Normans and even more importantly their lands back under his own firm control. Politics through marriage was cheaper and far safer than warfare.

The bloom of spring gave way to the heat of summer and still Judith struggled with her emotions. The heat of summer though, was not nearly as stifling as the routine of her life, but the wheel of time was about to make a fortuitous turn again, and that change was already in the air.

In the courtyard no person stirred to disrupt the shimmering heat. Judith sat alone with her thoughts, lost in heady dreams of what could have been, but 'twas not. A soft breeze arose, as if of its own mind and created a whirlwind in the dust of the castle common. To Judith it was an omen of the dry parched existence she foresaw for herself. Her youth and beauty, in time would whirl upwards and away, as did the turning winds of this small dust devil. It would be drawn into summer's sky and there it would dissipate to the nothingness of time, wasted and forgotten with little to show for its effort.

As Judith sat and wept in the confines of her home, her one true friend and life long personnel nanny, Annis, came to her side. Annis had tended the child since birth and regarded Judith as a child of her own heart. She knew of the young woman's dilemma and shared in her pain, for after-all the girl had complained continuously of late, and it troubled her immeasurably to see the child entrusted to her in such despair.

As a youth at Annis' knee, she had played and sang and been the light of the fortress Brittany. She had brought joy to all who had seen her, but in the short years since her moon cycles had started to flow, her gleeful light had slowly faded to a young woman of morose aberrant behavior. It broke the heart of her ancient Druid wet nurse, to note the change.

The teen years are hard on all people. Emotions run wild along with hormones, but when into the mix is added a presumed injustice, rebellion can be the result and it was so with Judith. She was quickly becoming untenable. Her parents were at a lost as to how to control her mood swings and horrid behavior. Something must be done!!

Annis reached an arm out and encircled the girl pulling her close to her breast as she had done so many times while Judith was still a child. She murmured for her Princess to be still, for the fates had not yet written her future, and things have a way of working themselves out it they were given enough time.

Judith, in the heat of her aberrant teen mood, threw the protective arm away and spoke in a harsh venom filled voice, *"What do you know old woman, you are no better than a stupid slave, stay away from me!"*

The elder nurse dropped her arms and turned to leave, her emotional fervor for this child severely bruised. Judith eyes caught the slump of her shoulders and downcast look on Annis' face and again experienced a mood swing. She remorsefully cried out for her nurse to stay. *"Please don't leave Annis, I'm sorry. It is not your fault that my life is in ruins."*

Annis was in a quandary; she knew that Judith ached for some change in her life, a way to alleviate her allotted path. The nurse also knew that an answer may be available for the girl, but she trembled to think of its potential cost. A moment of joy for a possible eternity of pain was a very high price. She drew a heavy breath and made her decision.

"*There, there now child.*" Annis said as she returned the aged arm to encircle Judith. "*All is not lost. There be ways, though dangerous, if you be willing!*" spoke the ancient wet nurse.

Judith's head turned upward toward Annis' face with a puzzled expression upon it. An expression that said, without words, please explain.

"*You have long known of the Runes itched in blue around my fingers nails and have oft asked of them. Though I have told you they be nothing, in fact they list my standing in the sacred order of the Druids.*"

Now Judith sat up more attentively, caught up in the tale her nurse was spinning.

"*You may not know, but we are an order as ancient as the first people. In us lies the power to change that, which would be, to an alternate course of events. Our oral histories date six thousand years back, and with those years come the knowledge of many things, things that others may think of as mystic powers. We are Celtic and more, for we are much older than the Celts. We were the Unetice or Urnfield of time immortal.*"

"*You may have heard of our circles of power, for our people have created fixtures of stone throughout the world. To the north, in the land of the Angles is a circle of stone higher than a man's head, which support cross stones that can only be moved by the Gods. It had been there a thousand years before the coming of the New Religion of the Christians and shall remain for thousands yet to come.*"

"*The circle of stone is our totem. It gives us power and is the center of our worship of this world and its relationship with the cosmos. Each year we honor it at the winter and Summer Solstice. From there we draw much of our power, for these stones along with other monuments scattered across our world, are always placed along the lines of power within the earth's structure.*"

"*When done correctly with ritual, we can even use the circle of stone, and it's energy fields to commune with the Gods of old. Arawn, Belenus, Brigid, Cernunnos, Cerridwen, Danu, Herne, Lugh, Morgan, Rhiannon and Taranis have all been said to speak within the circle of stones.*"

Judith looked to the elderly nurse and said, "*But Annis, I can not get to the great stones in the land of the Angles, 'tis to far. Why torture me with words and tales that can not help?*"

"*There be stones of power throughout the Druid world, not just in foreign lands. Where the Druid is, there shall he make his mark and perform his rituals. The lands of Eire have many as do the lands of the Norman. Very near here is a circle of stone dedicated solely to Cernunnos the Lord of Dark places,*" said Annis.

"*Who is this Cernunnos?*"

"*Some Christian converts have likened Cernunnos to their Devil, for he is a great deceiver, coming to man in the form of a half animal with horns. He will at times grant dream wishes, but always demands great retribution. Many have trusted him unwisely, only to learn that they were given over to Belenus for transport to the afterlife or otherworld.*"

"*So he is like the Christians Devil, and takes your soul to hell?*"

"*The Christian would have you belief so. They believe that you go to heaven or hell after this life, but we believe life there is much as it is here. Both believe in an immortal soul, but we believe that each can move from one to the next and back again through reincarnation, new birth or even dream quest.*"

Annis paused as if lost in her thoughts, and Judith reached out to her, placing her hands on the aged wet nurse's arm. Annis looked at Judith's hand as if she were in a trance and concentrated on the fingers of her hand, before continuing.

"*Five*", she said, "*yes five!!*" "*You know, the Druids consider the number five to be honored above all and base much of their lore and legend upon the magical elements associated with them. There are the five paths, the five families and the five signs of the Ogam Alphabet. They are symbols of the mystic center, used for divinatory reason and to send and receive messages from the powers of the light or even from the dark lords of the Universe.*"

"*So you are saying that the Druid align themselves with good or evil and are marked accordingly with runes which contain the five symbols?*"

"*Not exactly child, the Druid itself is neither good nor evil. The Druids of old kept these symbols sacred and had them tattooed upon their person. The place, design, number of Runes as well as the color craved into their flesh identifies them not only as Druid, but notes their place in the order of ascent. Each initiative receives the first along their fingernails and as their choice of paths become known, receive more in varies places on their body to denote their standings and trade.*"

"*I have heard some little something of the legends,*" Judith said, "*but it is not the way of my parents and most of our people no longer listen to the old gods. Tell me how can the ways of the old faiths help me.*"

"*Well my child, listen carefully and learn. There are only three commonly known Druid classes. They are the—1. Barbs or Bardos, 2. Vates or Ouateis, and 3. Manteis or master Druids.*

"*The Barbs are singers of songs and ballets. These keep the legends and family ties straight. They must recite from memory the oral histories. They are the custodians of the sacredness of mother earth and give voice to the visions reported by others. They also deliver eulogies and ceremonial rites.*"

"*The Vates or Ovates interpret signs and omens, read the sacrificial bones and relate natural phenomena to the events of the world both present and future.*

The third are the Manteisi. They divine spells and ceremony to accomplish deeds of benefit to the people of the Druid society and act as doctors to the people."

"*These Manteis or Master Druids are the most powerful of the three and it is from these, that the last two orders are drawn. The Manteis are the professional class in the Celtic order. They perform the functions of priests and teachers. They are ambassadors, astronomers, theologist, scientist and more.*

Once these have acquired enough knowledge and demonstrated their worth, they are said to ascend to the higher orders. Most are male, but a few are said to be women, though it is often hard to tell, since they are secretive and mysterious."

"*Each initiate must pass through one order to get to the next and there are few who live long enough to ascend to the fourth or fifth order. I myself have lived among the society for my entire life and have never met one of the ascended. Perhaps they be merely myth, only fantasy tales to spur on others in their life long search for knowledge among the orders, I do not know.*"

"*I am of the Ovates Order, though I have not practiced in a long, long time; I still know how to throw the bones and read their signs. We speak to the ancestors and prophesize. We are also known as healers. That is why your father kept me on as your nurse, though you no longer had need. We can read the future and if all else fails,* attempt to seek out the higher orders and through them change the fates; though 'tis said the cost would be high."

Judith said, "*I will give anything to change my lot Annis, anything!*"

"*Be careful what you say child, for the Lords of Darkness hear all! The leaders of the fourth and fifth order can conjure up all sorts of things, but tis a dangerous and chancy thing to evoke them.*"

"*Fourth and Fifth order? I have only heard of the three orders, who are these other two?*" quizzed Judith.

"*As with all Druid themes, the number five is also present in its priest. The top classes are much more mysterious to the people and dangerous to the priest who practice them. They deal in dream visions, and must practice extreme diligence, for good and evil appear much the same in the vision world and it is hard to divine the ultimate purpose of what is being seen and how to act. A dream event can predict true events or events which can be altered, and one must know the difference. One wrong interpretation and the fate of the people will change from a path of light to one of darkness.*

The Lords of light and dark recognize the power of these Druids and flow to them, trying to seduce them for their own purposes. It takes a truly strong human soul to pull power from the Gods without falling prey to their own wishes and whims; even giving voice to the name of these mysterious higher orders is forbidden."

"*Do you know any of the higher orders who can help me call upon the powers of light and darkness.*" asked Judith.

"*Yes my child, but the cost may be more than you can bear. Please consider carefully before asking me to set up a meeting,*" replied Annis.

"*Dear Annis, I must know the secrets of these Druids. Please take me to them that I might learn.*"

Annis shook her gray clad head and said, "*As you wish my child. First you must be prepared, for there is much to know and learn in order in evoke the rites of the higher powers.*"

Judith studied hard that summer and with an intense fervor. No longer did she appear a precocious child intent on self-indulgence. She had a new drive, a new purpose.

Her own destiny was now in her hands. A change could be wroth in her life and she could be her own instrument of that change. She must be diligent. She must succeed!!

Her parents noted her diversion from her domestic studies, but Annis appeared to have taken on the role of tutrix and that suited them just fine; as long as she behaved and did not bother them.

Judith learned quickly, but could not hold her excitement as she continually plied Annis for news of when she would be ready. Finally, Annis gave her the answer—

"On the first day of November the feast of Samhain will start. It is combined with the Feast of the Dead and the New Year of the Druid and Celtic calendar. It is a time when the veil between our reality and that of the Otherworld is most easily penetrated. It is also called the fire festival and it is the day when we must seek your pact with the Light or Dark forces."

"If we are successful, the Embolic festival or festival of Bridget, which marks the return of the light will bring your answer. It is held on February first. Some sign will appear to show that your dreams are firmly planted and taken root."

"On May 1st the celebration of the fires of Beltaine will mark your success, if it is to be. For this 'tis the season of the blossom, it is a time for renewal of life and the pacts that make it so. The youths of age will dance around the May pole to make Beltaine accept their coming time of fertility and adulthood."

"By August 1st, during the Feast of Lugh, you will have what you wish, or the pact shall be broken. For it is the time of the harvest and Lughnasad will see that you receive the ripe fruit of your effort."

Judith, whose face had been bright with interest, now brought her lips to a full pout and said, *"August! But, that's a life time away, Annis!"*

Not dismayed Annis replied, *"And that's only if you commit to your studies. Now back to work my impatient one."*

CHAPTER 2

▼

The Pact

On the first day of November, in the light of the late eve sun, Annis led the youthful Brit teen to a distant hill that overlooked a small wooded glade. There in an open area shown a slightly worn path leading toward a circle of stones. Here at the apex of the trail, the two waited for the evening light to move onward to nightfall. The quiet shaded wood, which held the circle and surrounded it, was surreal. Neither bird chirped nor frog croaked within its shade. No earthly sound of any kind disrupted its placidity. It was as if it this place did not exist at all.

Judith waited, then as the day gave way to evening, she unhesitantly moved away from Annis and down the path until she stood alone in the wood. Here, she timidly moved amid the circle of stone. She held her breath and looked around for signs of the spirit world, but none shown. The stones had the markings of the strange Ogam alphabet inscribed upon them, and with the fading evening light they seemed to glow.

The moon rose full and yellow in the clear cool evening sky, ascending to the tops of the surrounding trees to alight fully the circle of stone, and she knew it was at last time.

Judith reached for the pouch, which swung, from her waist. She pulled the small rune marked flask from its folds and drank the potion of heady herbs, which Annis had given her. She immediately felt weak and a little bit woozy. She steadied herself and tried to remember the text she had so carefully memorized.

At first in hushed tones then in a stronger voice, Judith carefully recited the words that Annis had taught her in the previous weeks..........

"Earth and stones, shining stars of the night sky, mother moon, tumbling waters, other—world magic and ancient wisdom flow to me thy servant. Bring forth the hidden inner knowledge. Let me see beyond the veil of time and distance. Allow me to travel thy mystic course that I might see the other Realm and know the magic of the Ancients, to there and back again to Earth. Let my soul fly as a bird to the sun or like a bat to the moon. I beseech you, let me hear the voices of the Gods and Goddess' whose essence reside in the trees, rocks and rivers of old."

The strength of the potion or the Druid magic took hold of her. And as the words of her chant ended, a shimmering occurred within the circle of stones. She suddenly found herself not in the dell with Annis at all, but at the entrance to a land she had not seen before. She looked in amazement at the new realm around her. Here was a place of strange haunting beauty, tucked between two hills. One rise appeared as the crouching beast described to her as the god Tor, proud and masculine with a mane of golden grass; the other seemed more rounded as if the breast of the female God Chalic even to the small darkish node, which adorned it highest point. Between the two, which she easily recognized as being so perfectly male and female, lay a mist-shrouded garden surrounding a stonewalled well and its Druid altar.

A priest dressed in dark attire with its head draped in the hood of the robe, stood near the well. The Priest bade her to come forward with a simple motion of its hand. Judith could not tell whether the shrouded image was male or female, for there were no outward signs and the priest had not spoken.

Judith was not afraid and that amazed her more, for she had expected fear to grab at heart and hold her once she was near the secretive priest of the higher orders. Somehow though, the well, garden and hooded priest exuded a sense of extraordinary peace, though one of deep resonant power at the same time. Peace and Power, thought Judith, a paradox of nature in the outside world, but here it seemed to fit.

Judith stepped timidly forward passing the perfect lawn and flower beds of the garden. There were low hedgerows and gnarled yew trees flanking the path that led to the well. The path sloped gently upward toward the wellhead on the rounded mound. A finely wrought iron cover depicting the ancient symbol of the vesica piseis protected the well itself.

Judith waited alongside the mute priest for what seemed an eternity, neither speaking nor moving. Time itself seemed to stand still. There was neither movement of air nor birds singing within the dell, just a reverence of solitude, a deafening silence enveloping her and the garden center.

From the air around Judith a voice now seemed to grow, reverberating from everywhere and nowhere at the same time. Perhaps it came from the surrounding air, or from within her very soul, for it permeated all. In the beginning it was just a feeling and then it became words as the vibrations grew within and around her. At first, she thought the voice must have came from the priest, but he or she had left; look as she might, she could not see anyone within the range of her view, nor fathom from where the voice had come. The disembodied voice was soothing however. It too, was neither male nor female, neither sinister nor benevolent and Judith could not tell how it spoke to her. Its words however rang clear, *"What seeks thou here?"*

Judith looked again around the dell to see if she could note any living soul, but none were present. Timidly she said, *"I come to seek the ancient ones, to make a request."*

She waited, but no one spoke in return to her statement. She continued more boldly raising her voice to be sure she was heard, while glancing cautiously around with, *"I wish to bind myself and my legitimate heirs to you. In return, I ask a pledge of Royalty lineage for them for a millennium."*

The mysterious voice now spoke again. *"This is indeed a bold request, with ominous fortunes for you and your descendents. One, which should be considered most carefully least it be granted."*

There was a pause as if the voice waited for her to change her mind, then it continued. *"If thou art sure and wouldst continue, first look into the well and tell me what thou sees."*

Judith lifted the cover to the well and looked within its waters. She stared long into its depths for what seemed like hours, trying to divine something, anything from within its darkened gloom. The placid pool gave off no reflection, not even her own. It appeared crystal clear but without bottom, and with none of the normal wells imperfections of slime or organisms within its depth.

At first she saw nothing else, as she stared deep within its fathoms; but then slowly, as if they arose from those very depths, there appeared two circles inter-linked one to another.

"That which you see," continued the disembodied voice, *"is a symbol. To the new Religionist, it means Christ and God. To the Greek, it is the Philosopher's stone, and mayhap to some questing Arthurian Knight, an inner vision of the Holy Grail. To some men, it may even appear to be the sacred vulva of the Druid Goddess.*

In truth, each circle depicts the union of the two disciplines, the two beings, father and son or even the two powers, the light and the dark, the Yen and the Yang. But to all, it is the emblem of their faith in a greater good.

If you wish to continue with your request, know this—it can be easily granted, as easy as the blinking of the eye, though for its cost,......you shall forever give up the redemption of this symbol to you."

Judith trembled for she knew it was a terrible cost, a future of heaven or a present of **Empire**. She took a deep breath. She had come this far and she must not to be dissuaded. She slowly nodded her head and said, *"Yes, I understand, but nothing will stay me from my course."*

"So be it", the disembodied voice said. *"Into this well, drop only the essence of life—one drop for each of your future whelps. You and they in time will receive that for which you seek,—if it truly be your heart's desire. But remember, only the essence of life may enter the sacred circles."*

Annis had prepared her determined student for this event. From the hem of her cloak, Judith withdrew a sharpened sewing awl and carefully pricked her ring finger. She squeezed the appendage to create three tiny droplets of blood, one for each of the children she desired to birth. Three crimson drops of blood dripped independently from the wound. Each fell in a slow spiral, striking the placid pool in different spots. The first fell at the well's edge, the second in its middle and finally the third upon the far side.

Judith watched as each created a growing circle, moving outward toward one another soon to touch and then overlap. They would make an interlocking image as the vesica piseis did.

At last thought Judith, her life was set upon a path of her own making, not controlled by her parents or others. But the wheel of time and its treacherous path now took a disastrous turn, for then suddenly the neglected needle slipped from her inattentive hand and also fell. She leaned out and snatched at it, trying to catch it, but it fell straight toward the growing efface of the nearest circle.

Judith cried out and turned to call to the priest, but the priest was no longer there, for suddenly another shimmering occurred around her and she no longer was within the Druid's secret garden. She found herself instantly transported again from one realm to another. She was bewildered, confused and disoriented. She must find the priest and discover how her clumsiness had affected the ritual. But the robed figure could not be found, for she now stood once again within the circle of stones in the wood near her home.

She quickly searched the landscape, but saw no one save Annis. She tried to step out toward her, but felt weakened. The Druid pact, loss of blood or Annis' heady potion must have worked havoc upon her. She swooned and started to fall, her arm outstretched toward the distant servant.

Annis, who had averted her eyes, least she see the events of the ritual, heard the cry and rushed to her Judith. She slipped carefully to the ground and pulled the prostrate form of the young Brit girl's head into her lap. As she circled her arms protectively around Judith, she said, "*My child have you come to your senses at last and decided not to evoke the dark lords.*"

"*Nay,*" said Judith woozily. "*I have been away for hours and just now returned to you.*"

"*'Tis not possible,*" spoke Annis, "*for you have been here the whole time. I had merely turned my back when I heard you cried out. You have not gone!*"

CHAPTER 3

▼

Bonds of the Pact

On the ninth full moon of the year 996 A.D. of the New Religion, Judith became a bride in a land ripe for conquest. She now knew that her mystic experience within the circle of stones had not been a swoon-induced dream, for she felt the power steadily growing within her. She carefully guarded her secret pact, but she now knew that she would in time, reach her destiny of an **Empire**.

She had drawn upon the power of a Druid priest of the 5th Order, using the rites of the Dark Runes. She had summoned the Lord of Darkness to her. She had offered herself and each of her eldest legitimate heirs souls in turn, for all eternity. Hers was the bargain, that in return she would receive the promise of a royalty lineage of the first order. To her and her legitimate heirs would come an **Empire,** one that would last for the next thousand years! In this she was secure. In this her knowledge was now secure.

At first, Judith had not been sure she believed in the success of the pact she had made, but in the second moon of 996 A.D. (February), she came to believe. Word arrived of the death of the young French Princess, Margaret of Paris. It had been only scant months prior to her arranged marriage with Richard II, potentially the fourth Duke of Normandy.

At court, the King (Henry) was giving a party to commemorate the coming event and all people of importance within his realm were at the gala affair. From the farthest reaches of the French lands and from the courts of the royals of the other nearby Monarchs, they had assembled to wish the two a blissful union. The Duke of Saxony offered a toast. He was from the northern lands of the Norse Germans. As each guest turned the season's best wine to their lips; the Princess gasped, then her glass tumbled from her hand and she slumped to the great hall's stone floor.

She lay amid the ruins of the revelry, her hands clasped around her slender throat, silent and unmoving. Her death was sudden and though Physician and Priest tended her, she was not to revive. Accusations flew rampant; 'twas either poison or witchcraft most suspected. From that day on Judith knew the truth of her dream, for the festival of Brigid had just begun.

Rumors ran amok as to the complicity of the dire deed. Whispers were heard and threats made, but no direct evidence found to implicate any of the Royals assembled. Richard appeared duly saddened at the lost of his future bride, but the King still hinted that he felt the treachery was of the Norman's hands.

Tensions became great between the Normans and the French Capetian King, for his suspicions grew with his remorse. Someone must pay for his daughter's death. Surly somehow the marriage arrangements were the cause of his child's untimely demise. Rumors of war swelled throughout the land. To protect their name, lands and lives, a war council of all the Normans and their kin was called; one that Judith gladly attended with her Brit family. As rulers of Brittany, and kin people to the Normans, it was important that they stand together against these false French accusations.

Once arrived at the Norman stronghold, Judith wasted no time. Here was at last her chance, one she would not pass up, even at a wake. She sought out her handsome cousin. She was there presumably to console him in his bereavement. It was not unnatural to do so, it was even expected. She finally found him in solitude, alone in the plush garden area of the fortress Normandy near Falaise.

From his deep well of thought, he raised his eyes, just to have them become hopelessly entrapped by the vision before him.

She had planned long and well for this moment. She wore a snow-white dress of sheer muslin, which carefully outlined the swell of her breast and thinness of her waist. She also had selected a delicate fragrance, which had been given her mother by the returning knights from Italy. This floated ahead of her on the evening breeze and added to her sensuous allure. According to the Knight that had appropriated it, it was the very essence that Queen Cleopatra had used to seduce Mark Anthony, a fragrance that had captured a heart and destroyed an **Empire**. Now Judith would try to use the same to build a new **Empire** for herself.

The fragrance had aroused the interest of every Brit knight of her home estate, for she had tested it well before selecting it for this conquest. She wore her hair long, adorned with a wreath of white dogwood blooms. The evening's setting sun captured her just right as she paused for effect in the garden's arched entranceway. Its light filtered through the shear material creating a shadowy outline, a sensuous promise of what lay beneath.

She paused under the archway, awaiting the effects of her planned approach to show itself. It must work for she had planned to long for it not to. She knew what the effects of her sheer gown would do, for her mother had often warned her of the way light would filter through. She had carefully tested the aroma of her perfume. She had spent hours framing her hair just so, to highlight her face. Now if only he were properly receptive!

Richard's eyes clung to her as she floated across the flagstones toward him. Her smile was enchanting, compassionate and even ever so slightly mischievous. It added to her amorous allure. Richard knew it was his cousin Judith moving toward him, for she had caught his attention before, but never like this. Never had he seen her or anyone for that matter, who radiated this much beauty and raw sensuality. The Greek Goddess Athena could not hold a candle to this vision. Gone now were his thoughts of the Princess Margaret. How could he have ever selected another over this woman as his bride? French titles and treaties be damned. **This woman must be his!**

Within days, a new alliance was forged within the Norman Viking Clans and with it a new marriage bond created. The announcement came the 1st day of May, with the start of the festival of the Fires of Bel, just as Annis had predicted.

The new bride was beautiful to behold. Her hair was now snow white with skin that was practically translucent. The transference of power within the circle of stones had marked a change in her. With the fulfillment of her dreams, she had become more poised, assured and womanly, but the yellow gold of hair was gone and the natural red rogue of her cheeks bleached white.

She was still striking beautiful, but pale as a ghost. That combination along with the blood redness of her lips and the unbelievable hourglass form of her body had made Richard weak in the knees. He had never seen a woman so excitingly exotic and his blood raced for her touch. In the weeks since their betrothal, he had scarcely been able to withhold himself from ravishing her at each of their meetings. But the Lady would have none of that. She made him ache for her and at times was ready herself to the point of pain; but still she resisted, for a wedding ring would be the cost of their union. Now though, the day was at last upon them, and there was a flush of heat in anticipation for the nights to come.

She wore braids of gold and silver in her hair, which brought her skin color to a splendor that none other could match. She was the perfect image of a Queen— regal, poised, delicate and beautiful; but for the time being she would have to settle for the title of Duchess.

She wore gloves of golden lace, which hid her new marks of the Runes. Annis had placed them there after the first signs of the prophecy came true. This and her dutiful studies (which she had continued) had made her an initiative in the order of Druids, and as such she would continue to learn its ways. These Rune signs encircled her delicate fingernails and marked her as a Druid initiate of the first order, a Bardo.

Only her chambermaids were privy to her secret markings and they were hand picked to keep the secret, but a secret of this magnitude could not be kept for ever, and her Christian maids were already calling her Witch and Sorcerer behind her back, for they knew that all her desires were too quickly coming true.

Hers was now the land of Normandy. It was part of ancient Gaul, a land fought over for a millennium by Goths, Visigoths, Romans and the German Franks. As Roman, when conquered by Julius, the great Caesar, it became part of the Roman province of Lugdunensis. It had received the new Religion in the 3rd Century of their Christ and started to push out the other older beliefs. In 911, the first of her people the Viking, or North men had arrived. Their chief Rollo took the land and was granted peace by the succession to him of it, by the Frank King Charles III (the Simple) in return for a pledge of mutual defense.

The Brit part of her bloodline had been forced out of the Misty Isles and to the shores of France by the Angles and then the Saxons, but now Brittany lay behind her. Her brother held claim to those lands. She now had Normandy and a bright future lay ahead. She had only to plan and scheme, for more lands must come to her if she was to create her **Empire.**

For the remainder of her life she lived as if Queen, and started her new dynasty in grand fashion. In the year of the new Religion 997 A.D., she begot a son whom she named Richard III. A year later another male child was born whom she named Robert and two years later a girl child, which she named Hawise.

All was happening as the God of the Circle of Stones had promised. Soon she would have all she had desired, husband, children and a legacy for her **Empire.**

Forgotten were Annis' warning that the God Cernunnos was a trickster. The wheel of time had turned, and it was now time for the bill to be paid. At the age of eight, Richard her eldest son, became ill with fever and he soon died. Judith could not believe it had happened, not to her. She sent for Annis and cried foul, for this was not in her pact.

Annis thought for a few minutes, then reminded her of the pin she had dropped into well disrupting the spreading circle caused by the first blood drop. This could have denoted her first born. Perhaps this unpurposeful act caused a break in the life force of her first born and allowed the trickster to gain from the accident.

This revelation brought a fit of rage to Judith. She ranted and raved and called upon the Lords of Darkness and Light to bring her son Richard back to life. In private as well as public, she raved and cursed the God Cernunnos for taking him to the Otherworld.

Though Annis tried to soothe her and even called upon the head of the local Druid orders to quiet her fits, Judith could not be quieted. She continued to openly shrill and curse of her unholy pact. Though the very aged Annis tried to contain Judith's voice and maintain her secret, soon all at Court became aware of her pact with the Lord of Darkness or the Devil, as the New Religionist called him.

Her husband's heart was heavy. The lost of his first born son and now the madness of his beloved bride left him heart heavy and weary of soul. Desperately he sought out the new Religion's priest. He had converted recently and now commanded them and their God to exorcise her of her demons. The priest went to work at once. Their attempts were thorough and exhausting, but to no avail.

In the year of our lord 1017 A.D., Judith's overburdened heart failed and she perished. Before her death though, she had called Richard to her and pleaded that he evoke the binding ritual to keep her spirit Earth bound. She made him promise to thwart the efforts of Cernunnos, for he would take her far away to the Otherworld, and from there she could not watch over him and their children who still lived.

Richard had not been raised as Keltic or Druid. He was of the Religion of the Viking with the lore of Odin. Nor did he fully understand the new God he had so recently embraced. To help him understand and gain the necessary knowledge of the ancient Keltic Gods, he called for Annis, the old nurse of his beloved Judith. She must explain what and why his wife had made this demand.

Annis said, *"My lord,' tis just the ranting of a grieved mother for her lost child. Think on it not."*

"What of this God Cernnunos of whom she spoke? Who exactly is he that he could take my Judith?"

"Cernnunos." she explained, *"The old religion says he is the god who sleeps down in the dark, moist, odorous underfoot. He awaits us, to put down our roots and take us to the Otherworld, at the Sacred Center, in the grove of allworld or Earth, Sea, and Sky. Here lie the worlds behind all worlds. Here the god and the Great Tree are One. His immense limbs wide spread, stretch into the distant sky and starry space. His massive trunk is the spine of the Middleworld. It is the heart of the Ancient Forest around which all life sprang and all worlds turn. At his feet is the Great Cauldron from which the waters of the five seas flow. From his bowels came all—the whispering wings of flighty things, and silent step of forest creatures, the first Ancestors of man, and the oldest of animals. He welcomes them and they gather around him: Blackbird—the keeper of the gate, Stag of the Seven Tines—the master of time, Ancient Owl—Crone of the Night, Eagle—lord of the Air and Eye of the Sun."*

"Cernnunos is the origin of primeval essence. He is said to wear a crown of antlers and is a master of disguise, a seducer of the dead. The one who ferries us to the Otherworld. Some think him a horned God, half man and half animal."

Richard drew a breath and cried, *"Lord Satan! You speak of the Devil? He is after my Judith?"*

Richard waited for not for her answer, but went straight away and called together the head priest of the new Religion.

After much urging, the priest of the Christian faith agreed, but Richard had to be sure and called upon each of the three religions priest in turn. Duchess Judith was thus bound to her tomb by rituals through the rites of all three religions. These acts, each promised, would bind her soul to the earth and not release it to Cernnunos. The Priest of the Roman Religion would not guarantee her soul's salvation but perhaps the Devil's work would be thwarted, at least for one more allotment of man's time—three score and ten years.

Annis nodded her head at the binding ceremony for if it worked, Judith's soul would not rest but roam the Earth freely. It would be her victory over death, for at least seventy years. Her dream spirit could roam the land to help guide the destiny she had so carefully bargained for her children. If it did not work, then Judith's pact must have been successful and she had still won.

CHAPTER 4

▼

Duke Robert a.k.a The Devil

Robert a.k.a the Devil was Judith's second born and now her oldest heir. As per the dark agreement, his lands grew with his age. When he sought lands in battle there was little or only nominal resistance, for all knew of the legacy his mother had begat, and fear grew within their hearts.

Throughout his life, though a Viking warrior leader who must fulfill his rites of leadership, Robert had tried to do good. He offered himself repeatedly to the Christian Church to atone for his mother's sins. Some even started to call him 'Robert the Good' or 'Robert the Magnificent'. However, behind it all was the knowledge of his mother's unholy pledge, and still his enemies in careful whispers, named him Devil.

Before the death of her father Richard II, Hawise, Judith's daughter and third born, was promised in marriage to her cousin Eudo, the Duke of Brittany. Eudo a.k.a Odo was Judith's brother Geoffrey's child, and heir to Brittany. Although first cousins, the marriage was arranged and considered a good one since all knew of Judith's pact with the Dark Lord and there were little hope of a stronger marriage bond.

Judith perhaps could have intervened and found another suitable mate for Hawise. He would need be one who was as powerful, yet whose blood was less closely akin. That would be a hard task. The fiefdoms of the Norman and Brit were the most powerful of the entire Continent. She knew that Robert could easily fulfill her destiny of **Empire**. What the witch needed of Hawise was a back-up plan. Brittany also needed an heir, it must be one who could also build Judith's future dynasty, if need be. The contract would be made. Hawise would be the new Mistress of Fortress Brittany.

With the years, Robert's **Empire** continued to grow, and held true to the contract his mother had made. The curse of his mother's pact though overshadowed his childhood and many of his childhood taunters openly called him a child of the Devil. Even he himself was not sure of the truth of it. For many times during his sleep he had dreams of his mother. The specter would gently coerce him toward her goals, and as he followed them he came to realize the truth of this unholy pact she had made. He reluctantly decided, as he came of age, that the only way he could end the curse was to never marry nor produce heirs. But the great deceiver, the Dark Lord, Hades, Satan, the El Sebob or Cernnunos in his many names had other plans for him.

A young man's hormones often dictate the course his life takes whether led by the Devil or not, and it was so for Robert, for soon the beautiful temptress, Herleva, came into his life.

It was the late teen years of his life, though Robert was a man near grown. By chance perhaps, or due to fortune's design, one day he rode down the road to Falaise giving his white steed some exercise. While trying to accustom himself to the armor he had recently been given. He discovered there beside the road, where the bridge crossed a turbulent stream, a girl with golden hair. She was busy washing out her clothing, paying no heed to the occasional travelers upon the road.

Robert spied the maid and paused his horse; he was full of himself as young men often are, and needed someone to admire him in all his new splendor, even this common washer girl would do.

The youthful maiden was facing outward, away from the road and intent upon her job. Robert cleared his throat and tried to think of something clever to say, something intelligent, a word or phrase to impress this young maiden of his realm. His throat sounds made the maid turn, but just as he was about to speak, his eyes beheld her face and the words suddenly would not come forth. He became the opposite of what he had attempted; not suave, not gallant, just tongue-tied.

She was a vision. A beautiful as none he had ever seen. A string of purple twine held her golden hair back and her dress was of woolen weave.

Not impressive garb, as any might see, but the way it adorned her frame with the water spray of the stream holding it tight against her delicately curved body took his breath away.

She in turn stared at the young man upon the huge snow-white steed. His new Knights armor reflected the noonday sun and glistened as brightly as a new star. The steed pranced and turned upon the rise where the road reached the bridge, fighting its bit and showing its spirit.

The young knight looked to be a vision that any young girl would dream of, but never expected to see. She, in her amorous scrutiny, saw not his awkwardness, just a dashing heroic figure upon a marvelous steed. She suddenly felt flushed; the roughness of her dress began to stimulate the orbs of her swelling breast. Her face grew redder; she lowered her eyes and curtsied, the hem of her dampened clinging dress dragging in the swift stream.

Robert finally came to himself. He smiled and lowered his helmet in a valiant salute and rode onward across the bridge, though his eyes followed not the road, but the vision in the stream.

No words had been spoken, but Robert was amour-ized. He had not thought of girls much since the last assemblage at his father's court. Those were silly things that giggled when he walked by. This was something vastly different. She was neither fane nor silly. She was magnificent. He must know more of her. He was in a word, smitten.

Robert arrived in Falaise and immediately sent for his servants. One of them would surely know of the girl. None familiar with the countryside could not, for she was truly the most beautiful girl he had seen in all Normandy.

Two days passed before Robert received word. "*She is not of Royal birth Sire, but the daughter of a common tanner. Her name is Herleva, my Lord, but she is known by most as Arlette,*" the servant said.

Robert was confused and distraught. His minds eye continually returned to the vision of her beautiful face and the sensuous allure of her frame so carefully outlined by the dampness of her attire. He had not meant to be so attracted to anyone, much less a common tanner's daughter. He had already made a pledge to deny himself marriage and the siring of children, for each would surely carry the curse of his mother on into the future lines of the family. He had decided that her pledge must stop with him. This attraction he felt must not mature.

But fate, and the wishes of Judith were not to be deterred. The girl unexpectantly appeared at the castle at the end of a fortnight with her father to deliver some new leather products. Robert saw her from the window of his room and again the vision of her in the stream arose, sensuous and alluring. The attraction was just too much. Affairs of the heart and loins had overruled man's sane thoughts for all eternity, how could he change that? He must talk to her. He had to touch her. Just once he thought. Surely a chance meeting, a rendezvous, could not hurt. Not just this once! He called his chamber servant to him and bade him to make it so.

The servant went to the tanner and told him that the young master wanted a special leather tunic made for travel and battle, one that befitted his station. He wished him to make a few for his inspection. Perhaps the young female assistant could bring one by on the morrow for review.

The tanner and his daughter both raised their eyes to look at the youthful Duke in the window above. The tanner looked then to his daughter and saw the gleam in her eye. Perhaps, he thought, this could turn out to be a chance for them to become more important. The boy Duke was not married; maybe his daughter would become the Duchess. It was not unheard of. Others had married into the royal line before. And even at that, these had not always been royals themselves. Somewhere in their background these of the royal family were just common men.

"Yes, let it be so," said the tanner.

Though unsure of how he should handle the situation once the plans had been made, Robert readily received her in his private chambers when she brought his new tunic. This initial trip was one of development, of familiar-ness, of awaken-ing by both, though neither dared touch. Each was determined to keep uncom-mon reserve least they lose all control.

Robert stood at the far side of his room while she was issued in. Arlette looked at him, curtsied and said, *"My lord, I have brought the tunic which you have ordered."*

"Thank you. You may lay in on the chair," Robert said, his eyes locked upon her face.

"But my Lord, thou hast not looked at it", she returned. *"Perhaps it is not to your liking. I—I could take it home and bring another."*

Robert's eyes remained upon the face of the beautiful Arlette and he was suddenly aware she had asked him something, but what? "*Yes,—yes,*" he stammered, "*that will be fine.*"

Arlette turned to leave. She was bewildered as to why he had rejected the tunic without even looking at it. He had ordered it, and her father had labored long into the night with it! Why must Royals be so obstinate?

Robert was confused. He had not understood, but he knew he did not want her to leave. "*Where are you going?*" he asked.

"*Sire why do you toy with me?* Cried the maiden. "*You said that you did not like it.*"

"*Oh, but I do!*" Robert stammered, as he took a step toward her. Thinking quickly he added, "*I just…I just meant that I wanted some others besides this one.*"

He reached for the tunic and their fingertips touched. The strange phenomenon of static electricity charged through them. Both drew quickly away as if burned and the tunic fell to the stone floor. What was this energy, which grew from their touch? Their eyes, which had been locked before the surge of energy, moved to their fingertips, as if to seek out the source of the electric energy. Then, recovering, each reached for the tunic at the same time and their faces came together. Their noses barely grazed. This time no sparks flew, but Arlette jerked quickly back, as if it had. She staggered and fell, landing unladylike and heavily upon her buttocks.

Robert smiled and then Arlette giggled. The tenseness of the situation became more relaxed and Robert told her," *I really like the tunic*". He extended his hand to help her to rise, and then finished by saying, "*but in God's truth, I ordered it only as a pretense to see you again.*" She reached out testing his touch for sparks, then took his hand and arose.

Arlette's face became red. She pulled back her hand and then laid the garment on the chair before saying, "*by your leave my Lord.*" She then fled the chamber and down the stairs for home. As she cleared the castle she looked back over her shoulder and saw the handsome Norman Duke watching her from his chamber window. She stutter-stepped, almost as if she did not want to go, and then she turned and continued her headlong rush for home, the garden hedge hiding her troubled escape.

That was the first of many meetings for the two and as Robert's leather tunic supply grew, so too did his desire for this maid. The embers of love flared and with it the smiles of a snow white female specter, which followed both Robert and his sister Hawise's every move.

There was no need for further action by Judith, for with the beguile-ness of the serpent; Arlette's belly soon began to swell with the product of her and Robert's uncontrollable lust. Whether true love, demon induced passion, or a normal human hormonal desire, their unions were a mixture of extreme bliss and yet utter madness to his tortured Christian soul.

When with her, he was possessed, when apart, forlorn. Forgotten in his desire for the beautiful Herleva, a.k.a Arlette was his pledge to end the cycle his mother had started with her pact to the ancient Druid god of the underworld, Cernnunos. However in rare moments of clarity he would remember, and it pained him. He vacillated between ecstasy and agonies, adrift in a torment of lust, love and despair. He would pledge his life and soul to the Lord Jesus Christ if only he could stop this unholy cycle.

Robert was beside himself when he learned of the pending birth, for he loved Herleva with all his heart, as did she him. However, the product of their yearnings would continue his mother's pact with Satan. What must they do?

Each of his court advisors had different advice, for they each had covertly put their eye upon the Duke's title and lands. If no heir was produced for the fief, then each of them stood a chance to inherit. Their suggestions thus ran from murder of the unborn child and mother, to birth and then castration of the child if he be male. These were unthinkable to Robert. Surely there was another way!

The priest of the three religions were summoned and asked for help. Advice that each freely gave—

The Viking priest said that in their religion, the God Odin was a son of Bur the first man and that he protected all men from the frost giant Ymir.

Odin in turned had vowed to protect the children of Njord the first Swede King of whom Robert was a distant descendent. Thus to harm the mother, Herleva, or her child purposefully, would be to call down a curse upon the Normans by the Gods of old.

The Bishops of the God of the New Religion pledged that their God and his emissary, Jesus the Christ, would protect the boy, if only Robert would seek them out. He continued by saying that the Christ child in essence had been an illegitimate birth and he had become the savior of the entire world. A child, any child, thus is a gift of God and must not be harmed.

The Druid priest agreed with the other two yet offered a hope. He said that the four weeks of the 9th moon, which marked the Druid festival of the Dark Lord, is upon us. It is the time of harvest and feasting, a time when the Gods are most receptive to sacrifice and prayer. Robert and his assembled priest should pray to the gods of all three religions for an answer. The Gods of man were after all benevolent in all religions, and with the powers of gods, a way can always be found.

Robert believed the priest of the three religions were in sync, and set their prayers in motion. He was a man of faith, faith in God, and faith that man must help the Gods to solve his own problems, thus he also sought council with his closest friends and relatives. The gods might offer answers, but in the words of the Christian—God helps those most, who help themselves.

The Viscount of Conterville, Herluin, a youth who had grown to age with Robert and shared his many adventures and trust, came up with his own solution to their problem. He had admired the beautiful Herleva since first they met, and was greatly envious of the joys she had bestowed upon his friend the Duke, so he offered to marry her. The joy and beauty, which she possessed, would be his. The grace, effervescent personality and eventually her physical desire, if not emotional, would also be his. So to would be the child that she carried. For Herluin it was a perfect solution.

Of course, Robert at first said that he would rather die than lose her love, but Herluin convinced him that the child, if fatherless would be seen as a bastard and without rights, if they were not married. If they were, then the Pact, which he so hated, would be continued. But if Herleva married him, the child would have a home and he could pass the titles of Conterville as well as his lands to Robert's son in time.

Robert could see no other way out and reluctantly agreed. To Herleva it was a betrayal of the worst kind, though tired of the vacillating emotions of her lover, she was not prepared for total rejection. She vowed never to speak or even look upon the Duke who had abandoned her love and its creation. Her father, the tanner, however was not distraught, for she was still to marry royalty in the form of the Count of Conterville. His own station in life would still be greatly improved, and since all knew his grandchild's true heritage, perhaps in time they could still lay claim to the titles and lands of the Duke of Normandy.

Thus William came into the world as the illegitimate son of Robert the Magnificent in the year of our lord 1028 A.D. However he was born to the house of Count Herluin and Countess Herleva in Falaise, Normandy. Hopefully, these sacrifices would allow the boy to grow up free of the curse of his grandmother's pledge.

Robert had no other children throughout his life. The loss of his one true love and her contemptuous disdain of him caused the Duke a lifetime of misery and remorse. He became celibate and pious with a steady endowment to the Church, an effort to seek forgiveness and absolution. He, instead of thinking of his lost, used his time in devotion of the acquisition of lands and titles for Judith's **Empire**.

The wheel of time continued to turn and the Viscount and his fertile bride brought forth other children of their own. Robert covertly spied on them, for he was no longer welcome at the estates of his old friend. He was still overlord of their lands and could have issued orders for an audience, but he could not stand to think of Herluin and Herleva together, much less witness it. He did though, note the two other children of Herleva and his ex-friend the Count Herluin. They, he knew all to well, would grow to become men with needs of lands of their own; a situation that might leave his own son destitute, without lands or title.

There must be an answer to this dilemma and the constant pain of his guilt. Perhaps in the lands of his God's own son, he could find an answer. He called his most trusted knights together and planned a pilgrimage to Jerusalem. There he would seek the guidance of the New Religion's God.

Piety and prayer, the hope of the forlorn, were given in plenty. Robert had an abundance of both and lavished it upon the holy relics of his chosen faith. But no answer came readily to his tortured soul. He spread his funds among the churches and their dark robed monks. Months passed and still no word was given. With a heavy heart and a much-lightened purse, the small band of Norman knights started for home. Robert's heart was still heavy and his soul still troubled.

Perhaps it was his disillusionment; perhaps merely an abandonment of hope, but Duke Robert became ill in Constantinople on the return trip, and while laying on his deathbed, a priest of new Religion of the man from Jerusalem came to him. Robert tried to explain that he had no gold left to pay for prayers, but he was waved to muteness. The priest, dressed in a snow-white robes, told him that he was totally absolved of guilt through his piety, prayer and pilgrimage and that he should embrace his child, for God had forgiven his mother's unholy oath.

"No man or woman," he explained, *"may pledge another's soul. It is for each of us to make our own destiny here on Earth or in the Hereafter. Embrace that which you have begat, for it is our one sure proof that God's covenant with Christ still exist here on earth."*

Robert's spirit if not his health was much lifted. He immediately called his knights to him and forced them to pledge their own oath to William, his bastard son, as the rightful heir and the next Duke of Normandy.

It was not a pledge easily given, for several still had designs on Robert's lands. But their duty was clear and if Robert survived, he would never again trust those who did not forthrightly give him their pledge. Therefore, each pledged his life to the new Duke, though William was still only a babe of eight years age. Some gave their solemn pledge with fervor and some with reluctance, but give it each did.

The solemn pledge had been given, but now with the Duke dead, many of the Normans were opening rejecting the bastard son of Robert the Devil. A resulting twelve-year Civil War erupted throughout the lands of the Norman, a war that gave rise to Robert's bastard son as a warrior-general capable enough to create an **Empire**.

CHAPTER 5

▼

Duke William

As a child William had often seen a vision which others around him could not. It was of a woman with white hair flowing over her white raiment. She would come to him in dreams or in visions and tell him of his future. She would talk to him and tell him what he should do and who he could trust; of how to train and what he must learn. She became a sort of dream world tutor.

William was never afraid of Judith. She had visited him since he was a babe and never spoke harshly nor tried to scare or harm him. To him she was as real as the men and women of his fortress home.

At first he had told others of his dreams, but they did not understand or marked themselves with the sign of the cross whenever he mentioned her. He did not as a youth understand their attitude toward her. The story was told to him and with age came wisdom and finally William grew to understand. That which is not real to others should not be mentioned. The new religionist would never accept his visions as anything but witchcraft and symbols of deviltry. She therefore, was to be a secret mentor, known only to him and his family.

William's life was constantly in peril during his early years and often at night his specter protector would come to him and advise him to move from one sleeping area to another. These nightly moves kept the Norman enemies off balance and the several attempts to assassinate him failed.

Unknown to William, the image also appeared to another child, Alan of Brittany. Alan was the third child of William's aunt Hawise and the ghostly apparition visited him as well. Judith had but two children and Hawise could bear her legacy as well as Robert the Good.

Judith had come to Hawise three times, but each had met with rebuke. She knew of her mother's pact with the Devil and was determined that God's grace would cleanse her of it, for Hawise was a convert of the new Religion. She sought out the robed Christian priest and asked them to exorcise her of the demon spirits of her mother.

In turn Judith visited each of Hawise's children, but only Alan Rufus seemed ready to accept her and her advice. To the others she became only an old dream, one that had repeatedly occurred in the sleep of small children.

The Witch did not want to scare her heirs, so she fled from the minds of those who would not accept her; but the pact had been made and sealed, and she would see it carried through ill regardless of the timid minds of these her heirs.

If her son Robert "the Good" refused to have heirs to carry on their line, then it would have to fall to Hawise, whether she wanted it or not. Judith had given up far too much to fail now. In death, her spirit was allowed to stay earth bound to ensure the fulfillment of the Dark Lord's promise. An **empire** to last a thousand years was promised and it would come to be!

Thus it came that the only person to whom William could speak of Judith with, was his cousin Alan of Brittany, but they had seldom visited each other. However, at the funeral of Richard the two had met and became quick friends. To them was given a gift, a second sight; to each a sense of things around them, which others failed to see.

Alan understood William's visions well, and even said that he had seen Judith in his own dreams. It became a secret shared by these two alone, and it brought them closer together than brothers; though they were often separated for months at a time, each was daily in contact with the other. Judith's dream visits helped, they allowed her to become an intermediary between the boys. If either sought Judith's help with transference of ideas or plans to the other; she would readily relay to them what the other wished. It was a way to communicate, one friend to another, boys who held a sacred trust, a secret only they knew.

At times the boys would let a word slip of what they knew of their cousin's affairs publicly, and the truth of it amazed the households of each of the royals courts. Those who learned of it, thought the boys knowledge of events in the others life a mystic gift, perhaps it was an attachment of their ancient Royal bloodlines. For many of the royal houses claimed the second sight. Alexander the Great had had it, as well as Charlemagne and Julius the Roman Caesar.

Alexander would regularly go into trances in which he was said to be in contact with the Gods. They would advise him in battle and Alexander was never known to have lost a battle.

Charlemagne was also blessed by the Gods and through them had created a Holy Roman Empire in France and Germany. Only through the intervention of the Gods could it have been possible, for many and diverse were the people who swore him allegiance.

Throughout his entire career, soothsayers had advised the Caesar—Julius; and had he listened more diligently perhaps the Ides of March would not have been his final demise, for this too was foretold to him.

Each had thus been guided through the intervention of providence, whether 'twas called soothsayering, witchcraft, gypsy prophecy, or second sight; it was accepted by most of those who practiced the three religions. If it was of benefit, or related to a friend; then it was divine. If it caused evil events, or was the way of an enemy; then it was called a satanic practice. It merely depended on the person.

Richard in his final days had called his Norman Knights together and entrusted the life and titles of his son William to them. Of those who never were to fail him, were his uncle and Arlette's brother Osbern, plus Gilbert of Brionne, who was Richard's second in command and lastly his uncle Eudo the husband of Hawise and father of Alan Rufus.

The drawing of the three was complete. William now had three trusted guardians to watch over him and his **empire,** at least till such time as he could become of age to ascend to the title bequeathed him by his father and necessary for his grandmother's plans to reach fulfillment. For a few years William and Alan were together through the need of Odo to care for William's welfare.

But the Wheel of Time rolls on, and occasionally its weight crushes others beneath its ceaseless motion. In 1040 rebel Norman lords made several attempts to kill the young heir to Normandy. In the struggles Gilbert of Brionne, Eudo of Brittany and Osbern of Seneschal were all killed, but dream vision warnings from his grandmother the witch saved William each time.

It became a topic of discussion throughout France. Many of the folk of the land pointed to the legend of Judith the Witch, and to Robert the Devil for William's miraculous survival. The stories of his escapes added mightily to his growing legacy of invincibility and those who opposed him seldom lived to realize their mistake, but the battle to keep him alive took a heavy toll on those dedicated to its pursuit.

Gilbert Brionne was found murdered outside of the young William's bedchamber. The room had been sacked, but the boy Duke was found safe the next morning curled up in a ball in a corner of the great hall, sleeping soundly, but safe.

A month later, Osbern was also killed in a struggle with would be kidnappers, again outside of William's bedchamber. But Osbern, or someone had managed to sound the alarm before he perished and the plot was foiled again.

The last of the three was a man to powerful to allow armed assassins to deter him, and he foiled yet another attempt. But Eudo of Brittany was found a week later poisoned in the dining hall where he had gone for a late evening goblet of wine. Again William was found safely concealed in the early morning light. No assassin it seemed could touch the charmed boy Duke, even without these, his trusted guardians.

Alan of Brittany came to his own that night also, for Eudo was Alan's father and it left Alan in line for the title to Brittany. He greatly rebuked Judith when next she came to him, for she could have forewarned his father of the dastardly plans of the murderers.

"*Why fair witch did thou not tell of these deeds afore they haped? Did it suit your foul plans for my sire to died so meaninglessly a death." Pray tell me why? Thou sayest ye are watching over me and yet ye let this misfortune fall upon my head?*"

The witch appeared solemn, almost to the point of tears. A specter though, cannot weep, even at her young grandson's plight. Would that tears could fall, she sighed, and then spoke.... "*My soul aches for your lost my child; but alas, I can not foresee things which do not effect my plans for you. I have tried to envision events of the future of the world at large, but the curse of my existence is to see only those, which favor my descendant's fortunes. Would that it were different, but 'tis not.*"

Arlette's other brother, Walter, came to William as a body guard and servant then, but he was no warrior and took to hiding William out with trusted friends whenever he feared another conspiracy was afoot. Almost daily the young heir would be whisked away to the far reaches of his realm. It was an inconvenience to his physical training, but Walter was an excellent tutor of the histories of war and the strategies involved. In these, William became well versed and as time allowed, he also learned of the arts of physical war.

One of the suspected conspirators, Ralph of Wacy, also became a self appointed guardian now, and leader of William's army of retainers. By then William was a 13-year-old teen warrior and unhappy with the murder of his prior trusted guardians, but what could he do. That night his dream protector told him a truth to which he would never forget. She said, *"Patience cures all. Keep your enemies close to hand......or at least within a swords reach."*

Three of William's trusted guardians had been ruthlessly slain, dead by violent means. One of them had been Alan's father, but each had died through the treachery of vassals related by blood to the boy's families. William's protectors had been ruthlessly murdered. Many of their kinsmen thought that they stood to gain if the child Duke of Normandy were to die. Eudo had only been a side effect of those plans, but now both boys had a reason to train, to hate and to become the optimal warrior. Theirs was a mutual will for vengeance upon, and destruction of those who had robbed them of their trusted guardians.

Their dream guide continually quelled their passions; she bade them wait, train for the future and learn, for those responsible for Eudo's death would pay in time. They did bide their time and trained very hard. Theirs was an effort born of hate, with a hunger for revenge; but those around them only saw the quick maturity of these youths. Men with a gift for the sword and a nose for the lessons of ancient battles fought, whether won or lost.

With their development in size and skill, respect for them soon followed. In 1042, William reached his fifteenth birthday and was knighted by the French King, Henry I. The king used this tactic to belay the pending struggle for the lands of this important vassal. The act also anointed him as a man grown, a man capable of handling his on affairs. The knighting came just in time for the most important tournament of the year. It was now time to repay the treachery of Wacy and his allies.

The Fair of Paris was his chance and William prepared for it well. Many regarded Wacy as the best mounted lancer and swordsman in all of France, if not the Continent. Four years in a row, he had won at the King's tournament, each time vanquishing his opponent ruthlessly.

This year was to be no different, except that both Alan Rufus and the youthful Duke of Normandy were entered. Wacy saw this as an open invitation to not only defeat the boy Duke, but to eliminate him without reprisal; for the tournament often ended with the death of one or more of the knights who chose to battle.

The cousins, William and Alan, each wanted to best Wacy, for Judith had made them aware of his treachery in the death of Eudo and William's other trusted advisors. It was common knowledge that their enemy was a master of both the Joust and Sword. However, he rarely would enter more than one style per year, for the effort was too much to compete in both, even for the most avid warrior. Unfortunately the junior combatants were required to enter first, the past champions seeded last. This allowed the past years champions the optimum chance of success. It lay to Wacy's choice, as to which of the cousins would come a chance at him.

Alan Rufus chose the lance and mounted combat as his entry of choice. William picked the sword and hand-to-hand combat. Between the two, at least one, if providence so dictated, would have the chance to meet Wacy on the field of honor.

To the elder champions go the best seeds and to this end Wacy chose the sword and personal battle, for he intended to end the young Duke's life. He had seen William's name listed among the combatants and thus made his choice. He had control of William's army; with the Duke's death he could also claim his title and lands. One quick swish of the sword and an **Empire** was to be his.

William won his first round without effort, clubbing the shield from his opponents grip and forcing his capitulation. Here there was no roar of approval, for the battle ended to quickly, leaving the downed combatant stunned. The contest was also too clearly one sided, although many in the crowd were amazed that the young Duke could have wielded such a devastating blow.

Wacy's first opponent was also hammered down, but no quarter was given. As the vanquished knight lay upon the ground, Wacy cleaved him upon the head until his helmet was rendered asunder and the man blinded. Wacy held his sword aloft in a gesture of victory and walked around his downed kill trying to get the crowd to yell their support; but those assembled held their voices silent, for his was not a chivalrous act.

Wacy in his second and third rounds had continued to wreak vengeance upon the head of his helpless opponents. Each round was quickly over. The second of his contestants had been carried from the field upon a litter and reportedly later died of his injuries. The third escaped with his life, but his sword arm hung uselessly at his side and would probably never be of use to him again.

William also continued to win, though his were more battles of finesse rather than strength; however he held each in equal amounts. He drew out the battles to both gain practice and hone his skills. To Wacy, the Duke was taking to much time and appeared to be struggling, but each time William's contest ended with an exhausted opponent, while the Duke had hardly worked up a good sweat.

Only two contestants now were left to fight for the prize, William and the traitor Ralph of Wacy. The two stood within the circle, swords at ready. Each turned and saluted the King and his entourage. They turned then to face each other. William brought his sword up to his face in the traditional salute of his opponent, but Wacy used the moment to strike. His sword thrust struck William's raised gauntleted arm and numbed it to the core.

William fell back stumbling with the onslaught. A roar of disapproval came from those assembled, but there would be no intervention as both men knew. This was a field of honor, even if one of the combatants himself was honorless. The winner might not be respected, but none would deny his right to vanquish his competitor at any cost.

The Duke caught his self and swung back with his shielded left arm to thwart the next cleave of Wacy mighty sword stroke. The stroke was so strong it made a dent in the Duke's shield and again forced him backwards.

Wacy was smiling beneath his masked face shield. This pup would soon be dead. He, Ralph Wacy, was destined to be the new leader of the Normans nothing could stop him now. He forced the young Duke back farther, looking for an opening in which to end it. His first strike had paralyzed William's sword arm just as he had intended, now to find a chink in his armor, a place for his weapon to bite, to hack, to bleed, to kill this minor player in a man's world.

William knew he was in trouble. He had expected treachery from this old enemy, but he had not thought it would be during the salute, not did he think it could leave him so open for attack. He must find a way to survive long enough for his sword arm to revive.

Wacy raised his sword again to batter down upon the hapless Duke's shield. William used the motion to crouch and bend his legs into a defensive position. Wacy thought William to be crouching in fear, but the Duke had other plans. He shifted his shield to cause Wacy's sword to strike a glancing blow only, then he thrust his legs mightily in an upward motion, striking the open chest plate area of his antagonist with his right shoulder and driving him back.

Ralph of Wacy was raised bodily from his feet by the attack and flung backwards so that his helmet struck the ground first, causing a buzzing in his head. He pushed himself up into an upright position, his head swimming and struggled to his feet. He raised his shield to receive the downswing of William's now revived sword arm. He knew he was injured, his head not right, for there appeared an angel in his view plate floating a few feet above the head of the Duke; a snow white specter in flowing white apparel, its face smiling. Suddenly the smile peeled away to reveal a fearsome image of malice and hate. A look of rage welled up, it suddenly flew straight at him. He raised his shield upward to ward it off, just as William's blade struck down with a terrible blow. The two moves proved disastrous for Wacy, for the upraised shield arm left the opening between armor and underarm open and into this crevice bit William's sword. Arterial blood spurted from the gapping wound that had nearly severed his shield arm.

Wacy fell back to the ground, his life's blood quickly flowing from his wound. The last thing he saw as his eyes clouded over was the mocking smiles of William and his specter protector. Judith was satisfied. Now both William and Alan Rufus could feel avenged.

The two youthful knight cousins clasped hands and looked to the ruined form of Wacy. This part of their revenge was now over. It was time now to finish the job, for Wacy had received help with his subterfuge.

William now set out to play a more personal part in the affairs of his duchy, ever guided by his secret mentor. But his attempts to recover the rights he lost during the anarchy, and to bring disobedient vassals and servants to heel inevitably led to more trouble. From 1046 until 1055 he dealt with a series of baronial rebellions, mostly led by his own kinsmen. Occasionally his lands were in peril of falling. He relied heavily had on Alan Rufus, but also ask King Henry for help. In 1047, the combined Brit, Norman and French forces finally defeated the rebels at Val-es-Dunes, southeast of Caen. The trials were over for now and William had prevailed; and in doing so had learned the ways of war and the right of might. At his side was ever his warrior-general and trusted cousin Alan Rufus. The strength of their arms and their uncanny leadership skills reeked havoc among their enemies. At times it seemed as if the two wings of their army functioned as one mind, or one entity, but with two heads. Pincher movements were enacted with an uncanny precision. Never were they caught unprepared or defenseless. It was as if the gods themselves guided the Norman and Brits every movement.

At the age of 18, William had started to enact his revenge. First he secretly secured the allegiance of many of his father's former soldiers and when he felt that he was strong enough, he had made his move. He had successfully executed the traitor Ralph of Wacy at the tournament and now he would arrest his traitorous men. Those who did not swear loyalty to him would be put to the sword.

Next William went to war with his cousin Guy of Burgundy to reinstate his control of that part of his inheritance. Guy may not have led in the treachery of Wacy's assassination attempts, but he had used the turmoil to claim part of William's lands. With the help of the French king, Henry I, they defeated Guy and forced the rebels to swear allegiance to William. The Duke was fearless in battle and recklessly led his men in each engagement, to the utter dismay of his men and the cautions of his specter protector.

Immediately upon hearing of the change in power among the Normans, other French provinces revolted under the leadership of William of Arques. The count thought that without the leadership of Ralph of Wacy and Guy of Burgundy, his would be an easy conquest of the young Norman's lands.

For four years, William repelled two of the Frenchmen's invasions and then moved forward himself, to push back against these French invaders. Each battle gave William more experience in both tactics and politics. For ten years the battles continued until he finally captured the province of Maine. These French people were at first unwilling to accept William's rule. Thus he quickly followed with the tactics he had used against his Norman enemies, slash and burn. In 1063 William's army ravaged the lands of his enemies and forced the people to accept his rule.

Fear of a devastated land and the death of the combatants, finally allowed William to gain control of his vast new empire. Those who opposed him ended up dead and their lands either destroyed or confiscated. Each time he or his equally adept cousin, Alan Rufus had personally led his forces and exacted his revenge. Now William's **Empire** stretched across the Continent from the English Channel to the Mediterranean Sea, the very heart of France.

William soon learned to control his youthful recklessness. He was always ready to take a calculated risk on campaigns, for an unseen force would caution him where to place his foot and most importantly how to fight the battle. He was not chivalrous in war, for his own kin had taught him that lesson through their actions. A leader must be decisive and fearless in combat. He also learned to show those same qualities in government, for he never lost sight of the objective. First he had re-secured the lands of his father, now to move on to his **Empire**.

The unending passion of their grandmother had helped to bring them this far; but Judith was not the only older female force in Duke William's life. For the one passion that his mother, Herleva, would not let him forget, was his ties to his religion. At present and in the coming future it would be the New Religion of the Christian, for the far-reaching power of the Church could not be denied. William would have to keep the other religions happy to solidify his position, but the new one, at least for now, held the power for his future. Alan however was spared the tedious affairs of state and need for deceitful moves in politics and religion. To him would come the complete leadership of their growing army while William attended to these mundane details.

To accommodate the Church, and his mother Herleva, William made his half brother Odo, the Bishop of Bayeaux in 1049 at the tender age of 16. This move helped to consolidate his control of the local church and kept him in good stead with the Papacy. He used funds from taxes to entice new Monks and scholars to the monastery at Bec. The most prominent of the group was one Lanfranc of Pavia, who was enticed to see himself as a vassal of Duke William, thus further strengthening his ties, and control of the local church.

With the church of France under control and respect for his rule growing in the Vatican, William turned his eyes toward the Angles and their Saxon rulers across the channel. If he were to solidify his plans for control of their lands, he would need an alliance of prominence there. Perhaps he could find a Lady of worth to whom he could marry; a titled Dane of Royal lineage mayhap, one who would give him an even better claim to the throne. But Judith would not have it so, for she had other plans for her grandson. It was not yet time to worry of the lands of the Angles, first a union to solidify his Norman lands, and then an alliance here on the Continent to create an even larger army of vassals for his military conquest abroad.

He would have to find another way to acquire alliances in the Misty Isle, and time was the factor, which led to a solution. The death of the Lady of Kent left her husband in control of a large fief. To the north of Wessex lay his lands and they would fit the bill perfectly. If they did not fall to him in conquest, then an alliance would create a buffer zone between William and the Danes to the north.

William began to formulate this new plan. His half-sister Adelaide might be the conduit. She was comely enough, and the Earl was said to be an older man with taste for younger women. He could marry her to this Earl of Waltherof and Kent. Their union would give William a firm base in the middle of England, should he ever have need of it. The Earl was an ambitious man though, and William knew that in time he would either have to use him or be used by him. That was the way of politics, still the importance now was for a family connection, and this could be an important one.

A contact was made and the union sanctioned. With the tie to the Isle created, William turned his eyes back to the Continent again. There was still work to be done here. He had too much land to control alone and again he looked to his mother's other children.

Robert, Duke William's other half-brother, became the Count of Mortain, a title that William gladly bestowed. As such he would control a large contingency of vassals, who could be called upon to assist the Duke should times make it so. These three, as the specter grandmother of William had decreed, would serve to create an atmosphere more conductive to the creation of his **Empire**. Though William's half brothers were not of her lineage, she would gladly use them in an effort to reach her ultimate goal.

After 1047, William began his move to spread his influence to events outside of his duchy. He did not pretend to fully understand the politics of the future, but Judith had not led him astray as yet. In support of his dues as vassal to Lord King Henry, he fought a series of campaigns against his former friend Geoffrey Martel (the hammer), Count of Anjou. It was a delicate affair, for the specter, Judith, had convinced him not to fully defeat Geoffrey, but only subdue him.

She advised him that this action would serve a three-fold purpose.

(1) It would help protect William's southern frontier from the growing power of the Count of Anjou.
(2) The King would be satisfied that William had faithfully fulfilled his duties as a trusted vassal.
(3) It would leave Geoffrey in position to oppose the King if need be in the future and much more importantly in a position to owe William his gratitude for not destroying him and taking his lands.

This was a stroke of genius, for in essence it would help expand William's influence into the province of Maine without need of occupation forces. A total defeat would have unnecessarily humiliated Geoffrey Martel. He, along with his powerful Duchy of Maine and Anjou, would be needed to assure William's future and Judith's plans for her heirs.

CHAPTER 6

▼

A Queen for a King

In midsummer of 1049, Judith came to William in another dream and whispered her next request. It was time for William to select a bride and produce heirs. He needed to marry and marry a woman strong enough to sire a Dynasty of Kings!

Duke Baldwin V of Flanders was a rising star in the affairs of state and more importantly he had a daughter named Matilda who was of age. The only problem was that she was not interested in William or life at the Norman Court. She professed to be in love with an Anglishman, named Brihtric, but this did not deter the Norman Duke nor his specter grandmother; for affairs of the heart, and the fancies of young maidens could be easily altered, if it was handled in just the right way.

Brihtric was the third son of a minor Lord from an old Mercia fiefdom. As such he had no rights to land or title. He had no interest in the church, for he favored the ladies excessively and had no interest of becoming a Knight, for he had neither the aptitude nor skill. His one viable vocation it appeared was to be a foppish seducer of woman who he hoped would support him in a lavish style of which he had become accustomed.

Rumors from the Isle indicated that he had been run out of nearly every court of the Saxon and Dane lords. Only Brihtric's royal family ties had kept him from the executioner's axe. Now he had moved on to the Continent and his eye had fell upon the dowry of the young Countess of Flanders.

William had also openly courted the short but comely Matilda for some time now. She though, became incensed that her father would consider her marriage to William, when she so clearly proclaimed her love for Brihtric of the Angles.

He was all that William was not. He had style in dress and manner. He whispered sweet words to her and seemed to dote on her every move. He never spent his time practicing the useless arts of war as did William, but instead plied the Lute and learned verse. Sure he had a reputation, but that was just jealous talk of lesser men.

Matilda's father had heard of the transgressions of Brihtric, and he was no fool. He wanted to order the worthless fop from his lands and would appeal to William to offer the knave no rest in all Normandy. A decree could be issued forth and Brihtric expelled from Norman lands. William's allies stretched across the Continent and each in turn could be pledged to refuse the cad access to their courts. However Judith learned of the plan and she feared the overt act would only exacerbate the situation. In her youth, she would have, and had gone to extreme lengths to satisfy her desires. She had no doubts that Matilda would do the same. Care must be taken least a single word or action alter the plans so carefully laid for William and this young Countess of Anjou. For a happy marriage between the Countess and her grandson was on the line. Thus she whispered a revised plan to William, one more dangerous and certainly more devious, but one that would yield the desired result if arranged correctly.

A rumor was started that a rich young heiress to the title of Czar of the Kievian Russ lands was recently widowed. These people were also of Viking descent, and might easily welcome a European Noble of similar bloodlines. A fortnight passed and talk of the Czarette became the buzz of the land and with each telling, as rumors do, the story and her allure both in appearance and fortune grew.

William was privy to Judith's plan and now it was his turn to lend a hand. He called Brihtric to him and told him to either ask for the Countess of Flanders hand or evacuate his lands on penalty of the sword. He said that he knew it would cost him the love of the maiden, but it would be worth the cost to keep her from the disgrace of an affair with a foppish Angle.

Next he approached Baldwin with a request to let Brihtric have audience, but to let his daughter secretly over heard the discussion. Perhaps Matilda's mother would let her stand near at hand. She could even hint that the discussion would be of a proposal of marriage between the two.

Now it was time and the stage set. In the trouble dreams of Brihtric, Judith inserted her plan. He could gain on both ends of this troubled problem if he were to offer a trade to Baldwin. Upon awaking, Brihtric set his own plan in motion. He immediately sent word to the Count of Flanders, announcing that he wished an audience. The trap was set, now if only Brihtric would take the bait.

It was a chancy plan; thought Baldwin, for this yet might backfire on them. If this scoundrel actually asked for his daughter's hand and he refused, William would end up with a most unhappy bride; for Baldwin had already decided that Matilda would wed William and be Duchess of Normandy whether she wished it or not.

A young heart can easily be captured, but just as easily shattered. If this game was to be played, then the deal must be handled just right. But now the cards had been scuffled and the hand was dealt, and it must be played out. On the next day's eve the players were assembled and the plan put into action. Baldwin met Brihtric in the great hall, while Matilda and her mother secretly slipped into the adjoining room. Baldwin knew they were in place, for he heard a slight creak as the door edged open, just at the moment Brihtric was shown in. The young page that brought Brihtric quickly fled leaving the two alone. All at Castle Flanders knew of the Count's hate for the Angle and none wanted to witness the carnage they expected him to heap upon Brihtric. The Angle sauntered forth, approaching the Count with confidence, but quickly stopped when the Count commanded.

"*Well be quick with it,*" gruffly spoke Baldwin. "*I agreed to this meeting, but I'll not allow it to take all night. Speak you mind.*"

Matilda held her breath. Now was the moment. Her mind was a whirl of Ideas, ways that Brihtric could confess his undying love and win the admiration of her father. It was at last possible that her daydreams would come to fulfillment, for if her father had even agreed to hear Brihtric, and then perhaps there was a chance for them. All her Anglo-Saxon love had to do was ask for her hand.

Brihtric cleared his throat. This was the moment when fortunes are made he thought. True he had been pushed from nearly every court in Europe, but in many cases he had made off as a bandit with ample funds received from either husbands or as here, from fathers. He never got rich, but it was always enough to survive till the next quest. Now, he thought, it was the turn of the rich and powerful Count of Flanders to pay, and he would make it as painful for him as possible. For he truly despised these husbands and fathers who would readily give up funds to save the feelings and reputation of their silly women.

"I wish to make a proposal," he began.

Matilda's heart fluttered with expectant joy. She looked around at her mother to see how this news would meet her. Her mother's face was strangely a mask of none emotion, neither joy nor fear. It was as if she had not heard Brihtric's pledge and still waited for him to begin.

"I know you are aware of my interest in your daughter and she in me," he said and then paused for effect.

With Brihtric's words, Baldwin stiffened and acted as to reach for his sword, which normally swung from his hip; but on this occasion, was not present, only a leather pouch swung from it place now. However the gesture was not entirely wasted on Brihtric. He paused searching for the right words before continuing.

"I know how you feel about me and my tryst with the fair Matilda," he began, *"therefore I wish, as I said to make a proposal......funds and transport to the land of the Russ, and the city of Kiev, in return I pledge my permanent absence from Matilda's life! After all, to me she is merely a meal ticket, whether here with her or far away with your funds. She is a ticket that I feel I can cashier at will. There is nothing you can do save kill me, and that would only make her hate you more and rile the ire of my family in the Isle. However if funds were available up front—"* He left the rest unsaid.

Matilda's mouth, which had slowly lost its smile, now fell open and then her eyes glazed over, and tears swelled their orbs. She turned and buried her face in her mother's shoulder and was quickly led away. Her mother was quick to remove her from the room, least some new word give her renewed hope. Matilda in her distress was glad to go, so that she would no longer have to hear her lover's betrayal. How could he have spoken so? How had she fallen for his lies and manipulation? She broke into a study torrent of sobs and clung tightly to her mother, as they moved toward the comfort of Matilda's rooms.

Baldwin's face had been one of stern controlled anger, but now it turned to a smile. For he had heard the soft gasp from behind the door of the adjacent room when Brihtric had made his request. He also noted that it was closely followed by the closure of that same door.

Baldwin took the leather pouch from his waist and threw it to Brihtric. Then he called for his squire and pointed at the Angle. He said, *"See that he safely makes it to the border of my lands. Turn him over to Duke William's man for the next leg of his journey. Tell the Duke's man to make sure he never returns to the land of Flanders."*

A month passed and the young Countess was continually in retreat. But the Wheel of Time and the affairs of state must move on and a meeting was arranged of the families of Duke William and Count Baldwin in which the arrangements of a betrothal were made. A royal gala was planned in which the marriage would be announced.

The party was an affair of state and most of the area Royals were in attendance. Succulent roast pig and goat were served with fresh fruit and an ample supply of the rich wine of Flanders. Talk was of war and treaties, births and deaths; the common news of the far flung provinces of which they knew. Jugglers and Minstrels performed during lulls in the conversations until the Count Baldwin of Flanders sounded his words for quieting of the revelry. He had an important announcement to make.

Baldwin arose from his seat at the head of the table and waved his hands for silence. *"Friends, fellow Royals, loyal Knights and beautiful ladies, I bit you welcome." We assemble here to renew our common pact of mutual defense and to rejoice in the good fortune presented to us by the gods. We must celebrate the bounty of our fields and our women's wombs."* He paused for a riotous uproar of agreement. *"For we have received an abundance of both."* Again there was an uproar of agreement. *"With that in mind,—my Countess and I would like to announce the betrothal and coming marriage of our child Matilda, to our Lord Duke William of Normandy."*

With the announcement, a continuous uproar resounded throughout the hall. Baldwin raised his goblet of wine and saluted those present, letting his eyes follow from one to another around the assemblage. William was smiling and also toasting the arrangement, but the newly betrothed Matilda was no longer at the table. With the announcement, Matilda had fled the room, her mouth pouty and her eyes filling with tears. William took note and followed, pausing only long enough to drop the ornate pouch of gold in Baldwin lap, one that Baldwin recognized as that given weeks ago to the foppish Brihtric.

Matilda's mother, the Countess rose to follow, but Baldwin stayed her with his arm. It was now up to William to comfort their child, or else the arrangement would never endure happily.

William caught up to his future bride in the garden near where his steed stood hitched awaiting his return. With long strides he easily reached her and spun her around in her tracks, to stay her flight. She recovered, her face still a mask of tears and slapped him, and then uttered between her sobs, "*I would rather become a Nun than the wife of a Norman Bastard*".

William was not prepared for her venomous onslaught. In his rage, William grabbed her and struck her across her tear stained face. She struggled to pull free, the effort tearing the bodice of her gown. The force of his retribution stunned her and she was immediately ashamed for her unthoughtful words. She grabbed the material of her bodice together to cover her ample breast, before falling weeping to the ground again.

William took in the scene before him, and then turned his eyes from the silky whiteness which shown at him. He was disgusted that he had let his rage get the best of him. He quickly mounted his steed, which was still tethered near the garden. He was prepared to leave, but instead whirled his horse in a tight circle, then glared at the fallen Matilda. Her eyes were red and the flood welled continuously up in tears. From his recent efforts, the amorous betrothal, or from her rejection by her Angle lover he knew not, but his words cut her to the quick.

"*Bastard, I might be, but until tonight I had always been a gentleman. To you my dear, I have offered an Empire and my eternal love. I had sought out a maid whom I would make Queen, and instead found you. Frivolity is not a trait that endears me. I want not a coquettish concubine as does your foppish Angle, but a regal Lady with enough fortitude, grace and stamina to help rule a land and sire future kings. Fail me and yourself in this endeavor, and yea shall have neither!*"

His words arrested her tantrumous mood, but the force with which he delivered them captivated her. Strange thought Matilda, never had she seen him so wrought with passion. She had heard others refer to him as handsome and virile, but she had never seen it till now. He looked so tall, so strong, so much a man as he rode away, his back stiff and straight, his steed prancing. Suddenly she felt a heat growing in her. Where she had been indignant, now she was enthralled and at the same time despairing, that indeed she may have lost something which she would forever regret. William must now see her as some kind of spoiled child!

Brihtric had no title, nor had he ever offered marriage. The Angle had played her for a fool, and perhaps that was exactly what she was, she thought. Now she had slapped the face of the most eligible man in the known world. Here was a man who had not played silly games, but been forthright in his ardor for her. Pray to the Gods, Matilda thought, that it be not to late.

Baldwin, an imperial vassal with a lineage back to Charlemagne, was in rebellion against the Western Emperor, Henry III of France. An alliance with Duke William would strengthen both allies, but could also cause some few other problems, for the new alliance would put William at odds with the King. To both he and William it was worth the trouble though, and the marriage went forward, luckily without protest from the now much docile and repented Matilda. The French King however was much disturbed by the growing power of both Count and Duke. The union of their two families would not be good for the Kingdom of France. War was an option, but in that he might lose. There must be other options. He would therefore call in all his markers in an effort to split the two. Perhaps the growing power of the church could be of use.

The Pope, Leo IX agreed to help. So in support of the Emperor, Henry of France, the Pope condemned the marriage as incestuous. True enough the two were cousins, though it was a distant connection and hardly worth noting. The world of politics though removed all stops.

'Twas said all was fair in love and war, and if a rift could be made between William and Baldwin then the Emperor would have a better chance of winning his constant struggles for control of all the lands of France, Norman and Flanders alike. Perhaps in this particular case, love and war were intertwined, and the division of one might forestall the other.

At the Council of Reims in October the Pope, in support of the King of France, made his decree. The marriage was declared incestuous, but William was not to be so easily dissuaded. He instead, listened to his ghostly advisor and married Matilda before the end of the year of 1053. Judith had convinced him that the Pope's objections were merely temporary, and they could with guarded guile easily repair the damage.

The wedding was the greatest celebration ever held in the lands of Flanders and Normandy. Though it may have been entered into timidly, in time the two became an amorous couple, renowned for their love and mutual respect. Now

William's Royal lineages were tied even closer to those of the old **Empires** and the scene was now set for the birth of a totally new one.

Judith was satisfied with the marital arrangement, now for her plan of reconciliation with the powers of the Papacy and the Western Emperor Henry. All alliances, including these two, must be firmly in place for her important future plans to succeed.

First Judith's voice whispered to William of Pope Leo's desire to create two monasteries at Caen. Through shrewd maneuvering and wise use of his tax receipts, William was able to convince the Pope of his penance. He did so by ordering the construction of these monasteries. This led the two to make a new mutual support agreement to one another. The Pope's previous objections were repealed. It seems it had merely been a misunderstanding of the true lineages of the two and now the Pope wholeheartedly supported the union. The Papacy now rejoiced in this Holy union. For in times of need, as Christian leaders of the World, they could together direct the affairs of the French people; through the gathering of riches for the church that would glorify the existence of God.

At last events were well in hand. Through guided diplomacy by Judith of her grandson William, there was now an entire continent owing assistance to Duke William. Brittany through marriage with his Aunt Hawise; Flanders through William's marriage to Matilda; Maine through guarded conquest; Anjou through mutual support treaty with Geoffrey Martel; King Henry of France—with William as his vassal, and lastly with Pope Leo IX through William's financial support of the Church.

Alliances were to be the backbone of William's new Empire building strategy, especially during these early years of his **empire**. William had not forgotten his other obligations to his Grandmother's desire—heirs for the throne. For no future dynasty could exist without heirs. To fulfill this requirement of Judith's plan for him, he and Matilda had thus far sired four sons and a daughter.

William was now a noted Christian leader of his **empire** due to his careful cultivation of the Church, but Judith did not wish that he should forget the other religions; for an Emperor must be accepted by all his subjects not just the Christian, and to be accepted by the people of a faith, one must understand the basics of that faith. To that end, in her dream visions, Judith would tutor William in each of the major faiths, as well as of his own heritage and the Viking lore of the first man.

"First there was nothing......The North Star of the Heavens and that of the Southern Cross joined together and made a Frost-Giant and called it <u>Ymir</u>. Ymir created other giants who ruled over the creatures of the white shadow, which spread across the night sky of the heavens."

"In time a Cow was created to feed the giants of the heavens. This was at a time when the earth was still covered with ice. From the cold of the heavens and the warm blood of the slaughtered cow came a new Giant, <u>Bur</u>, who had three sons. These four killed the first giant Ymir and used his hot blood to warm the frozen world below, which in turn released its' waters to also create the earth's seas. His lifeless body became the dry lands and his skull created the mountains that rose toward the heavens.

Bur's first son was <u>Odin</u>, the Lord of Valhalla. He and his brothers created the first men, from whom all mankind sprang."

Judith paused and watched for William to absorb her words, then finished by saying, *"You my child, will be as Odin! From your loins will spring a Nation and an Empire. One that shall be ruled over by your spawn for a millennium and beyond."*

William took her words to heart and set out to sire a family to be proud of. Matilda was his one true love, and to her he held in all fidelity. He vowed that no illegitimate heirs would he create to confuse his lineage, nor would he forsake the sacred vows of his Christian wedding. Never would anyone proclaim a child of his, a 'Bastard'. A name he had been forced to endure during his early years of struggle to become the rightful heir of Normandy.

William's first son, he named for his father Robert, a.k.a The Devil. The second for his grandfather and dream advisor's husband he named Richard. The third was named for himself—William, and was easily christened by his flaming red Viking hair as 'Rufus'. His fourth and last son was named Henry in support of his ties to the French throne. One girl child was named Adele, and even at an early age was dedicated to the house of his Aunt Hawise of Brittany. For Judith wished her lineage to transcend and encompass all details of the future Monarchy of the New Empire which William would create. Adele would marry into the family of Judith's other closely supervised grandchild, Alan Rufus of Brittany. Not to Alan himself though for they were to closely related, and Alan was too much her senior. Perhaps it should be one of Alan's nephews or cousins. But there was time enough to decide later, for now William was still virile and Matilda very fertile. In all William and Matilda had nine children, of who seven survived........'Twas enough, enough to ensure heirs for a future **Empire.**

CHAPTER 7

▼

Alan Rufus of Brittany

Throughout the years the Witch had appeared to William and his closest allies warning them of problems ahead and directing them in battle, as well as diplomacy, always to victory with an eye to a future **empire**.

William was not her only grandchild or project though, for her daughter Hawise was also a possible source of empire. Hawise, unlike Robert, a.k.a the devil, was not afraid to either sire children or produce heirs. She believed that if curse there be, it would reside in her male counterpart and not fall to her. For after all, she was just a woman without the hope of holding the reins of **empire.**

Without worry of demon curses, she would bring forth eight male children to her Brittany home. But unbeknownst to her, Judith had her eye upon each as they entered into the world and grew toward manhood. She carefully evaluated them, each in turn for the potential leadership the family would need if her dreams were to ever reach fulfillment.

Geoffrey was the eldest and an able statesman, well spoken and refined. Hawise foresaw a different future for him than had Eudo. When young the boys aptitude for war was tested and Alan Rufus easily outshined his older brother Geoffrey. Brian was a different matter; he was an outstanding swordsman and at an early age was able to defeat his younger brother Alan Rufus in their daily forays. With time though came a change, for Alan grew into an exceptional force in the matter of arms. Whether sword, lance or mace, it mattered not. He exceeded all the young men of court including Brian. True Brian was a close second, but not in Alan's class, for Alan it seemed was imperious to attack, knowing were to strike and when to defend at all times. It was as if he was charmed.

Alain Niger (the black), William, Richard, Ribald and Stephen, each also were taught the skills of war and learned their lessons well. But theirs lacked that crucial element that made them truly exceptional. Of all his brothers, Brian was the closest in camaraderie, but the youngest Stephen was the one to whom Alan felt most protective. Perhaps had he had children of his on this would not have been so, but the fates were to be different. In a future time Stephen was to become Alan's heir apparent.

Alan Rufus (the Red) was the third child of Hawise, and therefore grandson of Witch Judith. Through the demonstration of marshal skills, poise and assurance, his was the land of Brittany, to hold in title for his life's span, a noble and an important one indeed; but Judith had far greater plans for his life. Through carefully planning, he could be the backup heir to the **empire** she had so carefully set about to capture. His family, through him, would take a lion's share of the spoils of any future conquest. Therefore they must be closely tied to the new royal family just in case the Gods again broke their covenant with her and struck out against her favorite, William.

Alan's father Eudo had been a guardian of William's in the early days of his reign as duke of Normandy. The treacherous coup by the other Norman Counts had left Eudo dead, not by a sword thrust deep within his chest, as befitted his warrior heritage, but by the trickery of poison. As he fell, his sword had rattled to the stone floor, there to be found by Alan and his mother. Then and there, the youthful Alan had vowed to someday claim the sword and reap vengeance upon the cowardly murderers of his father. It was a blood oath by a Viking child. One that he had placed to the God of Thunder and the Protector of Mankind, Thor; and as such must be answered in due time.

Judith felt the pain of her grandchild, as he grew up without a father. She had made forays into his sleep throughout his life, singing sweet lullabies at first, and then becoming his advisor in the war games of a child's play. Though still youthful, she made a promise to the stricken child. In time, Alan would grow to wield the mighty sword of his late father to slash the throat of the vicious traitors who had conspired to take his sire's life. Time was their ally and time they had; for both William and Alan were still lads. They were boys who could be taught and trained, drilled and practiced to become the greatest fighters and leaders of men the world had ever known.

At age ten, Alan began his studies in earnest. His teachers were amazed at the boys thirst for knowledge and his drive to learn the military arts. The campaigns of Julius the Caesar, the exploits of William the Martel, Emperor Charlemagne and Alexander the Great were topics of constant study. Alan absorbed the facts and constantly asked questions of probable tactics and styles of each. The fighting tactics of the Moors of Spain and the ways of the Viking battle-ax were added to his lessons and drilled into his young head. The shield, as protection as well as a weapon with a sharp outer edge to use when needed was also practiced endlessly. The French long sword and Anglish longbow's uses were added as daily lessons. Hours of horse riding while fighting with lance and mace came, and he mastered each in turn as he matured into an able teenage warrior knight. Tempered by hard work, he grew tall and strong. But the long hours of training, which added strength and knowledge of war tactics, never quelled his deep burning desire for revenge. With the years, Alan had become the very image of a mighty Viking warrior. His prowess in strength and talent with weapons soon out paced the ability of his teachers to instruct. Though only a teen in years, he was becoming a man of vast ability in a world that could be controlled by men such as he, men of strength and wisdom.

The Witch watched his development closely and guided him when he needed it. She never let him forget the treacherous death of his father and the coup, which took the rest of his cousin William's trusted guardians.

Each time Judith made a dream visit, he would ask *"when?"* Each time her response was, *"Not yet, be patient, practice; for the time is coming and you must be ready."*

The sword of Eudo hung prominently above the main chair in the dining hall of Castle Brittany. Alan and his mother had removed it from the floor at Castle Normandy near to the hand of the poisoned Eudo. Since then it was kept safe as a symbol of the treachery of the world and their enemies. To the heir of Eudo who showed the greatest ability in arms would come this symbol and all it entailed.

The wheel of time rolled on and Brian and Alan come to be seen as the true viers for its hilt. But Alan's was the greater drive and even Brian came to readily recognize the true leadership of the redheaded giant who was his younger brother.

Each day before darkness gave way to the cold, pale dawn, Alan would be up, sitting on the stone battlements of his Brittany fortress home. Others might sleep, but his oath and desire for its fulfillment would not let him stay abed, so each day before the first stirrings of the Castle and its grounds, he would be here meditating and preparing. The only sound that would disturb the early morning quiet was the splashing of the swift flowing waters of the stream, which flowed round the castle's southern border. As he had so many mornings before, he would raise his father's sword to the spreading rays of the morning sun and pledge that revenge would not be long in coming. He would silently pray to the gods of the three religions to give him strength, and to Judith for guidance in his quest.

Soon the first stirrings of the day would bring forth the men who were to serve as Alan's sparring partners. A handful of men dressed in armor would venture out of the Knights barracks and take position around Alan. Each in turn would attack him with wooden sword, lance or mace, weapons designed for practice or mock fights. The battles had grown with the years. At first there would be but one; then in the latter years, it changed to two, then three. Now with the Red headed warrior near full-grown, a full half-dozen of the Knights would assault him and try to get his better.

They would circle him taunting with faints to draw him to them, but then to step back and let another try to stick him from the rear or flank. It had become an exciting early morning game for the retainers of Brittany, one in which all wanted to play. Occasionally someone would get hurt in the mock battles, but it was never Alan, for he seemed to always anticipate their moves even before they themselves knew what form their attacks would take.

As a child, these men would take it easy on the youthful heir to Brittany, but now each hoped for the new Earl to take it easy on them, and he did. Theirs was a camaraderie of friends with a deep affection for this hulk of a man-child whom they had trained. Each took pride in his prowess and would point out to the others that Alan had used one of their own tricks in his parry or thrust that day. The other boys of the Brittany clan, Alan's brothers, would take part at later times of the day, each to train in a style relevant to his age and degree of expertise; for the training was ever a necessity of life in these times of treachery. Men of destiny must be forever diligent.

Alan's chance came when he heard of the tournament of Paris. It was a time for the Knights of France to show their abilities and win the approval of their lords. William sent word via Judith, that at last the time had come for the two to begin their revenge. It must start with the defeat of Ralph of Wacy, suspected conspirator and murderer of Eudo, Alan's father. Wacy at present held control of William's army and if he could be dealt with at the tournament, then the transition would be easier for William, and Alan would at last have his revenge.

The Fair of Paris was their chance and the young Knights prepared for it well. Many regarded Wacy as the best mounted lancer and swordsman in all of France, if not the Continent. He considered himself a champion without equal. Four years in a row, he had won at the King's tournament, each time vanquishing his opponent ruthlessly. His fame on the Continent was thus well renown. It was up to the cousins to make sure that this, the fifth year, would be his last. Fate must reshuffle the deck and deal him a new hand. One of the royal cousins, Alan or William, must meet him in this year's tournament, for the final moment must belong to them, the last face he saw one of theirs. It was only just and right!

To Wacy this year was to be no different from any other, except that both Alan Rufus and the youthful Duke of Normandy were entered. Wacy saw this as an open invitation to not only defeat the boy, but eliminate him without reprisal; for the tournament often ended with the death of one or more of the knights who chose to battle.

The cousins, William and Alan, each wanted to best Wacy, but it was common knowledge that their enemy was a master of both the Joust and Sword. However he rarely would enter more than one style per year, for the effort was too much to compete in both, even for the most avid warrior. Unfortunately the junior combatants were required to enter first, the past champions seeded last. This allowed the past years champions the optimum chance of success, but the cousins thought it left it up to chance as to which would eventually face Wacy.

Alan Rufus chose the lance and mounted combat as his entry of choice. William picked the sword and hand-to-hand combat. Between the two, at least one, if providence so dictated, would have the chance to meet Wacy on the field of honor. As Alan's second and serving duty this day as squire, was his brother Brian. The two took time to prepare horse, armor and shield. Alain Niger, as Alan's younger dark-haired brother was called, performed similar duties for Duke William.

Alan drew a knight from the province of Alsace in the first round. He was an impressive looking knight with dark eyes and hair to match, a stark difference from the redheaded Brit giant he faced. They faced each other to take each's measure, and then saluted the King, who was watching closely from the grand stands. With a gallant salute to each other, they took their places at the opposite ends of the divider fence and prepared for the charge.

With the first lance, both men were struck on the near shoulder, breaking their lances. Alan and his opponent both came near falling from their steeds, but each in the end held on to the cheers of the crowd. Brian, (who served as Alan's squire) as he handed Alan the second lance, advised him that his opponent had dropped his near shoulder at the last moment to deflect Alan's lance from his chest. Perhaps if Alan held lower, then brought the lance up at the moment of impact, he might still strike the Knight's chest.

On the second charge, Alan won easily, unhorsing and disabling his opponent without permanent injury. The move had worked just as Brian had suggested, his lance had struck the knight dead center of his heavy armor and the force ripped the knight from his saddle bodily. The downed knight struggled to his feet, staggered for a moment and then bowed to Alan, an act that drew a roar of approval from the assembled crowd.

The second and third rounds came and went. Each a much tougher battle than the last, for only the best advanced to the next round. In the second round, Alan lost the temporary use of his right arm, when a glancing blow of his opponent's lance wedged under his armor and ripped a deep tear in the muscle on the first lance. Brian suggested he retire, but Alan was not ready. Somehow providence had allowed him to survive, surely he was meant to continue. He again used the move that he had used on the first opponent, and with his second lance he vanquished this opponent with a quick thrust upward of its tip just as it made contact with his opponent's shielded arm. The act unceremoniously de-horsed the knight giving Alan the sure victory.

The third round was also a win, but one which was devastating for Alan's steed. The first lance and second lances each came out even with both knights breaking their lances upon the other's armor without serious injury. In the third and final lance, the woozy challenging knight dipped his lance just as Alan made contact with his chest plate. The act unseated the knight, but Alan's horse received the full force of the deposed knight's lance. It splintered upon the steed's armor, but several pieces of its wood entered the mighty charger's chest. At the end of the round he stood blowing hard with a torrent of blood running from his chest wound.

Now it came to the finals with Alan's left shoulder deeply bruised and slightly bleeding, his faithful sorrel charger injured with a splintered lance embedded in his left foreleg. Alan looked to the steed's injury, removing the splinters carefully and sent Brian for water and ointment.

Alan knelt beside the injured animal and reflected on the day's events. With a sigh Alan decided there was nothing to be gained here. His enemy was not these valiant knights, and certainly not the freshly mounted one at the other end of the field. He had made it to the finals, as had his worthy opponent. He looked to his faithful steed, the blood dripping from his wounded foreleg. Brian returned and both again looked to the wound. Was the contest important enough to lose this valued steed? There was a short conference and a decision made. Alan removed his helmet and bowed to concede amid a timid outburst of applause. The red-headed Brit had come in second in the Joust.

Alan and Brian entrusted the care of the charger to a Druid healer and moved to the area where the personal battles of sword were fought. They arrived just as the final rounds had started. Alain Niger (serving as his Squire today) stood at William's corner and it was to here that they quickly gravitated.

Alain Niger immediately offered a update of the tournament to this point......

"Wacy in his second and third rounds had continued to reek vengeance upon his helpless opponents. Each round was quickly over. The second of his contestant had been carried from the field upon a litter and reportedly died of his injuries. The third escaped with his life, but his sword arm hung uselessly at his side and would probably never be of use to him again."

"William also continued to win, though his are more battles of finesse rather than strength; however he appears to hold each in equal amounts. Our cousin is a man of varied and vast abilities, yet he seems to hold himself in check. He intentionally draws out the battles. He says it is to both gain practice and hone his skills.

I have heard it said that Wacy thinks the Duke is taking to much time and appears to be struggling. But it is not so, each time his contest has ended with an exhausted opponent, while the Duke has hardly worked up a good sweat. Wacy has yet to see William's might."

Ralph of Wacy was glad the youthful Duke had made it to the finals. Now it was time for him to end the luck of this bastard child of Richard's. The two stood within the circle, swords at the ready. Each turned and saluted the King and his entourage. They turned to face each other. William brought his sword up to his face in the tradition salute to his opponent, but Wacy used the moment to strike. His sword thrust struck William's raised gauntleted arm and numbed it to the core.

William fell back stumbling with the onslaught. A roar of disapproval came from those assembled, but there would be no intervention as both men knew. The King would not allow it. This was a field of honor, even if one of the combatants himself was honorless. The winner might not be respected, but none would deny his right to vanquish his competitor at any cost.

The French King had personally knighted William. To intervene would be to admit that the boy was not yet ready to rule Normandy. The King was no fan of Wacy and even feared his ambition, but intervention would not solve his problem, just create more. If William was to be a true Norman Duke, he must prove it here.

The Duke caught himself and swung back with his shielded left arm to thwart the next cleave of Wacy mighty sword stroke. The stroke was so strong; it made a dent in the Duke's shield and again forced him backwards.

Wacy was smiling beneath his masked face shield. This pup would soon be dead; even now he shrunk from combat. He, Ralph Wacy, was destined to be the new leader of the Normans nothing could stop him now. He forced the young Duke back farther, looking for an opening in which to end it. His first strike had paralyzed William's sword arm just as he had intended, now to find a chink in his armor, a place for his weapon to bite, to hack, to bleed, to kill this minor player in a man's world.

William knew he was in trouble. He had expected treachery from this old enemy, but he had not thought it would be during the salute, not did he think it could leave him so open for attack. He must find a way to fight back, to shield himself, and to survive long enough for his sword arm to revive.

Wacy raised his sword again to batter down upon the hapless Duke's shield. William used the motion to crouch and bend his legs into a defensive position. Wacy thought he was crouching in fear, but the Duke had other plans. He shifted his shield to cause Wacy's sword to strike a glancing blow only. As Wacy's sword slipped from his shield to cleave the ground, Alan saw his chance. He bunched his muscles, and then he thrust his legs mightily in an upward motion, striking the open chest plate area of his antagonist with his right shoulder.

Ralph of Wacy was raised bodily from his feet by the attack and flung backwards so that his helmet struck the ground first, causing a buzzing in his head. He pushed himself up into an upright position, his head swimming and got one foot under him in an effort to struggle to his feet. He raised his shield to receive the downswing of William's now revived sword arm. He knew he was injured, at least temporarily. It would now be his turn to use defensive ploys till his head cleared. His head was not right, this much he knew, for though he had often seen sparks of light when struck on his helmet, there now appeared an angel in his view plate floating only a few feet above the head of the Duke. This was something new. It was a snow-white specter in flowing white apparel, its face full of rage.

As Wacy stared, the flesh seemed to disintegrate from her skull in savage imagery, as it also suddenly flew straight at him. He raised his shield upward to ward it off, just as William's blade struck down with a terrible blow. The two moves proved disastrous for Wacy, for the upraised shield arm, which he had used to deflect the spirit, left the opening between armor and underarm agap and into this crevice bit William's sword. Arterial blood spurted from the gapping wound that had nearly severed his shield arm.

Wacy fell back to the ground, his life's blood painting the ground red as it flowed from his wound. The last thing he saw as his eyes moved around the assemblage and started to cloud over, was the mocking smiles of William, his specter protector and three sons of Eudo the former Count of Brittany. Now both William and Alan Rufus could feel the satisfaction of being avenged.

The Tournament of Paris had ended in success, for Wacy lay dead at the hands of William. Both young Royals had now proved themselves valiant men, men to be reckoned with in a world controlled by fighting men.

The four young knights clasped hands and looked to the ruined corpse of their traitor kinsman. He had tried to play a game that even the hale of heart had found untenable, now the cousins would begin to gain control of the rest of the lands to which William had been bequeathed. This moment of revenge felt sweet, but there was still much left to do.

With William as Duke Overlord and Alan Rufus as his general, they set out to reclaim the lost lands of the Norman dynasty. In 1046 they began to deal ruthlessly with all sorts of rebellion. From former Norman Land-Barons to the alien lands that touched the Norman Empire, they fought a steady nine-year war. The worst of it was during the first two years with thousands of the combatants killed and still more wounded beyond the ability to continue their fight.

Ever the statesman, as well as warrior, William began to rebuild his army from a carefully coerce coalition. The French forces supplied by King Henry, to form a strong union of fighters, joined Alan's Brittany forces and William's Norman men. These additions slowly turned the tide and the lands of the Norman were restored. However it took nine long years of almost constant battle to solidify the Norman lands, but now those lands stretched again from the Misty Isles Channel in the North to the old Roman Sea in the south. The last of their enemies fell at Val-es-Dunes, just southeast of Caen.

During those years, William often returned home to help rear his children and sire more, as did Alan's brothers. Alan however, stayed in command of the ever-fighting armies. There need be someone always in control and ready to move at a moments notice to the far reaches of the **Empire,** and that time and time again fell to Alan. He was the only other man to whom the lands could be trusted and the only other man to whom their Specter Protector would communicate, a necessity which deprived him of time for a family of his own.

Alan's brother, Geoffrey took control of Brittany and governed it well, for he was an able statesman. To each of the other brothers came a time to fight and learn, and to assist their giant redheaded sibling. But for Alan it was a steady unending task. To them it was only temporary, a necessity for learning the arts of war.

After the fall of Wacy at the Tournament of Paris, Alan and William's combined forces had moved on their cousin Guy of Burgundy. The battle was brutal with heavy losses on both sides. But in victory the Brit and Normans allowed those vanquished to join the forces of the victors. It was a pattern that followed with each win. The defeated were given a chance for a new life, if only they would swear their allegiance to the new power in the land. In this way the regal authority of William grew, and the ranks of warriors in Alan Rufus army also swelled proportionally. It would take a man to maintain control of these new alliances, and that job also fell again to Alan.

William of Arques was the next to rebel, but he also fell to the growing force of Norman and Brit Knights, and in time so did the lands and forces from the Provinces of Maine, William's Empire continued to grow.

The Gods must at times have a sense of humor or at least a wish to throw the whims of fortune some ironic twists, for there appeared a shipwreck upon the

Norman coast and from its wreckage waded ashore a man who would be a major force in the trials of William's climb to **Empire**.

Harold Godwinson the brother of the Queen of Wessex in the Misty Isles of the Anglo-Saxon had come to the court of the Normans. He had survived a shipwreck in the Channel and was found upon the shores of William's lands. The maturing Duke had taken him in and with time had also taught him the methods of war. Harold learned quickly and even became an ally serving as an officer in the army of the Norman, French and Brit alliance for a while. His was a desire, if not need to learn the arts of war, and who better to learn from than the mighty redheaded Brit and his cousin the young Duke of Normandy and their allies.

Brian found something not quite right about Godwinson when paired with him on Alan's flank. But it was not a definite thing, nothing to hold on to; still he thought it noteworthy and mentioned it to Alan. Alan was not a man to take his lieutenant's words lightly, especially his own brother Brian's, but William had placed Godwinson and it was not for Alan to question William's orders. He advised Brian to not mention it again, but to keep a careful eye upon the Saxon. The Saxon must have felt their distrust, for with both Alan and Brian watching Godwinson's every move, it was not long before he found an excuse to sail for home.

The wheel of time was forever turning and suddenly it was 1063 and still Alan led the armies of the Normans. In the sixteen years since his pact with William to restore the Norman Empire while at the Tournament of Paris, Alan had never rested, nor had he taken time to woo, find or marry a woman of his heart. At times he thought of those things, which he had missed out on, a family of his own, children and a home. But Judith's constant dream visions and the never ending wars over acquiring new lands or trying to hold old ones were just to demanding.

His two older brothers had married and sired children, as had the two younger than he. In time so would Ribald and Stephen, that was a given, but for Alan Rufus it seemed there was time only for blood and war. He was now a man of his mid thirties. A time when most were turning over the arts of war to younger, more vital men; but still Alan led, for now it was all he knew. His brothers had each found their nitch in the world, and perhaps so had he. To fight and lead men in battle was his art and his life, at least as long as he won. That fortuitously had not been a problem to date, for through shrewd maneuvering and reconnaissance by Judith, he had never lost. Fear of his sword and the reality of his retribution kept his men in line and his enemies at bay.

War, war and more war, Alan's arm and Eudo's sword had soaked the lands with blood till by the mid 1060's there were none left to fight, at least not on the Continent! Those who had not revolted looked gravely upon the remains of those who had, and found solace in being called Norman vassals. So it was that peace settled upon this land, but now it was time to move on, for the Witch's cry could still be heard....

.... *"EMPIRE TO LAST A THOUSAND YEARS!!* ....

CHAPTER 8

▼

Edward the Confessor

Harold Godwinson returned to the land of his Queen-sister, Angland. He had learned much from the tutorship of William, Alan and Brian; so after swearing his oath to William, he sailed for the Misty Isles and reported to his brother-in-law King Edward the Confessor in the Christian year 1064. He had been a part of the vast Brit and Norman army and had seen what a power the leader of an Empire could wield upon the land. This power appealed to him, and if circumstance should allow, he would seek it out.

Both Norman and Saxon could trace their roots to Denmark's Danes and each of the three could lay legitimate claim to the land of the Angles, for former ties intermingled within the bloodlines of all three Royal families. To Harold this fact held promise for his own future.

Edward the Confessor was not an amorous lover, if Harold Godwinson could believe his sister. In private audience with Harold she blamed Edward's lack of sexual interest as the reason for her barren womb, and for her that was the only reason for marriage, to produce heirs for the continuation of her own royal line. If Edward could not provide her with those things, what good was he or any man? As in her self indulgent Godwin family trait, she also implied to Harold that King Edward could easily be replaced, if she was guaranteed a prominent place in any new Kingdom. As a widowed Queen, she would still be accommodated the amenities of Court and could seek out a more amorous mate, perhaps one more handsome, muscular and virile enough to sire heirs.

In the year that Harold had been at the Saxon Court, he had been a constant advisor to his sister's husband, the King. And as such, Harold watched the King closely. He needed to know if his sister's assessment of her husband was correct. Perhaps the King was one of those rare men who favored young boys over women, but Harold soon determined that that was not, at least overtly, the case. It appeared that the King was equally disdainful of both sexes; his interest was for constant confessions to the Church. He would spend long hours alone with the Archbishop of Canterbury in that repentful pursuit.

Harold's knowledge of the affairs on the Continent were of interest and perhaps even invaluable to the King and therefore he kept Harold close, much to the disapproval of the Archbishop. Harold was not sure why, but the Archbishop was distrustful of the two while they were in conference on the affairs of state. Often he had spoken reproachful of their closeness. Harold did not wish to create problems for himself with the Church, for he might have need of its power; and as such often initiated an offer to have the Archbishop present at all of his meeting with the King.

The newly built Abbey of West Minister was to be consecrated on Christmas Day of 1065, by the Saxon King. But King Edward, the Confessor's health had started failing soon after Harold's sister's confession of her true marital status. He, fortuitously for Harold, fell ill the day before the consecration of the Abbey of the West Minister and was unable to attend, much to the distress of the Archbishop. Instead, Edward sent his new trusted advisor Harold, a move that put Godwinson on good footing with the Witan (the Anglish Council of Lords) and the priest of the Christian Church, if not Archbishop Stignand personally.

Edward's health continued to weaken daily if not hourly, and as he lay upon his deathbed Harold entered the chamber. He told his sister Edith, that he needed to speak to the King. She nodded her ascent but made no move to go to the King herself. Harold moved to Edward and looked long upon him. Stignand, the Archbishop of Canterbury had just finished a religious rite, which Harold did not fully understand, but suspected it implied that Edward was not long for this world.

Harold Godwinson's was a strange family, with turbulent tempers and strong desires to attain fortune at all cost. His brother Swein was named for the Norseman King Sweyn. His family affiliations thus assured him a privileged life, but he was a true black sheep even among them. When Swein was twenty-four, he seduced or raped a young Abbess of the nearby Coventry Church and then laughed about it at the taverns along the roads. For this unusual sin, he was exiled, but after extensive political moves was forgiven and returned home. He then murdered his cousin, Beorn over a future heir ship to an Earl's fief in Northumbria. Again, he was exiled and again forgiven, but only on the condition that he did penance in Jerusalem. With the title to the Earldom at stake, he left there walking barefoot in order to show his new piety. However, he died on the return trip near the Greek capitol Constantinople, of a strange fever that racked his body. Some thought it a suspicious sickness, for his brothers did not wish his return. 'Twas said that many pilgrims with influential enemies in Europe had succumbed to similar fevers along this same route.

His father along with his younger brother, Tostig were also thirsty for power and each in turn allowed their ambitions to get them into trouble. They quickly seized the deceased Swein's lands, and pushed for others. This eventually got them in trouble with the Witan. In 1051, the entire family was deported over a blood feud in Dover. Fortunately for them, Harold's sister had previously succeeded in marrying King Edward, and now sat as Queen of the Anglo-Saxons. This had the potential to someday renew their prospects in the Misty Isles. This Godwin daughter had at least reached her desired destiny, but what of the Godwin sons, Harold, Tostig, Leofric, and Gyrth? Each had desires that must be quelled.

Harold now knelt beside the King's bed and reached for his hand. The King's hand came easily to Harold, but it was cold and stiffening to the touch. Harold immediately knew the truth—the King was dead!!

Harold looked to the Archbishop. He was busy consoling the Queen, and had not taken notice. The guards were also distracted. They were watching the growing numbers of dignitaries, mostly of the Witan, who crowded at the door. No one it seemed had noticed. Not one eye had seen the King draw his last breath. All still waited expectantly for some hopeful word. A light began to grow in Harold's mind. Why not? These fools did not know. It could be done.

Harold rose from his knee and leaned toward the King and at the same time saying, "*Yes my Lord. I am here.*"

He dared not look behind him, but he listened carefully for footfalls. None came, but a silence had settled over the bedchamber, as if each of those assembled was trying to hear the hushed tones of what was being said.

Harold leaned closer to the dead King's corpse and continued. *"Sire art thou sure?"*

Harold used his knee to jostle the bed so as to move it, as if the King himself had done so. He grasped the King's hand in both of his and stood there awhile before turning, then announced, *"The King is dead!"*

The Archbishop rushed forward and examined Edward's body. He turned to the Queen and nodded his head, as a solitary tear descended his cheek. Then he bade the visitors leave before he began the final rites.

Harold moved to the Queen, his sister, and kissed her on the forehead before moving into the antechamber among the waiting Saxon Nobles. She raised her head to him and said one word only—, *"Remember!"*

Saunwor the Earl of Wessex spoke and asked, *"What did the King say at the end?"*

"I hesitate to say", proclaimed Harold, *"for I am not sure others heard it."* He had the Lords ears now and he hesitated. Each was looking on with raptured interest. Harold paused for effect, and then said—*"He asked me to take the Crown and rule as only a true Saxon could. He said—all my kingdom I commend to your charge."*

Harold turned and looked back into the bedchamber of the King, as if lost in thought, but his ears were carefully attuned outward. He listened intently for whispers of how the Saxon Lords would take his proclamation, and as he expected there was much talk.

One voice said, *"But what of William and Hardrada?"* Another answered, *"They are not Saxon! We need a Saxon King for a Saxon land. I say good for Harold Godwinson."*

Numerous voices echoed the Lord's sentiments and Harold smiled. It had worked. The Witan (council of lords) would have to meet, but now it was a mere formality.

In the year 1066, on the twelve day of the year, King Edward the Confessor was buried within the newly consecrated church of West Minister Abbey. With the traditions of the time, a cry when forth throughout the land

....................**the King is dead, Long live the King**,.....................

and Harold Godwinson, brother-in-law of Edward the Confessor, was crowned the new King of the Saxons and anointed Ruler of the Land of the Angles and Saxons.

CHAPTER 9

▼

Omens of Doom

Harold had succeeded beyond his wildest expectations. From across the land came word of the support the lords would give for a Saxon King of Angland. Each Lord in turn sent his personal pledge of their support and loyalty. Most were happy that no Norman or Dane would be placed on their throne. No tribute would have to be paid to a foreign King, and more importantly, nor would lands have to be given over to a new Royalty. Privately though, many dreaded what the future would bring. Surely neither the Danes nor the Normans could possibly accept this change of fortunes for Angland, and war must soon come to the land.

Within three days of Harold's Coronation word reached his brother Tostig, who had been exiled in Flanders. Only hours later the news was relayed to Duke William in Falaise, Normandy. The news also soon reached Malcolm the King of Scotland, and it came to King Hardrada of Norway within a week. Each had coveted the Crown of Wessex and title to the Anglo-Saxon union, thus each began to make plans to secure it for themselves.

Tostig was the first to make a move. He petitioned his brother for the lands that he felt should have come to him years earlier. He asked for the Earldom of Northumbria, but Harold was not amiable to his request. His alliances with the Witan were still too fragile and thus he forbade his brother's return to the land of the Angles. With war in the future, now was not the time to stir up descent by transferring lands from one vassal to another. As of yet those lands were still loyal to the Witan and thus to their King. Harold could not afford to shake that tree yet.

In the months that followed both Duke William of Normandy and King Hardrada of Norway also sent emissaries to the Saxon Court. They though each petitioned Harold to resign, for each wanted him to do so in their favor. Each put forth his own claim to the throne based on family lineage and previous alliances, further William claimed Harold had promised his personal support to William for the very throne Harold had usurped.

As expected all offers were rejected, but the petitions themselves gave fair warning to the Lords of the Misty Isles that war would soon be upon them; and with it the time for them to make a decision as to whom they would support. The petitions also gave legitimacy to each of their future plans for invasions, and if successful each one's claim to the crown.

Northern Europe became a boil with men of arms preparing for war. Saxon, Angles, Picts, Celts, Danes and Normans began preparations in earnest, as did Harold's brother Tostig and his cousin Malcolm, King of Scots. It was now, not a question of war, but when and with whom. A Darkness was descending upon the land of Misty Isles and none could tell when or from where would come the light that might restore it again.

William's interest in England was derived from an alliance made in 1002. The Saxon King Ethelred II of England had married Emma, the sister of Count Richard II of Normandy who was William's grandfather. That placed a Norman Queen on the throne of Angland. When the Viking Norwegian Prince Canute invaded and slew Ethelred, he proclaimed himself King. To solidify his control quickly, he also forced a marriage with Ethelred's widow, (William's Aunt) Emma, the Queen. This forced marriage solidified Canute's hold on Angland. After his death, his and Emma's son Hardecanute took the crown. When Hardecanute died unexpectantly, the throne then fell back to the Queen's first son Edward.

Edward was Ethelred II's true son, and a Saxon, but also half Norman. As a child he had been severely abused in creative ways by his conquering Norseman stepfather Canute. To protect his life and future manhood, Emma had sent him to the Norman court for safe keeping from the Viking Anglish King Canute's cruelty.

Therefore, two of the former rulers of England, King Hardecanute from 1040 to 1042 and Edward the Confessor from 1042 to 1066 were William's cousins once removed, through their mother Emma. King Edward and King Hardecanute as children of William's great aunt gave him a royal connection to the throne, as it did equally to Alan Rufus through his mother Hawise. But Alan's wishes and destiny were not for the throne. He foresaw his to be a more subtle connection through lineage to the power behind the throne. Theirs was also a distant relationship through bloodline ties to the monarchy of Denmark. If the fates were kind, and Angland fell to them, then Denmark might also in time be added. It could become a huge **Empire** indeed, one equal to the glories of old Rome or even Greece.

Duke William had met Edward during Edward's exile in Normandy.

When the Dane, Canute, had killed Edward's father, King Ethelred and took his Queen; he had exiled King Ethelred's child. Edward (the future Confessor King of Angland), therefore came to the former Norman home of the new Dane Queen Emma. In those years, as Edward and William had together grown to adulthood in the land of the Normans, William had readily protected his introverted cousin from the childish taunts of the other Norman children; therefore a bond had been created. Judith, in her steady vision for future **Empire**, had guided William to become Edward's champion and thus the groundwork for a mutual support treaty created. Should the need ever arise for either—the pact was now made.

To William it meant a mutual agreement pact of future Empire between the Monarchy of England and Normandy. To all who knew of the pact, it was clear that the Normans would expected some sort of future reward from Edward, for his years of safe harborage. When Edward's marriage produced no heirs, it logically (at least to William) fell to the Normans to produce the next Royal heir to the Misty Isles. Judith had foreseen the possibility of these events and had planned for them,—thus the stage was set.

Now with war at hand, William sought to hedge his bet further. He sent word to one of his vassals in Rome to petition his Holiness, the new Pope Alexander III for help. With the death of Pope Leo IX, William's regard within the church had steadily grown by an amount at least equal to his continued endowments to its treasure vault. The wheels of success had been well greased through the creation of Abbeys and through increased funds allocated to the Church from taxes.

Judith, as a necessity, had ordained these in her long-term plans. Now it was time for William to reap the rewards of these careful and deliberate investments.

Six weeks after the last offer of the Normans for Harold to abdicate, Duke William sent an ominous message to the new King. A monk clothed in dark robes, although not overtly obvious from which faith, appeared at the Saxon court. He had no assembled entourage and was not herald at the gates, but seemed to appear from within the crowd without anyone noticing from whence he came. He carried a crooked staff with the head of a Boar carved at the hilt, a symbol not usually associated with Christian priest. His garb was of a usual enough monk, but something made him stand apart, perhaps it was the stylized Celtic Runes etched in his skin or his aura of power.

The priest waited patiently while Harold spoke to each who wished his audience. Harold had many important guests and wished to appease each; none had been, nor would be turned away this day. One never knew when the very one you anger, could be the one who might have saved the realm; and with war in the wind, Harold needed the good will of all his vassals—rich or poor, Lord, Priest or serf.

When his turn came, the priest brought his staff down with a thud, which stilled those few still remaining within the hall. His message was not loud, but could be heard clearly by all those present, and the strangeness of him made most press harder to hear his words. He spread his arms to bring greater attention to himself and waited for the hall to become totally quiet.

He said, "*I have been sent by my Lord Duke William. He is befuddled at the absurdity of you Harold, who has usurped his crown!.*" With this he pointed his staff toward the raised seat of the King, and waited for effect.

When no opposition came, he continued. "*He has sent me with the message that the whole of the known world will be brought against you and your Saxon Lords, if you do not abdicate. He also proclaims that the Gods of the three religions are all on the side of the Normans. He has predicted that if you, Harold, do not abdicate in his favor, that is to say Duke William's, that by Easter, (the holiest of Christian days), the Gods will send a ominous message. It shall be written across the skies in flames for all to see. It shall be sent to denote your betrayal. You, Harold, have broken a sacred oath; one that you freely granted to William just two years ago. A betrayal of this statue shall not be allowed to stand, Not by Man nor God!*"

Harold was stunned and for a moment said nothing. He then arose from his chair trembling with rage, and said, *"that is blasphemy, William would not dare attack England, nor will the Gods favor a bastard Norman over me, a true Saxon Royal!"*

The Priest stood unmoving, his hood masking his facial features, and continued—*"Even now Lord William builds a vast fleet and assembles his Knights. They are as the leaves of Sherwood, ever growing and increasing in their multitudes. Soon they will rival the stars of heaven in their number. Take heed least it become too late for you. Remember the Gods will send a message!"*

The entire court stood awe struck and looked at each other muttering among themselves, Harold had heard enough, he suddenly screamed an undistinguishable oath and called for his house guards. He ordered them, *"Arrest this false priest. He is Druid! Lock him away where no one will ever have to listen to his heathen lies again."*

Harold stood and announced the audience for today was over, and retired to his personnel chamber, further he issued orders; there would be no more audiences for a fortnight. For only a few days ahead was Easter, the sixteenth day before the calendars end of May, and he decreed that he must prepare for this holiest of days.

The words of the false priest worried him greatly as he sat and considered his options, for if he was truly a priest of the new Religion, then perhaps the Pope and God himself had turned against him. There was time for that worry later though. As yet, he still had two weeks in which to prepare, pray and seek guidance.

The following morning broke clear and it appeared a glorious day in the making as the King began to attend to the ceremonies of his office for this coming Easter day. The words of the priest revisited him as he worked; could they be truly prophetic, or just the rambling of one of William's lackeys. Perhaps he worried too much, but the words came again and again to his mind. It was as if the priest was inside the very head of the King repeating his ominous warnings.

Then in the late day evening sky, just as King Harold Godwinson prepared for his evening sup, a great shout was heard from the courtyard and every member of the household ran to see what could cause such a clamor.

There in the eastern sky was a streaking star with a longhaired tail flowing across the heavens. From the throngs of his countrymen came a call—*a sign, a sign—the priest was right—a sign!*

An hour later, with the comet still visible in the night sky, Harold called the captain of his guard and ordered him to bring the imprisoned Norman Priest before him. He would know more of his predictions and possibly of William's plans. This he would do or this priest would pay with his life. The guard returned only minutes later and proclaimed that the priest had somehow escaped.

The priest's untimely escaped was inconvenient, but it mattered not to Harold. What did, was the ominous message he had delivered. War was coming and Harold was not ready and this message of the Gods did not make it any easier. Harold did not believe in such nonsense, but his people might. What must he do?

The sky message stayed for a solid week in the heavens over Angland. No man within the realm missed the vision, but only those who had attended the court of Harold at the month's beginning knew of what ominous news it truly foretold. Harold ordered all who knew to quiet the rumors of its false prophecy, or face the sword. Somehow the word must not reach the masses and further frighten his already worried vassals.

What to do? Harold only controlled Wessex with his loyal Saxon troops. Although proclaimed King of the Saxons and Angles by the Witan, actually Edwin, the Prince of Mercia controlled the rest of England along with his brother, Morcar, Earl of Northumbria. Somehow Harold must strengthen his position with these two powers before the tide of events overwhelmed him. If only he had given those lands to Tostig, but that would have only caused other problems. It was better that it worked out the way that it did. But somehow he must obtain their loyalty and support, perhaps if he were to pay a state visit.

Harold called his guards and ordered them to quickly assemble a train for a state mission to the north. He needed to ensure their unquestioned loyalty. It must be a grand entourage in appearance without being offensive in nature. The trappings of grandeur were arranged and the train sent forth. The trip took seven full days, and arrived by February's end. The entourage appeared with lines of Knights in shining armor followed by the King's own standard barriers and finally the King himself attired in his Royal best.

He was at the gates of Mercia, arriving in grand splendor and awaiting the assemblage of the Earls. Here too was the fortuitous arrival of the Christian Bishop of Wulfstan, whom had personally crowned Harold only months before. Rightly Signund, the Archbishop of Canterbury, should have performed the deed, but he had still been in mourning for the loss of King Edward the Confessor.

The meeting began in a grand manner, but dragged on for a week. Harold was wasting valuable time with talk of mutual treaties, negotiations of rights and careful political posturing. It was not time he could afford, time needed to train and prepare his army. Somehow he had to speed up these proceedings.

Harold however, realized he must use his time wisely. Here was an opportunity to solidify his hold on all of England and acquire enough loyal Knights to help defend it once the opposition finally attacked. It just needed to happen quickly.

During the pressing arguments for a mutual defense treaty, Harold took notice of a young woman who occasionally spoke to both Edwin and Morcar as if a peer. When asked, the Bishop of Wulfstan identified her as Aldyth, the sister of the two Earls. At last, thought Harold, he had found the key.

It took Harold only moments to approach the two and speak of an arranged marriage between himself and Aldyth. All parties knew what this would mean. Such an alliance of families would place the two on equal footing to inherit the title to all Angland in an uncertain future. Harold Godwinson himself had laid his claim for Angland based upon his sister's marriage to the former King. Now Edwin and Morcar foresaw that either of them could follow suit should their sister marry King Harold Godwinson. It was a quick solution.

The marriage was quickly arranged. The Bishop of Wulfstan performed the ceremony and it was consummated within the day before Harold's hurried departure.

Aldyth was proclaimed Queen of all Angles and Saxons; a title that she was happy with, one she thought was destined to grow. Now, at last thought Harold there was a chance to weather the storm of the war to come.

Harold's supposition was that his position was now secure, but it was not necessarily true, for the two brothers were not to be so easily forced into Harold's war. Each well knew that if Harold was defeated and killed, then either of them could make a push for the crown. With their sister sitting on the throne as Queen, they would have a legitimate claim. As far as Harold's war, they would fight, but only to protect their own lands from invasion. The weaker Harold became through war, the stronger their chances to claim the entire prize of **Empire.**

CHAPTER 10

▼

Tostig and the Danes

In April, Harold's outlawed brother Tostig departed Flanders. William's father-in-law, Count Baldwin of Flanders, supported him with men, equipment and ships. With a fleet of sixty ships and these supporters he set out to raid, terrorize and plunder England's southeast coast. Duke William and Alan Rufus knew of Tostig's plans, but they made no pretense to oppose them. In fact it fit in well with their own plans, for it would keep the Anglo-Saxons harried, while the Norman fleet was built and fitted out for war.

Using the time-tested tactics of his Viking ancestors, Tostig, applied a hit and run strategy. Tostig's fleet became a symbol of terror to the hamlets that dotted the Anglish Coastline. Anytime a dragon ship was seen, the women and children would gather what goods they could and ran for the forested hills of the interior, for the raiders took all and burned what they did not personally want, be it food, goods or women. For months, in this way Tostig kept Harold's army ever moving and growing tired of the chase. The Anglo-Saxon army became spread across the southern coastline in an effort to delay him long enough for the King's fleet to surround him. But Tostig was a shrew tactician and not easily trapped. As the pickings in one area would become depleted, Tostig would move rapidly on to other areas. From the southeast, Tostig's fleet moved on to the rich lands of Harold's wife's brothers. Here he entered the river Humber and began to ravage the inland areas of Northumbria and Mercia. These should have been his on lands, and from them he would exact his greatest revenge.

But Tostig, here, had made his first miscalculation and it was a fatal mistake, for the Earls Edwin and Morcar were not in the south with Harold protecting the coastline as Tostig had expected, but were sitting at home with a full accompaniment of knights and armor.

By now it was mid-summer and the river was running low. Tostig's ships were dragging bottom with the heavy weight of their plunder when the Earl brothers struck. At a point where the channel undercut a raised bank, the Scots covertly amassed. Here the depth of the river would bring Tostig's ships right under the overhang. Edwin's men lay atop the bluff with huge rocks, cut timbers, and long-bow men. Morcar hid his own archers on the far side in the bramble, which grew in profusion close to the water. When the middle ships of the flotilla were under the bluff, the brothers struck. The results were devastating; the ships were splintered and ripped apart by debris from above, while the onslaught of arrows significantly reduced Tostig's forces, and they were easily defeated.

Of the sixty Dragon ships and 1200 men with which Tostig had entered the river, only twelve ships and 150 men were able to flee rapidly enough to reach the sea. Gone were Tostig's hopes for a foothold in the north. Forty-two dragon ships and a thousand men lay crush, dead and sinking in the shallow shoals of the Humber River, the river ran red with the blood of these invaders and the dead drifted in piles along the sandbars in the rivers currents. It was a massive victory for the forces of Northumbria. With virtually no loss, they had ripped Tostig's forces to pieces. These at least, would never again come to harass the people of York.

The news reached Harold and he greeted it with relish. Now there was one less gnat at which to swat.

Tostig had managed to survive, but was devastated by his loss. He now reassessed the situation and turned his remaining ships north to Scotland and the protection of his half brother by blood, King Malcolm. Here he would receive a much needed refuge and time to study for his next move. The goods he had amassed in his months of raiding lay in wait for his return and now that he had few left with which to split them, he would be considered a wealthy man, but Tostig was not interested in wealth alone. What he wanted was power, respect and lands of his own.

Malcolm, though more than willing to offer his rich kin refuge, would not help Tostig to reinvade the south. That would put him at odds with the powers of the Saxons, Normans and Danes; and it was not a move he wanted to make, at least not yet. He was well aware that it was entirely possible that he, Malcolm himself would someday be able to take complete control of the Misty Isle. Once the numbers of combatants had been sufficiently trimmed down by the coming war, he could make his move. Malcolm's strategy was to wait and maintain his meager forces in tact. Much might be accomplished with these few, as other events unfurled. It all would depend on timing and the fates.

Malcolm had only finished his last war eight years ago. Then he had been known as Malcolm Canmore, a chieftain Prince of the Moray district, faithfully serving his father, King Duncan I. He would still have had that title and designation had not fate stepped in. Mac Beth had murdered Duncan in 1040 and claimed his throne. The Dane, Malcolm waited, and time and madness took its toll. In 1057 Malcolm was able to kill his father's murderer, Mac Beth, in fair battle; but it had taken time and patience. This play for power in the south would be no different, patience and time—that was the key to a Scottish **Empire.**

Tostig's failure with his half brother, the Scottish King Malcolm III did not deter him, for he then contacted Harald Hardrada, King of Norway, with whom he had been previously in contact. Here was another waiting army who, if approached right, might move to help him secure the English Throne; and if it came right down to it, he would give up the throne for a shot at revenge on the head of his hated brother Harold the Usurper. If need be, all he wanted was the return of his Earldom in Northumbria. Here again his acquired wealth greased the way for him and the pure blood Vikings lined up readily for a taste of the spoils. Tostig knew the young men of the North would readily sign up for an adventure to acquire such riches for themselves, for that was the old way of the Viking. Many of the youthful warrior class were ready to test their metal against the Anglish, as had their fathers and grandfathers before them. Their ancestors stories of wealth, plunder, maidens and glory prepared the way.

Their King, Hardrada had secured a brilliant career as a soldier. He had served as general and had fought for the King of Norvogod. He also had spent some years in the service of the Empress Zoë in Constantinople. In 1042 he had a falling out with her over the division of war spoils and returned to Norway. He arrived a rich man with a fearsome reputation and soon convinced his brother Magnus to give him half of the vast Norwegian Kingdom to rule in return for half of those spoils. Then in 1047 when Magnus died, Hardrada became sole ruler of the Danes, however some of the Danes would not accept their new King easily, and for the next 12 years the King had a bloody civil war on his hands, one which depleted his amassed fortune and took the best of his fighting men.

In 1063, King Hardrada decided to sue for peace. Though he had not succeeded in uniting the Danes, he signed a peace treaty with King Swein in 1063. This King, Swein and his predecessor Ulf, were his cousins, as well as cousins of the new King of the Anglo-Saxons, Harold Godwinson and that fact added to Hardrada's desire to take Angland from him.

A new generation of Viking men had now grown up in his land and they hungered for adventure. If an alliance with Harold's brother Tostig was needed to secure all these things, then so be it, after all theirs was a complex family affair, with confusing family lines and loyalties.

King Harald Hardrada was still bitter over his loss to Swein and its treaty of peace that had split Norway and created Sweinland. He also thought his own claim on the throne of England to be as viable as any other considering his family line. Therefore he quickly agreed to help Tostig, but asserted that the crowns of both lands of Norvogod (Norway) and the lands of the Angles would be united again,—under him.

In 1038, when Harthecanute was still King of Angland, he and King Magnus of Norway had made a pact to hold the two kingdoms in trust for each other's family should anything happen to either line. When Canute's son Harthecanute had died without a direct heir, the throne of the Angles should have come to the heirs of Norway, not to Edward the Confessor, or so thought Hardrada. Since he, Harald Hardrada, was the younger brother of Magnus; the throne, he decided, should have been his by default, but at the time he was still embattled in the Danish Civil War. Now all he had to do was reestablish his rights!

Tostig agreed to Hardrada's terms; the Anglo-Saxon throne was Norway's to command, but for his assistance Tostig wanted the renewal of his family's title to Northumbria. This would solidify his rule of his former lands plus bring about revenge on the forces of the brother earls, Edwin and Morcur who had devastated his flotilla on the river Humbria. Tostig's family ties would add greatly to the legitimacy of Hardrada's rule, so the two readily agreed, Northumbria for Tostig and **Empire** for Hardrada.

The stage was now set, and King Hardrada would not be denied his rightful place in history. The Dane King quickly made contact with his magnates in the Orkney Islands, and also with the court of Malcolm in Scotland. When he had his armies organized, he would invade. He asked only for Malcolm's non-interference, while he ordered his magnates in the Orkney's to supply men of arms in his assistance. If he could catch the Usurper Harold in the south trying to protect the coast from the Normans, theirs would be a quick victory in the North.

The early winds of the fall of 1066 were upon the shores of Norway and the Danish King loudly proclaimed that the winds of Odin would lead his troops to a victory greater than any Viking had ever known. True to his word the Anglo-Saxon ships at the Isle of Wight were scuttled in the fall gale, which also rapidly blew the Danish ships southward. At the same time, these same winds deterred William's Norman fleet from sailing north across the channel and interfering with the Danes early strike.

Tostig stood forward on the helm of the second Dragon ship as they sailed rapidly southward upon the winds of Odin's breath. He would soon have his revenge. The Usurper King and brother of Tostig, would at last pay for his treachery in denying him his true lands and titles.

Two hundred and forty ships were at his command. The King had trusted him to lead this mighty Viking armada into battle. With these men, he could scale the walls of any parapet, or wade the depths of any moat to accomplish his goals. These were his men, men born and breed for fighting. These men reveled in war and lived the life of true full time warriors. Their well-sharpened razor-edged battleaxes would crush the shells of the Anglish armor and cleave the heads from Harold's puny retainers. The might of a pure bred Viking was legendary and he knew that this would help the Dane forces to intimidate the Anglish in the battle to come.

The Shetland and Orkney Island Vikings joined the fleet in route and swelled their ranks. Never had Tostig seen such a fleet and army assembled with just one objective—the body-less head of the traitor Harold. These additional troops swelled the flotilla to over three hundred shiploads of fighting men, an army 6,000 strong.

The fleet struck the coast first at Scarborough and Northumbria. Here they found little resistance, and the plundering of Vikings of old took hold of the excited men. The spoils of war were theirs; goods, gold, women and blood came to them in abundance. The towns were stripped and then burned to the ground. The men who resisted were put to the sword, their Saxon women's wombs filled with Viking's seed. How dare they put up even this feeble resistance to Tostig's

Viking hoard, he thought. Word would now spread; resistance would mean total destruction to the enemies of Tostig!

Reaching the ships with their booty, the men made ready to move on. Tostig took them where his own ships had failed. They would sail up the Humbria River, reaping revenge on those who had foiled Tostig's last foray here. The rivers now ran deeper, yet Tostig had learned…and sent runners ahead along each shore to ensure that no trap had been set. This section of the river's land fell quickly to the Viking's sword, and then Tostig led them next up the river Ouse. They sailed as far as possible, to the village of Riccall. Here they off-loaded and took what spoils the hamlet offered.

For two days they prepared with chain mail and armor for the coming battle in the capitol of Northumbria, York. The people of the land were torn and divided in loyalty between the two forces, for most were Danes or of Danish descend themselves. Some even had close family members in Hardrada's forces. However the devastation inflicted by the invaders thus far had convinced most that they must indeed resist the invaders or they stood to lose everything.

The Earls Morcar and Edwin were both in York at the time and they again send forth the call to arms. The battle with Tostig months earlier was just a prelude to the coming battle. However it had served as a practice call for the men of Northumbria. Once again, York must be protected from the ravages of foreign invaders. They had been victorious once before, with little personal cost to their on men. Now they must defeat this new army of North men at all cost.

Soon a vast army was erected of Nobles, Knights, Squires and peasant farmers. These assembled men moved out to catch the Vikings on the open ground of the lands south of York, for they did not want the coming battle to lay waste to their capitol city. This time there would be no ambush, no easy victory. This time it must be by force of arms that they protected their homes, lands and families.

Morcar and Edwin had managed to assemble a force of four thousand Anglish, Danish and Scot supporters. It was an impressive force, but word was that the initial forces of the invading Vikings had numbered over six thousand. But over a thousand had to be left behind to protect the fleet and the spoils of war already captured. This brought the numbers to near parity and the Scots thought they held the home ground advantage. These facts, along with their pride in their last victory and a new determined army arranged in a well-ordered defense, might just win the day.

The two determined armies met at Gate Fulford, about a mile south of York. Here would be decided the future of Northumbria. A ghostly vision was said to have drifted across the moors and along the streams in the early morning mist. It was a woman in the raiment of a specter that drifted with the fog and mist, an observer of the battle to come. Some though she was an angel of death, here to take home those souls destined to travel on to the next world this day. It was a poor sign for those who must struggle and die here today.

Morcar reached the area a few hours ahead of Tostig and Harald Hardrada, the Norwegian King. Here he found the defensible areas he sought and quickly set about to deploy his men. Morcar's recon men had told him of the vast numbers of the approaching Viking hoard. He knew that only through proper selection of sites could he possibly hold the line here and save his capitol city of York.

He located a marshy field between the Ouse River and the old Roman road the Vikings were following from Riccall. Morcar formed a line whose right flank was anchored on the eastern shore of the river, and then stretched across the Fulford meadow to the road. From there he stretched his men outward toward the marsh as far as a man could stand and fight without bogging down. The defenders lines were now established and Morcar set about reinforcing them several men deep.

The approaching Vikings saw the prepared defenders and spread out to match their formation. Under the determined leadership of Tostig and King Harald Hardrada; they formed up parallel to and facing the assembled defending army. The veteran warriors were brought to the center, where Harald himself was located. The second best were to form up on the firm ground nearer the river with Tostig. The least experienced troops, those from the Orkneys, were sent to the boggy field area under the leadership of Orre Eyestein. There they would only have to hold their own ground, while the center and right would be used to crack the defenders line. Neither force could out flank each other because of the natural boundaries. Here it would come down to who the best warriors were. To Tostig and Harald this was a given. They would prevail, for none were better warriors than the Viking.

With a roar of shouts and oaths, the two fronts clashed together. Men were hacked and stabbed, maced and lanced, fighting for their lives and that of their friends. The defenders along the bog started to gain ground on the green Viking Orkney troops advancing there, while the other two areas were locked in a virtual deadlock. The fields were a mass of blood and gore, as nine thousand men met with steel and shield.

Slowly the tough Scotsmen on the left next to the bog started to push the inexperienced Eyestein and his Orkney Vikings back along their entry track. The home defenders knew where the firm footing was and many of the hapless inexperienced Orkneys were soon mired to their knees in the bog. Once down the Scot, Saxon and Angle broadaxes were brought to bear on the Danes exposed necks. It was a bloody slaughter.

As the situation along the bog began to become desperate, a finger of mist seemed to slowly arise from the swamp. Harald and Tostig both saw the misty image of the white specter arise and hover there. With a swish of it smoky arm it seemed to point a finger toward the bog where the embattled green troops fought.

Tostig's eyes moved lower to encompass the losing battle on that flank and immediately sent word to Harald. The Norwegian King quickly ordered a splitting of the troops on the right. These on signal spread out toward the center. Here they would try to hold the left and as much of the center as they dared, and still maintain themselves against the Saxon, Angles and Scotsmen. With the center reinforced, Harald took his personal guard and wheeled upon the unsuspecting Scots who were harrowing his green Orkney troops near the bog.

The result was devastating to the advancing men of Morcar. Being struck so unexpectantly from the flank by a vastly superior force, caused the home front defenders, who had been steadily advancing, to now be caught in a vise. They were quickly squeezed from the side and again from the front as the Orkneys recovered. It was now the defenders turn to die and they did so in large numbers as they were pushed into the waiting bog.

Where they had been moments before wreaking havoc on the greenest Vikings of Harald and Tostig's army, now the tables were turned and they found themselves mired in the mud up to their own knees. With quick whips of broadsword and axe this arm of the army of Morcar was destroyed. A meager few survivors thrashed through the bloody mire of the bog to the distant sounder footing a full quarter mile away. Now, however they were out of the fight. It was miles around the bog to either side and to wade back through the bloody bog would have only invited sure death at the hands of the vigilant Vikings.

The morale of Eyestein's green troops, most from the Orkney Isles, was now greatly revived and they joined in the battle at the center with the vanguard of the invading Viking hoard with great relish. This success on the flank proved to be decisive, for the warriors of Norway had held on in both the center and along the river flank. Now with the addition of the Orkneys, they were making vast headways into the groups of embattled defenders.

The Orkneys and returning vanguard of Harald's center were too much for the still struggling defenders of York. First the wing of Vikings at the center, reinforced by the Orkneys and then toward the river rushed over the hapless Anglish. Soon the entire Anglo-Saxon line had collapsed as the defending soldiers who still lived, fled in a mass of disorder back toward their capitol city. Over three thousand of their brothers lay dead. The fight was lost.

Across the bridge and onward toward York the Vikings pushed, giving no quarter as they advanced. With quick swings of their mighty broadaxes they dispatched both the weakened and wounded indiscriminately as they rolled over the remaining hapless defenders.

The battle was soon over and the people of York offered no resistance, as the victorious Vikings entered the city. The residents knew that further resistance would only bring on total destruction of their city and all its inhabitants. Where thousands of strong men of war had left the city, marching confidently forward, now only a few hundred remained and these were suddenly in no mood for combat. It was only a matter of terms, if King Harald of Norway wished to offer any to the defeated city.

Tostig had gotten his revenge for the destruction of his earlier fleet two fold, and the lands upon which they now trod would soon be his to command. Now if they could only do to his Usurper brother, Harold as they had to these Northern provinces.

Tostig took stock of the city and its lands, with an eye toward the future. He gave word to Hardrada to spare as much of it as possible, for these were now his lands and his peoples. The less they destroyed, the less that would need rebuilding.

King Harald Hardrada's terms were simple. The town would meet no further harm, nor would it be looted, if they would agree to three simple terms:

1. Accept him as sovereign King of all England and Norway, with Tostig as their Earl.

2. Assist them in their upcoming struggle with the Usurper Harold in control of the south.

3. The town would give the Vikings 100 hostages of prominence, so that in the heat of the coming battle, no one would again change sides.

The town's people had little choice, agree or die! They reluctantly accepted the terms. They knew that they were now subject to further war from the south and King Harold the Usurper, but the battle of Fulford Gate was over and their army destroyed. What choice did they have?

For King Hardrada and Tostig, the north was secure, and the pledge given, on this Wednesday, the 20th day of September in the year of the Christian lord 1066. The hostages were to be brought to Stamford Bridge and placed into the hands of the victorious Vikings five days hence on the 25th. Also on that day would the surviving soldiers of the earl's armies to arrive for induction into the Viking hoard as reinforcements of the Danish Army. It would swell the army of their new sovereign by about five hundred warriors.

To keep his mighty Viking marauders at bay, King Harald marched them back to the waiting ships at Riccall. In five days, if his demands were not met, then his men would get their chance to loot and plunder with impunity. For the present however, his orders were for them to rest, tend the wounded, recuperate and ready themselves for the coming final battle with Harold Godwinson and the creation of their new Danish **Empire.**

CHAPTER II

▼

Battle of Stamford Bridge

News of the Viking Fleet's attack and the burning of Scarborough were speedily brought to King Harold Godwinson, who was at present in London reviewing his options. The messenger reported the attack as starting on Friday the 11th of September. It had taken the messenger nearly five days to make the journey to London and he pleaded for speedy assistance from the King.

It was now the 20th, and Harold feared Scarborough had long ago either surrendered or been put to the torch. If he left at once, even with a forced march, it would take a week. It would be to late for the town's relief. Perhaps though, he could trap the invaders near York; but to do so he must act quickly.

From London to Scarborough was 200 miles as the crow flies, but for a moving army it would be much longer, at least 250 or more. The couriers who had brought word had taken five days on swift horses to cover the distance. How long would it take his army to assemble and return via the same route?

Harold must have more information; a wrong move now could spell disaster to his fledgling crowned state. He assembled his fastest messengers and sent them out to the four winds. Each had a two-fold quest, to call on the loyal and rally them to the lands defense, plus bring reconnaissance of the possibility of any other attack from Harold's many enemies.

It was a tough situation. If he rushed north with his men, then the Southland would be left open to the Normans of Duke William, or even the Vikings themselves if this was just a feint, or a ruse; merely a raid and not a total invasion.

King Harold's advisors knew that William's window for invasion would be typically closed by the end of September, for the fall storms would not allow the ships to easily cross the channel northwards thereafter. No ships and certainly not a fleet could possibly cross until late November and maybe not till spring, when typically there was a lull in the southward push of the northern winds.

Harold knew his cousin William would come, but when? Already he was late, for Harold expected an immediate invasion after he had taken the throne. Instead the Duke had fooled him, sending the young hawk Tostig to harass him along the coast and waterways. Tostig had made him spread his forces out in an umbrella along the southern coast, but that would not keep him for defending against the Norman army, In fact it helped, for Harold was able to keep his own fleet in the channel seeking out either Tostig's flotilla or William's invasion fleet. It made no sense; Tostig was as a mosquito biting at the side of the lands of the Angles—his England. What could Duke William be planning?

As Harold slept that night, he had a dream. Its' story was simple enough. A vision, an Angel perhaps, had come to him with advice.

The specter whispered convincingly into his ear, *"If Duke William and his Normans had not come by now, then they would wait until the weather improved, perhaps months. They must be at present reinforcing their numbers and creating an even larger fleet. They could not possibly attack before November or December. Yes, the Normans could wait; while to your North is an army you can attack and defeat now. You must eliminate one of your enemies at a time,"* she whispered. *"The Earls Morcar and Edwin have dealt with your idiot brother, Tostig. Now it is your turn. You must be decisive. Show the world the might of King Harold Godwinson of England by defeating the hoards of King Harald Hardrada of Norway, now while you still can."*

Harold woke with a start. *"Yes that must be it,"* he muttered.

Harold sent forth his couriers. The segments of his army must form up as one. It was time to march. His forces, which were bivouacked at Coventry with the Lady Godiva and those at London near his own estates, must unite. The Vikings of the North had to be destroyed at once. The Normans could wait till spring. It was simple! Why had he waited so long to decide? The dream vision had now slipped to the rear of his mind. To him, his alone had been the decision, and his was to be the glory of a major victory against his enemies.

The Dukes of Northumbria and Mercia, who were his brother-in-laws had not agreed to fight with him against the Normans, but the invasion of the Vikings into their lands would surely change their minds. When he arrived to support them, how could they not do so in return? His earlier plans, to unite them through marriage to their sister would still pay off.

Harold sent word to the remnants of his storm battered fleet of ships to move with all due haste up the eastern coast of Wessex in support of his land troops. The channel and the Normans could wait, for now they must hurry north.

Harold's minions brought the word of the anchored Viking fleet at Riccall as the English army force-marched northward. Only two miles from there, was the township of Tadcaster. It was strategically located on the old Roman road, one that the Anglo-Saxons were using to rapidly push northward.

Here Godwinson sent out couriers again. This time they were to move around the Vikings and give notice to Morcar and Edwin of the King's arrival and assistance. The locals had fled before the approaching English army as if afraid of them, for in truth all previous armies whether friend or foe had laid waste to their lands, stole their goods and abused their women. To Harold this was nonsensical for they were his people and all they owned was already his to do with as he pleased. Surely they would not flee from him. Mayhap, Harold thought, they assumed his men were the invading Vikings and not the loyal defenders of the land, men of their King, for he himself acknowledged that their was little to tell friend from foe in the attire of his and the invaders men. There only visual point of reference was their pennants or colors and these were stored until the battle ensued.

Within hours the couriers came galloping back into the encampment. The news could not have been worse. The Vikings had defeated the armies of Morcar and Edwin. The North had fallen.

The collection of intelligence was coming swiftly now. Harold was soon fully informed of the defeat at Fulford Gate and the sub-sequential events at York. His was the only army he could depend on to defeat the marauding Vikings. Volunteers were hard to come up with within the area, for the men of this land were now confused as to where their loyalties lay and most were either dead at Fulford Gate or had fled. Of those who remained, most were of Danish descent and Morcar and Edwin had pledged their word to the invading Norsemen at York. Was not the sacred word of an Earl a bond to his Knights and serfs alike?

Harold could not allow their assumed pledge, sacred or otherwise to interfere with his plans now. He ordered the impressments of what locals could be found into his service. These, with a little encouragement, readily informed him of the passage of the Vikings back to their waiting ships at Riccall. Several men of the defeated forces of Morcar, who had been forced across the bog, now were straggling in to join the King's army. These informed Harold that the Viking hoards were, as yet, still unaware of the English Army's arrival.

This was excellent news, and with it Harold immediately quartered off the roads leading to and from Tadcaster. No word of his arrival must leak out to the enemy before he was completely ready. Small forces of Knights and their squires were sent out towards the shires of York, Ulleskill and Wharfe. These were to block those roads in the dead of night to solidify his ring of silence.

In Wharfe, he learned of the remains of a small fleet of loyal ships still manned by the sailors of Morcar. These he could easily secure if the need should arise, to either bottle up the Dane fleet at Riccall until his own could arrive, or to use for his own escape by sea should the coming battle go awry.

For the time being, at least throughout the night, his was an unknown presence in the area, and until his men could have a precious few hours to rest and recuperate from their forced march; he wanted it to remain so.

Viking sentries were said to guard the roads, which led into and out of the anchorage at Riccall, but all presence of the invaders was gone from the surrounding countryside. This was good news. A surprise attack at the main body of invaders would not be possible at their Riccall encampment, due to their advanced guard, which held the roads; but it left the rest of the country open for a possible ambush.

The 100 hostages, he learned, were to be delivered at Stamford Bridge on the following morning. Harold's mind was a whirl of thought. *How could that help? Perhaps an attack somewhere in route! What if he could arrange for a surprise reception for the Viking hoard and their bloodthirsty leaders? Perhaps it would be enough for his 6,000 men strong army to catch them unprepared, and that would tip the battle in his favor. A surprise flank attack on the Vikings as they were approaching Stamford Bridge seemed appealing. However, he reasoned that since they were expecting a peaceful meeting, the Viking would probably be too strung out to make a surprise total enough to ensure total victory. A long line could be cut, as a snake into two parts with a perfectly executed slash into its middle. But this serpent had fangs on both ends and once Harold's forces were in the middle, it might coil around them and squeeze. The two severed ends might then be able to flank and surround his forces. That would definitely not be advantageous.*

What to do? Harold was in a quandary as he ordered his army to quietly move out on the night of the 24th. With as much stealth as an army of six thousand could, they managed to reach the shire of York under the cover of a cloudy moonless darkened sky. It was a slow ten mile trek, but they encountered no one, neither friend nor foe on the deserted Roman road of their route. Thus, things were still looking favorable for a surprise attack, as they tromped into the tense, beseeched city of York and brought her fully awake.

Harold quickly asserted his empirical authority and informed the leaders of his plan. Little sleep would be gotten this night, for an attack by their King on the morrow would be a break in the terms that they had only days before agreed upon with the Vikings.

Morcar and Edwin were split on how to proceed. They had given their word to the Danes, but now that their own King had arrived and issued his Royal orders, they were honor bound to comply. Either way they were set to lose. If they fought and lost, the Danes would have no mercy. If they refused, then their own King would probably have them beheaded as traitors.

All knew what either option could possibly mean, a complete destruction of their lands and ruthless slaughter of their people. Theirs was but one chance. They must fight alongside these English, and this time defeat the Danes or die trying. The morrow would bring a desperate struggle. Victory or death was their only option.

Previously they had brought 4,000 men to bear on the 6,000 invading Vikings and had lost decisively. Sure they had killed a few hundred of the invaders, but had lost thousands in the effect. Had Godwinson arrived a week earlier it may have been a different story. They may have even been victorious. They would have had 10,000 men to throw into the fray against the Danes. But now those numbers were gone. The new English army and the invading Danes stood at near parity. The few Saxon-Scots, which could be reformed up from the York survivors, might tip the scale, but only the morrow could tale.

Harold needed to be rested and as sharp as he could be for the early morning battle, but still he feared the treachery of these people of Northumbria. To him they had already belied their assumed loyalties by agreeing to Hardrada's conditions while men still lived to fight. He gave an order to secure all entrances to the shire and death to any who tried to leave before his trap could be sprung.

With the coming of dawn, Harold rallied his forces. He dispersed his few new recruits throughout his loyal troops, with orders to watch them closely. By impressing all men of Northumbria old enough to wield an axe, he had swelled his ranks by another thousand men, though some were mere boys and others peasants without war skills. These new recruits he did not trust though, and an order was given; a sword thrust or battle-ax blow to any who tried to flee or refused to fight. With renewed resolve and a troubled army, the Saxon King led his forces northeastward toward Stamford Bridge. It was only eight miles away and the English army held to the old Roman road for the first seven. Then at Helmsley Gate, just out of sight of Stamford Bridge, which was visible from the road ahead, he waited in concealment.

The Viking Army leisurely approached for the meeting. They were sure that they were meeting a defeated and demoralized people. Though always physically ready for battle, theirs was a lack luster attitude of superiority. Most were as at ease as if they were marching down the paths of the Fjords of home. Only two-thirds of the Norwegian Vikings had come for the expected formality of the hostage exchange, a force of perhaps four thousand. The rest had stayed to rest, tend wounds and guard the ships and their gathered plunder.

The Vikings assembled on both sides of the bridge, which spanned the Derwent River, and waited for the arrival of their promised hostages. This September day was extremely hot and the unsuspecting Vikings had left much of their heavy personnel body armor at Riccall. None wore heavy armor; some even had forgone their suits of mail for this formality of surrender. Many others also proceeded to stack their shields and weapons under the trees, which flanked the road, or against the abutments of the bridge, anything to reduce the heat of the day on their Northland accustomed bodies. They need not worry of attack, for the funeral pyres of their former enemies still burned. It had been an over whelming victory and the vanquished could not possibly have rebuilt their numbers yet, if ever. This was a subdued land. Three thousand or more dead Saxon-Scots would be near the total population of adult males in this northern province of the Anglo-Saxons. Who among them was left to be feared?

Harold stood in a cluster of trees on a hill over viewing the scene below; his men were hidden in the swell between his rise and that of the Vikings. It was a narrow valley filled to the brim with heavy armored fighting men, men ready and eager to reap revenge upon these Viking invaders.

The Danes had, in their lack luster attitude, set up a poor defensive position. Many were now unarmed and lounging in the shade of the oaks which lined the riverbank. They waited as if for a coming parade at a country fair. Harold smiled. He had seen enough; the natural barrier of the river split the unsuspecting Viking forces and neither could easily reinforce the other.

Harold ordered his line of troops forward across the ridge that had hidden his presence. The rising sun suddenly was caught upon their shields and the sparkling glare reflected downward upon the assembled Vikings. At first the Vikings thought it was the townspeople bringing the hostages. Then from their ranks rose a warning as the English rushed down the hill upon their divided forces. Those resting under the trees ran for their weapons. They must have them before they could form up into any kind of a battle line.

The surprise was total; the Viking forces were divided on each side of the river, and on each side of the road. The smaller force of the two was caught on the side from which Harold attacked.

Tostig ran forward and tried to organize his Vikings quickly into a defensive ring. He yelled for King Hardrada to pull back, and not force the fight here. It was not a defensible position. The King refused to yield. He had already defeated this squalor once. They could not summon enough men to stop him now. The King had yet to realize that this was a new army, with superior numbers.

He turned his men to offer battle and for the first time saw the ever growing number of men, not the vanquished Anglo-Scots as he expected, but fresh well armed King's troops. They were quickly filing down the ridge upon his poorly armed men.

To late King Hardrada saw his peril. At once he ordered a messenger, Eyestein Orre, south to call upon the remainder of his troops at Riccall. This would be the decisive battle he had foreseen with the Usurper, but he had not expected it to be now. He must hold until his reinforcements arrived, then this usurper would pay in blood. Orre hesitated to leave with the battle at hand. He had failed once to hold the line at the bog days before and he hesitated to abandon his men now, but the King had given an order and he must obey. He must hurry or miss the final end of their push for Angland and the glory of victory.

Hardrada's mind assessed the situation. He knew he could not turn and retreat now, for it would leave his flank and rear open. With his men poorly armed they would be overrun by the rising tide of Englishmen pouring down the hill. With his best men to the rear, facing the coming onslaught of Englishmen, Hardrada ordered his men across the bridge to form a defensive mass on the other side.

With the rearguard struggling to hold the bridge, Tostig and Hardrada tried to move the rest as a battalion to a ridge some 300 yards southeast of the Derwent River. Here they would make their stand and hope to providence and Eystein Orre's fleet feet to deliver them.

The elite rearguard was soon overwhelmed with the force of the Englishmen's onslaught. They fell to a man trying in vain to slow the advancing tide. No quarter was given, as all knew of the slaughter visited upon the men of York only days ago. It was now time for retribution.

Once over the bridge the English spread out in an attack formation several ranks deep extending out along the river's bank. They stopped here, reassembled and waited as their King looked up the ridge at the poorly equipped Vikings who held the high ground.

Tostig and Hardrada finally had burst free of the trees along the river and into the bright light of the meadowland, swords swinging. Tostig's throat was hoarse from yelling; the fever of battle boiling up in his bloodlust, as Anglish Knights harried their steady retreat. Suddenly they were free and moving up the hill to their waiting comrades.

King Hardrada knew that they must immediately form up and make a stand. All of his years of training convinced him that continued retreat would leave him open to assured defeat. He must form up and hold till his reinforcements arrived. After the way they had dealt with the weakened and wounded Saxon-Scots five days earlier, he knew that he could expect no quarter in the present battle. Their only chance at life for another day was victory.

Hardrada formed his few men who had shields into a shield-wall at the front with the rest of his men settled down behind to avoid the hail of arrows he expected, although none came. Godwinson had not called up his archers, but forced a frontal assault. His early defeat of the Viking vanguard at the bridge had given him confidence. He calculated the opposing surviving numbers and decided that their shield-wall would have been an effective defense, had they larger numbers; but he decided a quick decisive frontal assault would end this battle before reinforcements could be called up. King Harold Godwinson ordered it so, and with a rush they assaulted the hill and the weak Danish shield-wall.

Hardrada's booming authoritative voice was lost in the din of noise around him that followed, the clang of metal on metal, the thud of ax against shield. The rolling meadow was quickly alive with determined Saxon and Dane, indistinguishable except for the shape of their shields, hacking at each other and screaming their defiance. No strategy had been planned for this event, and even if it had, it would be now gone. Those Danes under Tostig who'd survived the push up from the river and to the hill now turned to meet the onslaught of the Saxon line head-on at Hardrada's side.

Tostig slashed to the right with his mighty sword as the first of the enemy rushed his ragged line of Danes. A young Saxon boy, no more than fifteen seasons of age, met his fate as Tostig's sword moved forward and bit his neck. There was no time for pity though, for two others replaced him and the battle continued.

Tostig used his shield to bash at the shoulders of an enemy on his right, even as his sword found the soft underbelly of another ahead of him. He heaved up mighty with both sword and shield, throwing his enemies backward. Their fall created a temporary void in the enemy lines and into it step Tostig. King Hardrada was to his left hacking forward also. Their men were tired to the bone from the previous day's battle and they were weary of mind for this day's march had already been long. Sword and shield, if shield they had, were battle-heavy as blood and sweat filled their eyes and covered their bodies.

Vikings expected this, but to battle without armor against a fresh, well-shielded foe of superior numbers was something else. This weariness they had felt before, and for those who lived, they would feel it again, but for the moment it was severely taxing.

Tostig shouted encouragement to his loyal men, as he kicked the sword hand of a lunging Saxon away from the King. Hardrada had not seen the thrust or else he was tiring to quickly in the suffering hear to care. The Saxon had been intent upon skewing the King and had not Tostig acted quickly would have been successful in piercing the royal robes of King Hardrada.

The Viking Royalty's face was bloodied when next Tostig looked. It could be the blood spray of an enemy or perhaps with the King's own gore, he could not be sure which. Tostig's shoulder was also slashed and was now bleeding, but thanks to his chain mail, it was not deep. There was no time to rest; he turned from his King's bloodied face to hammer a Saxon's nose with his sword's hilt. The man had gotten to close for Tostig to use his blade, but now the Saxon fell back allowing room for his blade to turn and follow.

"*The line,*" Tostig shouted to his men. "*Keep the line!*" Only by standing shoulder-to-shoulder in their thinning ranks could they hope to stay alive. Had their runner reached the reserves yet? If so would they arrive in time? Tostig spared a glance to the see if the raven flag was fluttering at the Saxon rear, a sign of his reinforcements arrival, but none could be seen.

The battle surged around the hill as Tostig's blade again gained momentum. How long had they fought? How long could they continue to hold out? His men were fierce fighters, but the Saxons surrounded and outnumbered them. At this point, Tostig did not want to know by how many.

Slash a long bearded enemy here, defend against a swinging ax there, push forward and fall back; it was a steady battle just to keep moving in any direction. He and his men were grunting with effort as their living numbers slowly diminished. His sword arm was suddenly forced downward by a paring ax stroke. His sword was forced all the way to the ground, but he recovered and brought it back swiftly upward, cleaving between the legs of his Saxon attacker. He whirled in time to sever an extended neck, just as the next Saxon body pushed forth against his shield. A blade reached his backside causing a searing pain as it cut deeply. He stumbled, the enemy's blade lodged in his chain mail, ripping it from his attackers hand. He fell forward, the blade hanging from his back. He managed to turn and reached the now unarmed Saxon. He repaided the thrust with a whip of his own sword, severing his opponents up lifted sword arm, which had reached out to retrieve his lost weapon.

The situation was quickly deteriorating as the Danish line was slowly folding in upon its self. Tostig looked to King Hardrada, he now lay prostrate, dead in a puddle of his own blood, a broadax blade extending from his torso. A yell came from the river and the reserve troops of his Viking hoard swarmed onto the field. At last the relief column had arrived. Tostig raised his sword to signal, and then attempted to fight his way to them. He tried to voice his cry so that his men would see help coming and rally, but his voice failed him. He felt another stroke of a blade to his unprotected back. He wheeled to face this new enemy, but his legs would no longer work. He knew he must move, he must fight, it could not end like this!

He was with the Viking hoard; they could not fail. Tostig staggered, all senses were gone. A trail of blood formed at the corner of his mouth. Death's veil of darkness reached out to him, enveloping him. He felt himself falling, but there seem to be no ground under him, only an endless tumble into total darkness. In his dimming vision, he realized that Valhalla was now upon him. His lips formed words, "*Damn you brother*," he whispered and then his lifeless body slowly fell to the waiting blood soaked meadow.

With King Hardrada and Tostig dead, a roar went up from the Englishmen and they charged the hill as if on signal. Their heavy armor protected them from the waning blows of those they assaulted, while their own slashes ripped easily through the weary tunic clad Viking defenders. These Vikings had put up a valiant fight and were still valiantly struggling when Eystein Orre and the reinforcements arrived. But, Orre was to late to save King Hardrada or Tostig, both died at the top of the blood soaked hill surrounded by innumerable scores of dead Viking and English alike.—He had failed his King again.

The site brought Eystein Orre to a halt with his men close upon his heels. They were breathing heavily from the long run, and spread across the field is a long straggling line as their eyes beheld the ruined bodies of their King and his new General. Four thousand Vikings had arrived a few hours ago, now only a handful still lived. The fields though were still crawling with thousands of able-bodied Englishmen. Eyestein had mustered nearly a thousand more Vikings and with these he now stood.

Eystein waited only until the stragglers were near, then he yelled, "*by Odin's horn*", and then he rushed the English, who were still intent on the slaughter upon the hill. The remaining Vikings on the hill rallied at the sight of their kinsmen, even though their leaders were dead. They broke into several small circles. Back to back they fought, the pile of dead ever growing larger of both English and Viking.

Eystein's men fought to reach their beseeched companions and for a while held against the onslaught, but the fates were not to be with them this day. They were still outnumbered over four to one. That along with the lack of armor, unaccustomed heat, the surprise and now loss of leadership was just too much to overcome. Eyestein fell near the body of his King, at last satisfied that he had done his best and fought to the last.

The Vikings were lost, destroyed beyond their ability to recuperate. The few survivors finally realized the futility of the fight. Now with the last of their leaders dead, they broke and ran in a staggering line from the field. They fled, as best they could for their waiting ships at Riccall, leaderless, demoralized and most without weapons.

From the English and Scot groups again great shouts of joy could be hear, but these were quickly stilled as the victors began to look around at the death and destruction which had been wrought unto this place.

The English Army had at last prevailed, but at a very large cost. The field was littered with the remains of the once proud English Army of six thousand. The Scots of Northumbria had also suffered mightily, for both Edwin and Morcar lay wounded among their dead and dying comrades. They were being quickly attended, but many of the still living would die in the aftermath of this battle.

The Anglo-Saxon King Harold felt both elation and remorse. He had met and defeated the greatest invasion army Norway had assembled in many a year, but he knew that he still had the Normans to contend with. He must rest, recuperate and rebuild. He just hoped that the Gods would give him time and enough fresh troops.

To the south, the assembled sailors and soldiers of the once 300 ship strong armada of Norsemen, began to scuttle the main part of their fleet. They then took 24 of the remaining long ships with all the survivors who had found their way back and slowly sailed for home. They had lost over 5,500 men in two days of fierce fighting. The greatest Viking Army of all time had suffered the greatest Viking defeat of all time. Their dream of a Danish **Empire** was forever lost.

Harold and the remnants of his army returned to the joyous revelry of the city of York. Their new king had saved them, and their regards for him grew. Harold had found the remains of his brother Tostig and brought the ruined body with him to York. Traitor he may have been, and a constant thorn in the side of the new King, but Tostig was still his brother and he wanted him buried within the walls of York's Abby. The first empty plot they found would do for Harold's love of his brother had its limits, but it was the way of the Christian to place family in yards of an Abby's bury.

King Hardrada's remains were placed in a small river vessel with sword, shield and axe. Then piled high with fuel rich materials and set afire before being pushed adrift on the river's current. The King, Harold Godwinson, stood upon the Derwent River Bridge and watched the ceremony. It was not Godwinson's desire to honor this invader, but Hardrada had been a Viking King and the native people of this, his northern lands, wished it so. He had after all honored his own traitorous brother in death, should he allow less for Hardrada, the kin of these who had helped to defeat the invader?

The remaining Viking dead were gathered into large piles and disposed of in huge funeral pyres. The people of the countryside went immediately to work on the task, for the season's heat would not long allow them to delay. The English and Scots were attended to as their religions dictated by their friends. Some had been Druid, some of the Viking faith, but many were Christian of these honored dead of the winning coalition, and each received the blessings of his own faith's funeral rites.

The only thing to which Harold found unusual about reports on the varies funeral rites, was that each whether Christian or Pagan, reported seeing a specter, a pale ghostly image, which moved over the battle field dead, as if searching for something. When asked to describe it, the more credible witnesses said it was a mere mist from the river; floating across the field, neither good nor evil. Others referred to it adamantly, as the Death Angel of their own particular religious orders, come to escort their souls home.

The battle was over, what Harold had a need of now was a rest, for both body and spirit. The remnants of his army also needed time to recuperate and heal from the battle. His ties to the northland were at last secured via this victory. The political loose ends needed to be tied up, but there was time now for both. The enemy had been met and vanquished. His lands were safe, at least till the storm season came to an end and the fierce Normans could amass their army from the continent. But that could be weeks or even months away. For now he needed solace.

For four days he rested, then on the first day of October he received the worst possible news. Near Pevensky 250 miles away, ... **the Normans had landed** *!!!!!*

CHAPTER 12

▼

Battle of Hastings

The call came early on a morn of the ninth moon. It was at last time. The winds had changed as Judith predicted and the fleet's sails would soon fill. This day of our lord the 27th of September 1066 would live throughout history as the date of the rise of a true monarchy, if Alan's Specter-Witch of a grandmother was to be believed. A trumpeted horn sounded assembly and the Norman army sallied forth to answer the call of their Lord, Duke William. As vassals, it was their duty. It had been so for hundreds of years. One must answer the call and defend those to whom they owed their loyalty.

They assembled along the shore in the morning mist twelve thousand strong. Men came from every corner of the land, seeking fame and fortune; the spoils of Medieval War. With horse and shield, sword and battle-ax, with armor and suits of mail in tow, they moved down the beach to the waiting longboats. Six armies of the continent, the Normans, the Brits, the Anjou's, the Maine's, the Flemish and the French; all securely pledged to Duke William as his trusted vassals.

Alan looked upon the long lines of assembled men. The endless years of pre-paring had at last culminated in this very moment, and all was as it should be. Years of training and sacrifice were about to lead him onward to reach this his final destiny. He had no doubts in the inevitable outcome, for that was his way. He just hoped that it would be quick for he was no longer the courageous teen of the Paris Tournament those many years ago. For him the time of promised reward was growing shorter with each day.

The square-rigged ship mast shown through the mist, which shrouded the shore. As the knights advanced, the outline of the boats slipped into sight, each adorned with the mighty headdress of its dragon protectorate. It had taken months to build and assemble this mighty armada of warships. Ports were visible along the sides of the assembled fleet, each with its long oar raised in salute to the approaching knights. With the promised winds these would not be needed, but they were a part of a proper Dragon ship and as such stood ready.

For a moment Alan thought he saw the image, which had been haunting his dreams most of his life. The Witch, Judith of Brittany, who had sold her soul to Satan to pave the way for this day appeared to be floating there among the misty vapors. Perhaps he only imagined her, for of late she had abandoned him and conversed only with William. The two cousins had been together these last few months, supervising and training their invasion forces and Alan learned of the Witch's wishes only through William of late. According to William she had been away from him also much of the time, and had only recently returned with word from the North.

The image appeared again, though it was only a swirling mass of morning fog with hair as white as snow, but it beckoned Alan and his train of Brittany soldiers forward in an urging motion, as if impatient to see her unholy pact with Lucifer come true.

Alan's steed's nostrils flared suddenly and he snorted into the mist as if he too saw the ghostly image. A piercing neigh ran out and the charger reared on his hind legs, pawing the vapors and scattering them out and around the entourage, as the shroud of her form dissipated into the waiting mist.

Alan's squire Lathor, who followed close upon the steed's heels, reeled, cried out and tried to flee, but Alan's brothers and his Brittany Knights who followed, had closed in around Alan in a protective shield. None had seen the image, but the rearing horse and the cries of the youthful squire had brought them forward in a rush, for many were the rumors of treachery within the Norman ranks. There had been much talk of the possibility of ambush by the Usurper Harold's minions.

The Normans had known of this possibility of war for months now, as they waited for sanction from the Pope for their invasion. William had been promised the lands to which they sailed by the former Saxon King Edward the Confessor. But upon his death the usurper Harold had stolen the crown. Now they would dethrone him and return the crown to the rightful line of Viking Norman Royalty.

Now the moment was at hand and the eager troops assembled with their horse and shield, banners and armor. As third son to the Aristocracy of Brittany (Eudo and Hawise), and cousin to William the Bastard, son of the Duke and Duchess of Normandy, he was compelled to lead his vassals and those of his family into the coming fray; even had not Judith, his Witch Grandmother, induced a childhood pledge of Alan.

William and Alan had planned long enough. Their recruiting was over, the tedious preparations made. The years had made them seasoned generals and master tacticians. They and their lieutenants knew how to use cavalry, archers and infantry to their most efficient purposes. William's flag ship the *Mora;* lay in waiting at the head of the 600-ship armada. It was time to embark.

The day began before sun and the 2,500 chargers were crowded aboard their stock ships, while Alan and the other leaders of the mass of knights filled the remaining dragon ships. Loads of prefabricated walls were also placed aboard some of the ships. These would be for quick formation of palisades and fort walls to protect the disembarking Normans, should the English army be waiting. No detail had been overlooked. No chance would be taken to interfere with the formation of **Empire**.

Alan looked to the distant shore and shaded his eyes to see if the beaches were free of waiting Saxon soldiers. Although Judith had foretold that they would be far to the north fighting the legions of King Harold Hardrada Vikings, Alan was not sure he believed everything of the dream tales told by his deceased grandmother. She had not foreseen the death of his father, and that was something for which he would never forgive. Perhaps she had miscalculated here also.

Alan surveyed the area. He had already carefully inspected maps and details of the old Roman occupation. All seemed as it should. The bay off Beachy Head was wide enough for maneuverability of the Norman fleet and the shore was flat, just right for the landing of the shallow draft Dragon ships. On the cliffs above to the east and west were the villages of Pevensey and Bulverhyte. Pevensey to the west held the remains of an old Roman fort and it was to this area that Alan had directed his men to assemble. Here Alan had decided to set up his headquarters and advised Duke William and his second Lord FitzOsborn that the area needed quick fortification to serve as the main barracks for their leaders.

Alan watched as the *Mora* touched the shore and Duke William jumped from its fore deck to the land's sandy shore. He stumbled forward in the loose sands and came to rest on one knee. Whether the fall was by accident or design, Alan could not tell, but William grasped a hand full of the sand and cried loudly for his men to hear, "This is my promised land, here I shall build my **Empire**."

The Hastings peninsula is bordered on the west by Pevensey lagoon and on the east by the River Brede. Each is a formidable barrier for anyone who would try and attack William's landing force. At high tide, the portion of the Brede that formed the lagoon would be one-quarter mile wide at its western end, at Sedlescombe, and widening to a mile or more as it approached its junction with the Channel. Hastings, situated almost in the center of the peninsula on the coast, is about 10 miles from Pevensey. About two miles to the west of Hastings lay Bulverhythe Lagoon, which has many small rivers and streams that feed it and helped to enhance the natural defensive terrain of the Norman landing site. The old Roman maps had proved their worth to Alan, if for no other reason than to find this defensive harborage in which to land. Hopefully the others, which showed old Roman roads, would also prove helpful in the campaigns ahead.

For three days, men and supplies continued to unload and assemble upon the beach without opposition. Mounted squads of knights moved inland to scout for resistance and approaching armies, while the temporary fortifications were made to the old Roman fort, which Caesar had built here nearly 500 years before. The walls of prefabricated timbers were in place before dark and surrounded by the army of Norman knights. All was as planned.

William's squires searched for the leaders of the various bands of Norman knights and called an assembly within the new fortifications walls on the fourth day. As always he knew the details of what was going on around him at all times. Most of the men thought him an uncannily strategist, but his cousin Alan knew the truth, as always the witch had his ear.

William outlined the details that were occurring to the north as if his own eye was upon the events as they happened. "*The Norsemen of King Hardrada and the followers of Harold's own brother Tostig, were far to the north and engaged in a mighty life and death struggle. In York, at Stamford Bridge the waters of the River Derwent were running red with the blood of Viking and Saxon alike.*"

Most knew that William had Norman sympathizers living in England. Some might had given word of the events happening at Stamford Bridge and the condition of Harold Army, but William and one of his generals Alan Rufus seemed to know much more. To the men who followed them, it seemed as if the Gods whispered in their very ears.

King Harold Hardrada and his Norsemen had invaded only a week earlier than William's Normans. With the aid of Tostig, they wanted to push the Saxon army out, before the French Normans could get organized and establish their own claim to the lands of England.

William loudly proclaimed, "*The Danes are predestined to fail. It is written in the stars that England will be ours to claim. It is just another step in the creation of our mighty Norman Empire.*"

"*In mid September, the Danes landed on the Northern English coast. There, as it was ever our Viking ancestor's way, they sacked the villages of all they crossed. Their destination was the shire of York to the south, but they tarried. Tostig, with his retainers, united with the invaders and together they quickly overwhelmed the sparse English forces blocking the road to York.*"

"*Harold had split his forces to be ready to move in either direction. He knew to fear the power of you my Normans. He feared we would arrive first and thus placed a larger number of his Knights to the south. When word came of our Dane cousin's encroachment into York, Harold had no choice. He swung his forces north, picking up reinforcements as he forced marched his troops.*"

"*The lessons learned fighting at my side to quell the rebellions in France, now have stood him well. He moved his men in a perfect pincher style movement and caught the Danes unprepared. They, as is their way, were still celebrating and looting the lands they had conquered thus far.*"

"*I had taught this traitor well, for the speed of his advance allowed him to surprise the Danes while still in camp at Stamford Bridge on September 25th last.*"

"*With their backs to the river, King Hardrada's men had no room to maneuver. A fierce battle ensued with hand-to-hand combat, which ebbed and flowed across the bridge back and then forth. Finally the Norsemen's lines broke and they sought to escape with their plunder in tow. Here the real slaughter began. The English army rolled over the fleeing Norsemen. The town's peasants, as well as the advancing English Army attacked the wounded and slow. No quarter was given and King Hardrada fell, followed soon by Prince Tostig. What remained of the Norse army ran for their ships and sailed for home.*"

"*So devastating was the destruction visited upon the Danes, that only twenty-four of the original two hundred and forty Dane and sixty Orkney ships were needed to ferry the survivors home. But the English were also heavily mauled and they now need time to heal and rest."*

"That my friends is something they will not have. We could force march and meet them in route, but we will instead wait here patiently for them to come to us. It will tire them out more and spread their supply lines out to thinly for them to help in this battle. The tricks that this usurper learned at my side will not help him now, for I have many more that he has yet to see."

"I ask of you to deal with him and his as he has done with our distant kin, the Danes. Neither ask nor grant any quarter, for they have demonstrated that they will do the same of us."

William waited for his words to settle among the leaders of his troops. He half expected someone to question his knowledge of the events far to the north, but no voice was given. Too many times in the past his prophetic words of the outcome of events far away had been tested, and each time the truth of his visions held true.

Alan looked on and listened without comment, for he too knew of the events to the north. This was William's time to shine, not his, so he kept silent. Let the King make the show, it would be to Alan that would come the long fight ahead. As always he would be the one to end the fight and still any future rebellious.

Duke William held aloft the Papal Ring sent to him by the Pope who had already proclaimed William the rightful heir to England when he had excommunicated the Usurper Harold.

"At the most holiest of times, I had sent an emissary to the traitor Godwinson. It was a last effort to save his miserable life and soul. But the Usurper refused my man. God himself then sent his messenger, a comet raging across the God's sky. For a week, the Lord's messenger was evident in the heavens, but still Harold would not heed. Let him know that the whole Christian World and all the Gods in heaven be for me and against this despot. How can he stand against God and the might of the Normans? The power of my Dukedom shall hence be turned into a great Kingdom," proclaimed Duke William. *"And in that kingdom each of you shall share as befits your effort here in this conquest. It is so ordained by God!!!"*

The stomps and cheers of the assembled army drowned out the rest of William's speech from Alan Rufus' ears, but he knew already the tale of the events as they had really happened.

One of William's vassals, the Norman, Robert de Guiscard, had conquered most of southern Italy and helped to secure the Papal States for the Pope. Robert de Guiscard, at the height of his victory in Italy, had received a visit from an unearthly angel with long flowing white hair who had commanded him to speak on behalf of Duke William. It was little enough for the Pope to support William after Robert had saved the Vatican for him. After all, an Angel had appeared to proclaim it—**Just and Right** that Duke William become King of England. He would be a powerful Christian vassal to the Pope at the far reaches of Northern Christendom.

Far to the north, Harold Godwinson had departed York at the first dawning of the sun on the first day of October. Taking all of his knights who could ride and what few surviving volunteers from his brother-in-laws lands who could still fight. He rode back to London as quickly as possible. It was a marathon for the bruised and crippled army to move so far, so soon after the devastation of the Vikings. But, in four days the vanguard had arrived and Harold set about creating a new army to meet this new threat.

The more severely wounded Knights and the infantry came at a slower pace from the Northern battlefront. They gathered men and supplies as they came, spreading the tales of their great victory in the north. The troops of the southern earls were gathered and Godwinson's army slowly started to rebuild. Daily new green local troops swelled their ranks as the slower moving veterans of Stamford Bridge most of them on foot, also filtered in.

The small fleet of the Northern Earls at Wharfe and Harold's own fleet that had been flanking the eastern coast in support of Harold's push on Northumbria and his attack on the Viking Hoard, now received new orders. They must immediately sail southward to bottle up William's own fleet in the channel and stop his re-supply and the arrival of any additional Norman reinforcements.

Harold set out to meet the encamped Normans with a tired but strong army of nearly 8,000 men. He sent word to all who could muster, that they were to meet at Hoar Apple Tree farm and there, to set up a defensive position along Caldbee Hill and the Sentlach River on the south side of the hill.

He knew the Normans would have superior numbers, but if he could command the high ground and his shield-wall held (a tactic he had recently seen tried), he stood a chance. Once the Normans were forced into retreat, his returning ships could smash their vessels and forever end the Norman threat to his lands. Then he could start to build his own Saxon **Empire**. With both William and Hardrada disposed of, his was to be the most powerful army in all the Northern Lands of Europe.

A fortnight passed without Norman movement, as they awaited Harold's army. Many of William's retainers were impatient, they believed in the easy victory and wanted to march on London now, but still William waited. Days passed without movement and the men began to grumble. Why did they tarry when the way was clear? Had William at last lost his senses, or his nerve? Had the clarity of his visions at last left him?

William kept his own counsel though, and only spoke openly to Alan. Daily he would approach and ask if Alan had word. Both knew of what he spoke, but Alan had had no dream vision visit by their Witch specter of a grandmother. They must wait!!

Most of the Normans passed the night confessing their sins to the Monks of nearby Abby Fecamp. They received the communion of the lord's body in the evening service, as all knew their hour was close at hand. Others foraged for food along the countryside. The peasant population had fled ahead of the Norman army and anything left of use was being taken.

In the dark of the night, as the owl called and spread its wings in search of prey, Judith finally returned to them. To each in turn, she came into their dreams. First to William and then to Alan, her unearthly image seeped into their quarters as mist upon the moors. She entered their mind as they slept and carefully laid down her plan of attack. Each movement must be precise, all depended on how each would react in the final hours of crisis ahead. Properly done and the victory would be overwhelming. It would be as none could have imagined. The Landed Royalty of the Angles as well as that of the Saxons would be swept from the field and victory would be assured to the Norman.

The morning broke clear as the Duke came from his tent. He held aloft his mighty sword, a prearranged signal that bade his squires to assemble the lords and they their men in turn. The time had arrived and finally William would order his troops forward.

Taking his vast army, he moved eight miles east of and around Pevensky bay. This placed his army just north of Hastings. Here was an area just east of the friendly Norman Monks of the Abby of Fechamp. They had known of the Normans' arrival and had kept a running tally of their enemies, adding important intelligence as to the numbers and placement of the assembling Saxon army.

As the rows of Norman Knights moved forward their faster moving scouts ranged in and out of their ranks reporting that Harold's Saxon army had positioned itself in a typical battle formation; Archers to the front, Infantry in the center, and Cavalry in the rear.

King Harold Godwinson and his remaining loyal brothers Leofric and Gyrth had taken the high ground position along a ridge. There they had amassed their men eight deep along an 800 yard path. Their numbers had been diminished considerably by the battles to the north with the Vikings, but they hoped their tight bunched masses would deter the 12,000 approaching Normans and somehow break their charge.

William smiled and looked to his cousin Alan. It was as foretold. The enemy troops were placed in position just as Judith had said. Now to the bloody business ahead!!

Alan Rufus with his brothers, cousins and Knights of Brittany held the left flank along with the contingencies of the Counts of Anjou and Maine, a force of about 2,500 men. William and his Norman Knights of near 3,000 along with his half brothers, Richard—Count of Mortain and Odo—Bishop of Odeaux, held the center. The Flemish and French groups with nearly 2,500 more moved to the right flank. The nearly 4,000 support and reserves held ready and assembled to the rear.

Each of the forward ranks contained three different major divisions commanded by relatives and loyal supporters of William. The archers with longbow and extra quivers of arrows came first, then the infantry armed with spears, javelins and swords; the last were the cavalry, though they were not always deployed in this fashion. It all depended upon the situation as the battle unfurled. The trumpeters would announce the changes of each group and its final makeup.

The two determined groups, Norman and Saxon, stood and looked at each other for long minutes. A chilled October wind from off Channel blew the color standards. The pennants ripped in the wind, but no voices were raised.

Like others around him, Alan looked sharply for some sign of weakness, some point at which to aim their attack. But there was none, just a solid mass of entrenched Saxon warriors. From the ranks of William's men came the song of Roland, a mighty hero of old. Then as it died down, Alan heard a 'thump' and looked to see his younger brother Stephen pound his shield with the butt of his sword. Brothers Ribald and Brian took up their shields and emulated him. From around Alan Rufus the noise grew. It built to a thunderous crescendo, as his entire wing of the army took up the beat. The roar was then in turn taken up by William's Normans and it quickly spread to the Flemish and French troops.

The Saxon troops in the distant appeared to stir, looking from one to the other and then to the rear, as if readying to turn and flee; but a harsh shout by the Saxon lords stilled the action and once again they settled into formation. They held forward a solid almost impenetrable wall of shields, waiting.

William moved his Charger to the front, turned to the assembled troops and waited till the noise stilled before saying, "*Today you fight not merely for victory but also for survival. If you bear yourselves valiantly you will obtain victory, honor and riches. If not, you will be ruthlessly butchered as your Norsemen brothers were just days ago—In Victory there is glory—Death leads to Valhalla or Heaven—Defeat leads only to disgrace, torture or slavery should you survive.*"

"*In front of you is an army and a hostile land blocks your advance. Behind you, there is but the sea, where the enemy ships even now gather to bar your flight. Know yea this, the English are not famed as fighters, many times their lands have fallen to the sword of their enemies and they easily accept the yoke of the foreigner. That is why they slaughter their defeated and wounded enemies, for they fear even the weak and wounded.*"

"*Know yea that the vigorous courage of a few men armed with a just cause and protected by God and Heaven, shall prevail against this host of common Englishmen. We shall prevail, though the fight may be long and costly. I ask only that ye' be bold, that none shall say that a true Norman ever yielded, and today Victory shall gladden your hearts.*"

William's white charger moved to the front of his assembled army. It's highly polished body armor flashed in the sun, as if the sun's rays themselves were coming from him. William raised his lance and pointed it at the entrenched Saxons on the ridge and with a roar the army surged forward.

Suddenly Saxon arrows filled the sky and rained down among the charging mass of knights and foot soldiers located in the center. With an authoritative voice, William yelled, "*Shields*", and as one they were upraised to form a protective barrier. The shields caught most of the feathered missiles with a loud clatter upon their metal hides.

The Norman archers with bows and arrows had formed the vanguard, followed closely by the ranks of infantrymen with spears and javelins, while the cavalry divided into wings was placed at the rear away from the Saxon archers.

In return to their initial volley the sky became black with a hail of death, as the Norman archers answered by unleashing their own long bows. Then, with a rush, the mad plunging Norman steeds surged forward among the Saxon men. It was hack and thrush, as men fought with sword and shield, mace and battle-axe. The Normans were valiantly trying to blast a hole through the solid shield-wall of the English.

The heavily armored mounted Norman cavalry cut a swath through their enemies as they rushed headlong over the kneeling shielded archers. These had no time to retreat or reset their bows for another volley. They were crushed to the ground by hoof and sword as the Knights moved onward to the waiting Saxon infantry.

The Normans, true to their kind, were a race of men inured to war. In truth, they were seldom happy without it. They were fierce in rushing against their enemies bodily, but where their strength sometimes failed, their guile would often succeed, and it did here.

The battle surged among the entrenched Saxons, with death being handed out on both sides. Both sides fought with the ferocity of desperation. For a time no one seemed to be winning, then with the blast of a Norman horn, the Knights of William began to fall back. They retreated in a mass, protecting themselves with raised shields from the renewed hail of Saxon arrows.

The Saxon Knights roared their joy at the Norman retreat and rose up from their massed formation to charge down the hill with a rush of adrenaline, anxious for the kill. With the Saxons hot on the heels of the slowly retreating Norman's front, a second horn sounded and the Normans turned, for their flight was merely a ruse. They then fell upon the suddenly entrapped advancing Saxons.

The massed Saxon strategy may have carried the day, but William's ploy had brought them out in a straggled line, which failed them. Alan's men moved in a classic flanking motion from the left and the Flemish men moved in from the right. Now the embattled Saxons, who had charged down the hill, were being attacked from three sides and losing on all fronts, as they vainly tried to retreat and form up again.

A ditch near the apex of the hill began to fill with the bodies of the dead and dying as the Normans forced the Saxons into an ever-tighter circle of defense. Now the field was littered with the remains of the Saxon men who had only moments before surged eagerly forward to meet the Normans that they thought had been retreating.

With the errant Saxons destroyed, a short lull now took the battlefield and each camp tried to regroup during its pause. The Normans rearmed their archers with arrows from the supply wagons and new horses were brought up for those lost in the opening battle. The Saxons too took time to regroup and reform their shield wall and mass formation of troops strategy, though there were considerably fewer of them to amass.

The second attack came at noon and each group proceeded as before. This time however there was no feint and the Normans moved steadily onward pushing the enemy into an ever-tighter circle of entrenched men.

For hours the encircled men struggle and died, ripped apart by battle-ax, thrust through with swords or skewered with lance. Gone was the cool of the early October morn. The rising heat of battle and the weight of chain mail and armor started to take a heavy toll. Even men who had not been wounded began to swoon from the hours of effort and heat of battle.

Alan now employed a new tactic, as his men pushed tighter upon the Saxon front lines. He ordered his archers to aim high and send their arrows not at the shield wall as before, but into the rear ranks, which were unprotected. The effect was immediate and devastating. The rear areas were unprepared and many of the officers were killed in the first volley. The archers of William and the Flemish saw the effect and also launched their arrows into the rear. Harold's brother, Leofwin was felled with an arrow to the neck and Gyrth was mortally wounded. The Saxon wall was shifted to try and protect the rear, but it only left large cracks in their slowly disintegrating shield-wall. The Normans rushed the breaches and fell among the Saxons. The result was devastating. In some cases whole battalions died to the last man, as their backs were unprotected in their rush to reform in protection of their leadership.

Both Norman and Saxon were throwing themselves into the fray now with reckless abandonment. Now the surviving Saxon archers were short on arrows and took to throwing and rolling rocks down the hill upon their enemies. Javelins, which had earlier filled the air, were ripped from the bodies of the fallen and used again and again.

Alan Rufus had led his men into a breach and stubbornly continued to struggle. His arms were weary from slashing through the Saxon bodies. Blood covered his body and that of his horse. He blinked in a vain effort to clear the red froth and sweat from his eyes, only to have it be instantly replaced by more. He shook his head; he must clear his vision and urge his men forward. They could allow no time for the enemy to retreat and live to fight again. It must end here, where it had started. The studied battles of old and the warnings of the Witch had told him this truth. Where men were given quarter and allowed to retreat, they would eventually return and fight again, no matter how long it took. Victory must happen today and in this place. It must be complete or there would be no victory at all.

On the rise ahead, Alan could see the last of the Saxon stronghold of men. They were formed up in a tight circle of their dead and dying Knights, horses and infantry. Their living numbers were slowly diminishing, but other scattered groups of loyal Saxon fighters were trying to reach them.

Now was the time. Alan summoned his remaining strength and called for a charge. He slapped his spurs into his tired horses sides and it responded gallantly. Suddenly his faithful charger faltered. It staggered, tried to catch itself and then collapsed with a Saxon lance deeply embedded in it chest.

Alan jumped from the dying steed, pulling his father's old faithful broadsword free as he hit the ground. He went to his knees, but recovered just in time and slashed out, cutting the hapless Saxon infantryman, who had wielded the lance, nearly in half. He surged up and forward without looking back. There was no need. He relied on the strength and trust of his men to follow him in his final push without question. He had trained these men and knew them well, where he went they would follow—if they could.

Three of his lieutenants were his brothers Ribald, Stephen and Brian. Four others were his first cousins, Hascoit Musard and three of his brothers. All knew what it would mean to follow this hellcat into battle, and the dire repercussions, if they did not. His visions had always been true to date, and he had shared the revelation of today's outcome to all his men before the onset of today's battle.

William to Alan's right, was now on his third steed, as the chargers fell from under him mortally wounded. The enemy Javelins and Arrows sailed by him as if he were charmed, as indeed many thought him so. William's bodyguards fell around his feet dead or wounded, but he continued unscathed slashing away at the entrenched enemy.

The embattled English King Harold and his brother Gyrth's trumpeters sounded the call for their surviving Saxons knights to rally around them and hold. There was always hope of intervention from God, though most knew that the Christian Pope had already excommunicated Harold.

Soon there was only an island of fighting men left with Harold at the center. The ground was now stained red with the destroyed bodies of Saxon warriors and Norman Knights, a virtual river of blood ran around the feet of the trapped King of the Saxons.

As the ring of fighters tightened, Alan saw William urging his charging steed forward. Its legs were drenched in blood clear to his hocks, though none of it was his own. It reared and pawed at the enemy, a mighty warrior in its own right. Behind him came Eustace, the Count of Boulogne and Hugo of Ponthieu. Giffard and a full band of mounted knights followed them closely, fighting to stay close to their Norman leader.

Alan knew that he and William were ordained to dispose of Harold together. Judith had been sure of it in her message, but if it were to be so, Alan would have to hurry, for William was moving forward. He was almost upon the hapless Harold.

Suddenly an arrow sailed over the heads of the remaining Saxons and Harold was struck in the eye. He tripped and fell across the body of his dead brother Gyrth, then rose with the arrow still piercing his skull, swinging his sword wildly. He appeared as a raging wounded stag, striking out madly in all directions. Usurper he may be, but Harold was a still a warrior, a half Norman himself and the Berserker blood was now flowing strongly in his veins.

From the outer circle, William reared his charger and jumped in among the embattled English. His steel tipped lance rose as he bore down on the hapless Harold. At the same moment Alan rushed across the entrenched circle of men cutting a swath of ground clear with his mighty broadsword. Three English infantrymen rose to meet his charge, but were ripped apart by the might of his swirling blade.

William's lance and Alan's sword found human flesh at almost the same instant and the resulting carnage was horrific to see. With the lance run through his body and into the ground beyond, an arrow protruding from his face and a broadsword stroke, which near cut him in half, Harold's remains slumped to the ground. Ivo de Ponthieu, one of William's trusted knights continued to strike and hack at the dead body, severing Harold's head and limbs, while screaming crazily at the top of his lungs, though the rest of the field had quieted.

Alan reached the man and threw his arms around him, pinning the young knights own arms to his side until he too quit struggling. William sat his horse impassively looking down at Alan and Ivo, and then turned his steed around scanning the wasted hill. At long last the senseless slaughter was over.

For a week the Normans build funeral pyres and filled the skies with the smoke of their burdens. The Saxon Royal families had been, as predicted, virtually destroyed along with thousands of their followers. The Normans too had lost men, but theirs were few when compared to the mass of dead Saxons, which lay strewn upon the field of battle.

Some few of the Norman Knights had died in the failing light after the battle, as they chased the small remnants of English who had survived. Their blood lust was not easily quelled and its pursuit had cost them greatly. The lands here were a sharp contrast of crevices and deep ravines and the mounted knights on their tired steeds often fell among them to lie broken and dead in the waning light. It was not long before William saw their peril and called a halt to the pursuit of these miserable survivors.

Most of the Norman leaders and their men were resting now, awaiting orders for further contest to come. And come they did; for to the north in Londonshire, another legitimate heir to the throne, Edgar the Atheling, was said to be holding an army in reserve; and throughout the land other small tyrants started to look for their chances to grab a piece of **Empire.**

CHAPTER 13

▼

Rychemonde Immortal

The Roman Legions under the Caesar, Julius, had conquered Brittany and the land of the Angles as early as the year 350 A.D. in the Gallic Wars. But by 450 A.D. they were abandoning it and moving southward back toward their embattled homeland, a land besieged from within and without. The assassination of Caesar along with a revolt of varies nobles and the invasions of barbarians from north and east had taken their toll.

Brittany, in France, had been a part of ancient Armorica, and became known as the province of Lugdunensis within that Roman Empire. It received its name of Brittany in about 500 A.D., when the Britons were displaced by the Angles and then the Saxons in the Misty Isles and forced across the channel waters and there they settled.

The Romans had given much to the peoples of Angland. They had build roads and temples, given laws and united a divided people. They had also enslaved the population, but this at least was not something new or different. It was the way of the land and most peoples of the world had been slaves at one time or another. It was just a matter of whose turn it was to be the masters.

Both Brittany and Angland were lands sought by many, for they were lands rich in soil and close enough to the sea to make them easily invaded, a place desirous of by many.

When the Romans left, the land soon was again divided into small warring states of minor kings. Then from near and far came a new wave of invaders. They raped, plundered and took, as each in turn attacked the indigenous peoples throughout the land. The Picts and Scots attacked from the North, the Irish and Norsemen from the seas to the north and west. From the east and south, other Vikings who had settled in Saxony among the Germany tribes and of course still to come were the Norsemen or Normans of France.

The Jutes from Denmark took part of Kent and the blend became a permanent part of their culture. The Angle and Saxon Viking tribes made steady head roads into their conquest of the Misty Isles over the next century especially along the east and southern coast and they too were blended in.

Over the next century from 560 to 613 they pushed the true Brits and Angles to a small area on the west coast called Wales. From there, some Brits sought to escape the yoke of the Saxons and moved across the channel to new lands on the continent, which they called Brittany. Now with Alan Rufus at their head the Brits had returned. The King's family may be known as Norman, but Judith had promised that the legacy of the land would be Brittany, a name from the family of her daughter Hawise and her grandchild Alan Rufus.

In the 8th Century control of the Misty Isles moved to Mercia and in the 9th Century to Wessex under the Saxons. In the latter half of the 9th Century the Danes pushed from the north in an attempt to control all of England. Those areas that it conquered became known as Danelaw. Danelaw was more than the land though; it was also a code by which the land was ruled. It promised fair laws for all, enforced equally whether Lord or Serf, an idea, which stemmed in part from the old Roman ideas, but grew with time.

Alfred the Great, followed by Edward the Elder and his sons, were each successful in pushing back the later interlopers and enlarging England proper. But the Celts and Danes in Northumbria, and the Brits still in Wales continued to harass these Anglo-Saxons for the next two hundred years.

In the eleventh century the Danes struck again. Sweyn, King of Denmark and his son Canute, with their Viking warriors swarmed over the land and took control. They then created a short-lived dynasty. Though they planned to make it much longer, the fates would not have it so; for upon the death of King Canute and his oldest male heir, the throne reverted to the Saxon leader Edward the Confessor, a son of Canute's Norman wife Emma and the late Saxon King/Ethelred.

Thus the land was a blend, not truly Saxon, Angland, Pict or Celt. It was a melting pot of the northern people, a true blend of cultures. Now it must try to accept the French Norman and swirl him into her blend.

After the week of rest and recuperation following the battle of Hastings, Alan Rufus, the leader of the left flank of the mighty Norman army was selected to lead his Brittany Knights forth to quite the rumbles from the north. As he expected, his was to be the way, and the force, by which the northlands would be quelled. William's trust in him was absolute and the eye of the Witch was ever upon him as it was upon William himself.

England was now a Norman state, but the north refused to readily accept the rule of King William the Conqueror. Alan Rufus' loyal forces were in tact and ready, so William ordered them forth. If the Saxon and Dane lords would not accept William, then there would be nothing left for them to rule either. William's only order to his dream-linked cousin was subdue them and lay waste to their land. *"The first you clear shall be yours"*, he told Alan.

With might of arms Alan moved on York and laid waste to it as resistance dictated. The only lands to which he spared was the lands of his new confidant, the Lady Godiva of Mercia. From York he moved on to Newcastle, there leaving farms as well as estates in total ruin. The building and crops were burned, farm animals slaughtered and every man old enough to wield arms was put to the sword, if there was resistance.

Control must be complete. There must be no revolts to call them back to this land again, for the dream maiden Judith had ordained it so. Judith laid out the campaign, names were given and sites selected. The rebellious found only pain, destruction of their homes and death. Judith's last word on the subject was to beware the youthful Lord of Loxley. But search as he might, Alan found no one who knew of a young Lord Loxley. Loxley was only a smallholding near Sherwood in the province of Mercia and was held by an old Saxon and his three homely teenage daughters, surely no threat to the Normans now, or even in the known future. Rarely had Judith led her grandson astray, but as she had often said, the future is not always clear. Perhaps Lord Loxley was someone in Alan's distant future.

It was Alan Rufus' destiny to rule this land. As foretold by Judith, once these lands were quieted, to him would come the lands of York watered by the turbulent river Swale. Here upon this mighty rise overshadowing the land, would Alan build his future, a **rich mound** upon which a man could establish his base of power.

A month later the entire north was under the control of the new leaders of the land, the Normans. To those whom had resisted came only death and destruction without quarter, for a lesson learned is worth repeating. A dead enemy could never again rise up against the victors.

The people of this land were tired of death and destruction, for the Danes had no sooner left than the Normans had come and all of their able men were now gone, dead in wars of conquest which mattered not to the common man. In two days of battle at the hands of King Hardrada and Harold the Usurper the north-lands had lost nearly 15,000 men hacked and bludgeoned to death. Another 10,000 of Saxon and Norman had died at the battle of Hastings. It had been a bad week, one that would take generations of lives from which to recover. This shortage of fighting men was to be both a problem and a blessing, for it reduced the number of local antagonist, but their absence invited foreign influence.

On Christmas Day in the year of our Lord 1066, William I, the Conqueror was crowned sovereign ruler of all England. Few of the Saxon lords had survived the months of struggle; first with Tostig, then with the Norsemen and now the Normans. The survivors of the Witan counsel had no choice, they must accept Norman rule or die. The dynasty that was to become Judith's **Empire** had at last begun, though drenched in blood.

Still small uprisings came and went in the new land and each kept Alan and his Brittany Knights jumping. In 1067 in the hill lands of Marcherland along the Welsh border, one such problem erupted. Renegade Normans plundered the lands of the Thane, Edric the Wild. In return Edric and the Welsh Princes of Bleddyn and Rhiwallon sacked the new Norman lands at Herefordshire.

Edric the Wild's lands lay in this Welsh Marcherland in the counties of Shropshire and Herefordshire. Before the Normans took England at Hastings, Edric was the Bishop of Worcester's shipman, or commander of his fleet. Edric had been at sea when Hastings fell, thus was not an enemy to whom the Nor-mans felt they needed to deal with. He had not raised arms against them, so he was left alone, as was the Norman custom. Now things were changing, though truly it was not all Edric's fault.

Then, Gytha, the Anglo-Saxon mother of the dead Saxon King Harold, started an uprising in Devon. She was distantly kin to the new King, but her son had been ruthlessly dealt with, his body coming home to her in pieces. For this she could not easily forget or forgive. In all five of her children had given their lives for a chance to control this land. If she could muster help, she would reap revenge on these Norman interlopers, and perhaps claim it for themselves.

Further Edgar the/Etheling had escaped to Scotland with his family and a few of the remaining Saxon royals. At present he was not a threat, but when looked at in a future tense, he might yet cause problems. If not dealt with soon, he might well return with a new Dane army.

Alan knew that he must stamp out these troublesome spots, for a Nit will grow into Lice. All they needed was time. With this in mind, inevitably each time Alan advanced upon a rebellious region, he did so with an aim to punish. His army burned, looted and lay waste as they went. In all times of the past, when he had compassion or given quarter, the situation had turned on him. He was determined to not let it happen again. This did not make him popular, but rather feared.

In the fall, two of King Harold's sons by an earlier marriage, who had moved to the Northeast coast of Ireland, returned and raided the western part of the country. Here the Celtic Cornishmen often joined them in arms. Theirs was not a welcomed raid, though for the people whom they raided were generally folk of Saxon stock who lived peacefully in these areas. The raids gave ample reason for the locals to accept their new lords and their protection. Indeed many locals eventually joined the Norman garrisons in repelling the Saxon raiders.

To control the areas William called for the creation of fortifications of stone in the form of Castles. Alan Rufus' was one of the first to arise and his was built to last through the ages. **Rychemonde** was its name as foretold by Judith. The locals spelled it with the English flair to make it the Castle **Richmond**, and it grew to be a stone fortress that dwarfed the tiny shire of Swaledale.

He built a thirty-three foot high Keep so that he would have a vista, an unobstructed view of the surrounding lands. A courtyard came next with walls ten foot high, to protect the defenders of his new lands. In secret he also had a tunnel carefully concealed within the floors of Scolland Hall. It was attached to a natural elongated cavern that stretched toward the river below. Should the time come when his forces failed to hold the land, he or his heirs would have a means to escape, if heirs he ever had. This was a trick the Brits had learned from the long years of hiding his cousin William from the dangers he had endured during his adolescences.

When the tunnel was finished and air holes drilled to create the necessary flow of fresh air, Alan again had the tunnel sealed. Soon no one would remember of its location, even if rumors kept the story of its existence alive.

Alan continued work on his home, adding a wall here and stair there. He decorated the walls of his Castle with Herringbone and then created in the southeast corner away from possible attack, a Gold Hold tower. Here he would amass his wealth and keep it safe for the generations of Richmonds to come.

Richmond Castle was a true work of marvel and it stood proudly above the turbulent River Swale. Throughout the shire it became a symbol of the power of this new lord of the land. It was a symbol of a change in the fortunes of **Empire.**

CHAPTER 14

▼

The Legend of the Lady

Lady Godiva a.k.a Godgifu was in her time a patron of the arts, equestrienne, and known tax protestor. She was in a position of power from 1040–1068 A.D. in the lands which fell to Alan Rufus de Richmond in the south of Yorkshire.

An arrangement was made with Godiva while she was still a mere teen, though a voluptuous one. It was to be a marriage of convenience and with it, Leofric expected to better control the indigenous population of his lands. The days of the old Celt and Pict royalties were long gone. Now the Saxons controlled the land and to them belonged the spoils, including the rights to the most alluring women. For Godiva, it was a chance to again gain power for her family and in doing so, to better protect her peoples and their interest.

However, though Godiva the beautiful Celt noblewoman of Coventry was to be chattel, through a forced marriage to the Saxon Lord Leofric, Earl of Mercia; he did appear to truly love her.

He considered himself a pious, religious Christian man, and had never been unloyal to his previous wife, nor did he expect to be so with this one. But unfortunately he was also ruthless in his taxation of the serfs within his fief and here he came into conflict with his beautiful young bride.

He became deeply enthralled with the beauty and spirit of his young teenage wife and though married and given conjugal rights, was ever trying to win her true love. This was something he assumed she could never give to him, an older man and not of her own people.

Godiva knew that Leofric wished to own her both body and soul. She also knew that for the good of her people she should comply, but that did not mean she need make it to easy for the Earl. To her it became a game of wills.

For Leofric, a taste of the youthful Lady's charms was not enough. He must possess her entirely, body and soul. But he recognized her game for what it was and it was one in which he could as Earl afford to play. For the time being at least he would do so with relish.

In 1043 Leofric had an abbey built for Ste. Eunice of Saxmundham. Ste. Eunice was a martyr from the old Roman days. He had been flayed to death for hiding Celtic religious relics from the Roman Centurion invaders. He was a hero to Celts and a heroic legend to his beautiful young bride. To win her approval and to add to her respect, if not love for her husband; he began construction of the church and its grounds in memory of Ste. Eunice.

The abbey became the largest most impressive of the area, but taxes were needed to pay for it. The imposed rates infuriated the teenage wife of the elderly Earl. She saw not the purpose of his construction, but rather the suffering it caused her people. She tried to plead their case to him, but was unsuccessfully. He was in a quandary. He must have the taxes to create the Abby. It was to be an everlasting image of his love for her, but the act of creation in itself had enraged Godiva.

"Women," though the Earl, *"what was a man to do. He be damned, if he does and damned if he does not".*

As money became tight, with the need to import stone and artisans, Leofric had starting taxing everything, even down to and including the dried manure used for fertilize as well as fuel. When Godiva tried again to talk to him about reducing the taxes on her people, he fell into a bout of raucous laughter—to the point of falling off his stool at the local pub and injuring himself. The fact that he was roaring drunk at the time may have assisted his laughter, but to the young Godiva it was a slap in the face. For this he would pay. He had humiliated her in front of the manor folk and she would repay him in kind, if only she could find a way.

She could withhold conjugal rights, but she knew that would not be effective, for the morning sickness was already upon her and she knew she was with child. But, until he relented she would not tell him of the life which they had created within her. This game was not over.

The argument over heavy taxation of the people became a classic war of wills between the two. She would nag and he would ignore. The stress of their battles became a stress upon the entire manor and its lands and people.

Godiva quickly tired of issuing her unwelcomed request on behalf of her people, and finally threatened to resort to a form of protest guaranteed to arise his interest. At last she had decided upon her next move, a protest; only for this one she must be quick or having a growing girth would cause the effort to be wasted.

She had become quite the equestrienne since becoming the Earl's wife. She started seeking the pleasures of horseback riding rather than the touch of his amorously demanding hands. To show her rage and make her point, Godiva threatened to strip nude and ride through the streets of Coventry in the full light of mid-day. She said it would show the degree of harm the heavy taxes had on her people. They had to provide support of her husband's greed, to the point that it's weight literally took the clothes off of their back.

The Earl saw her pledge as a weak effort to again coerce him, a threat as part of her games, one in which there was little chance of success. Little did he understand the zeal of his angered teenage Celtic bride!

It was late August on a Thor's day, and not cold for Godiva, though she shivered at the indignation she must endure to make her point. She had two maids in waiting riding fully clothed flanking her and slightly to the rear. These maids were to protect her virtue should any try to debase her sacrifice. It was not needed though, for reportedly her people would avert their eyes to keep from profaning her protest on their behalf.

The Abbess of Easby, her trusted friend and advisor, had tried to dissuade the young Lady of Coventry, but to no avail. She did however, issue orders to protect her as much as possible.

The Abbess had forbade even one eye to turn upon Godiva on penalty of God's wrath, for her sacrifice, she explained, was not for her own gain. Hers was rather for her people, their protection and their faith in her as their Lady.

Godiva sat straight and properly erect in the saddle with a look of composure on her face, confident, defiant, and as unashamed as possible. Her hair was down and done in two large braids, which flowed down her front to protect her nipples, and the roll of her breast. It was little enough cover, for she wore no jewelry or other adornment. To do so would have belied her protest. The three moved slowly through the streets, neither looking right nor left.

It was reported to Alan Rufus, upon his acquisition of the title to these lands, that a blind man who now served in the Abbey was struck so the very day of Godiva's ride. He had, as boys would, failed to heed the Abbess' words and looked longingly at the naked beauty before him. The boy, Tom, had only an instant to ogle her beauty; for at that very moment he was smote blind by God. Now he serves his years repenting in the service of the church that her husband had built. To the best of his ability, in his diminished capacity, Tom the Peeper, as the village knew him, and by providence as Peeping Tom tried to repent his error.

Tom had no easy time of it at the Abbey, for unbeknownst to him, the Abbess, Lady Godiva's friend and advisor was a strong hater of all men, for it was she who the young Saxon Swein, brother to the former King Harold had raped and dishonored publicly at the local taverns a few years earlier. For this reason, if for no other, did she gravitate to the protection of the young Godiva; who had been forced into a marriage with the much older Saxon Lord, Earl Leofric.

The ride took no more than a quarter of an hour to traverse the shire's main square, though to Godiva it seemed an eon. The rough hair of the steed rubbed her nude bottom raw. Perhaps it was this or the herbal brew which the Abbess had given her to calm her nerves before the ride, or even the wrath of God; but during the trip, her stomach began to cramp and a slight spotting occurred. It was as if her moon cycle had suddenly resumed. When she questioned the Abbess, she was told not to worry for it was a common enough thing, a slight blood flow early in a pregnancy could mean nothing. However during the night that followed, the cramps intensified and a small bloody mass of perhaps two or three inches was expelled.

The Abbess held Godiva to her afterwards. Her arms carefully encircled the young Lady and she smoothed her long hair, while gently whispering words of condolences. She called the miscarriage a blessing of God, but Godiva was devastated. She saw it as a punishment for her overt act and she decided to go into seclusion. At the Abbess' insistence she moved within the walls of the Abby and then she swore the Abbess and her nuns to complete secrecy of her maternal loss, and each firmly pledged their compliance.

Taken aback that Godiva would go through with her protest, and possibly a little ashamed that he had forced this incident to fulfillment; Leofric withdrew the new taxes he had imposed. He waited for Godiva to return and gloat, but she came not. Even his request for an audience with her was declined through her new protector, the Abbess. Three weeks passed and in a final plea, he withdrew all his taxes upon the people of the shire, save those on the wealthy, a tax on horses. These he said were necessary to run the affairs of the district. He told the Abbess to inform his young Celtic bride that she had won her battle and with this capitulation, it established a legend, of the Lady and her service to her people.

With deep love evident in his change of heart, and as part of the requirements of their new understanding, Godiva returned to Leofric; but never was he to be told of their mutual loss. Godiva and Leofric resumed their marital ties, but the relationship between her and the church became even closer, for the Abbess was now ever at her side.

Leofric became ill shortly thereafter of a mysterious stomach ailment and though treated by the herbs of the Abbess, he soon died. The Lady Godiva now ruled in his stead, a Celtic Noblewoman in control of her people's ancient lands. These lay at the junction of two lands, Wessex to the south and Northumbria to the north near to the shire of York and now on the lands of Alan Rufus de Richmond.

Time passed, and the pains of loss of both child and husband faded, but the fame of the lady grew. She became known as an angel of mercy to the fledgling Christian church that grew in the land of the Saxons, as always carefully guided by the possessive Abbess. Godiva absorbed herself into her people's welfare; perhaps this would make amends to the Gods for her loss of Leofric's child.

With time her beauty did not age, but rather matured. She was of the mid 30's by the time of the conquest of the Normans, but her regal beauty surpassed those of more tender vintages. Without the weight of children, her waistline stayed trim and her breast firm and high, though she would have gladly given up those things for the blessings of children.

Many where the local Lords and Knights which sought her hand, but few found favor, for encouraged by the Abbess, the lady had decided she had received enough of the pawing and privities of men. Hers was to be a celibate life. Although she ached for the lost child, she vowed that never again would she let men get control of her beloved people and lands. She, if ever need be, would prefer to be the seducer, not the meek helplessly controlled woman as befitted her time.

Though desireless of the affection of men, such was her fame and allure that Washingborough soon became more than just a manor. It became herald as the most receptive estate in the land and one of the most important administrative centers in the country. With importance came financial worth and Godiva's purse grew. Her manor house and grounds expanded to overshadow Lincolnshire and also Nottingham, which were the next closest manor estates. Even in York, her fame as the mysterious benevolent widowed mistress of her lands was known.

In an age when few wanted the new Religionist, she foresaw through her advisor the Abbess, the growth of the new religion and assisted a monk named Hough with a house and a new Abbey. This she called St. Peter in Barnwell. Thus, she had wisely aligned herself with the Priest and Priestess of the New Religion and the power it exerted on the known world. If this religion must overshadow that of the religions of old, she wanted to make sure she was one of those who embraced it early on. She too made repairs to the Abbey at St. Edmunds and its bury grounds in Suffolk. With each work of the church, her power within its structure also grew, as did her confidant, the Abbess'.

CHAPTER 15

▼

'AMIER'

(To love)

Godiva's lands had grown rich in power and prestige and she was not about to give them up. She had managed to survive through the governments of Canute the Dane, his son Hardacanute and then Edward the Saxon-Norman Confessor, by use of a mixture of luck, guild, and exceptional political skill. She had built her lands to her liking now, and would not easily see them destroyed or herself overthrown in the war, which was to come. To that end, she decided that she must make a pact with the winner before the war even started.

To support the reign of anyone of the three viers of the title, she must make sure that they would win. Failure could cost her those lands.

William I, the Conqueror had a good claim to the title, but the Dane King Hardrada had a strong army waiting in Norway to push his claim. The Saxon lords of the Witan were equally determined to keep Harold as King so that they might in turn keep their own lands in tact.

The Lady's benevolence to the church had caused her due notice and within its structure, her fame grew. She might now use some of that notoriety to her advantage.

Godiva first sent her agents to the land of the Norman Monks at Pevensky. They were a secluded order and one in which she could trust to keep her secret.

There she left a message to be sent to Duke William upon the first ship sailing south. Her message bade William welcome as the rightful King to the land of the Angles. She stated that his was the right to rule, as all knew, and she would support his acquisition, in whatever meager manner she could.

Next, she sent a messenger north to the Danes. She said she must get word to King Hardrada of Norway at the earliest possible date. Godiva signed her name with the title of her office and lands, and sent it forth. No further message though could be sent, for to do more would be to invite disaster and her words must never be used against her and her people. Verbal oaths of allegiance, especially through a third party, could be easily denied. She must not allow herself to be caught in an untenable position with any of the potential players in this drama.

Now for the new King Harold. What could she do to ensure his trust, yet leave her clear of any complicity should the English fail?

She sent word to the new king, Harold Godwinson, explaining that she knew of his dilemma. Her messenger committed the words to memory, for even here Godiva wanted no written account of her offer.

His words were these, "*My Lord, the Lady wishes you to know that she is aware that your enemies are at the gate. The Danes are to the north and the Normans to the south, each poised to invade our beloved England.*

As Lord General and King, you must be able to defend our lands from either direction. In your wisdom, if you should decide to, perhaps you could house your troops midway between. There they would be ready to rush at a moments notice to defend the realm from these despicable foreign invaders, and if her humble manor and lands would be of assistance in this cause, then she bides you to feel free to appropriate their use. She said that she personally holds no army of Knights to place in your service, but she could at very least supply room and board to your brave defenders of the land."

Troops of the new king had come steadily to the lands of Lady Godiva and with them the master of these Saxon Knights. King Harold, himself had arrived, but Godiva found nothing of the swarthy usurper that she could admire. She played her part as hostess well, but kept as far away as possible from the men of this king. Though willing to supply them with the food of her land, she offered no retainers to assist in the coming struggle for England. In all personal dealings with the new King, she kept the Abbess close at her elbow, a chaperone that even a King would not easily dismiss.

Harold had been a widower and known womanizer before his marriage of Aldyth, but to taste the pleasures of this Lady of Coventry, he might rile the displeasure of the Church. That would be one more problem, and he had enough of them already.

Now in the time of the first moon of the New Year, 1067, with the battle of Hastings over and a new King upon the land, Godiva was glad she had hedged her bet by playing to all the magnates of the wars, which had spread across England. Now Hardrada, the Norwegian King was dead, followed by Harold, the Usurper King of the Saxons; and a new power was upon the land. Hers had been a successful game until now, and she would continue to play as long as her lands and people were the pawns of such fortune.

Earl Waldheof, the new king's Norman nephew-in-law, now held the lands of York and to him she would have to look. If she could convince him of her loyalty then surely William I would leave her in peace. She privately sought him out and relayed her pleasure that he and his Norman wife Adelaide would be her neighbors and fellow Lords in the new King's realm.

The Earl was not impressed with Godiva, for he considered her a mere vassal of his, and a woman, which made her of no importance. Perhaps later, she might offer a night or two of distraction, but for now he was not interested. His young wife, Adelaide still quelled his hormonal lust.

He had quickly dismissed Godiva, but let slip that the fortunes of their new king were not decided yet and to Waldheof himself might fall the entire kingdom. This he thought might keep Godiva appropriately awed until he tired of Adelaide and had need of the Lady of Coventry's obvious delicacies.

The revelation of Waldheof's designs on the Crown came as a surprise to Godiva. She was a shrewd woman and planned not to be caught up in any formal revolt against either power. To her, the game must be played out so that she could remain in power regardless of the outcome of these contestants.

Godiva sent out her emissaries again. She must know more. There was just too much at risk. It would be best, she decided, if she could align herself with the house of the King in some way or another. He was the new power in the land and the fool Waldheof would soon be ousted, if she were any judge.

The King had two half brothers, but one was a Bishop and the other too heavily involved with affairs in France; perhaps a Lieutenant, or loyal leader of his army. It would have to be someone of Royal lineage, if she was to keep her titles. Her age was not a detractive, for she was only thirty and five years and still a fine figure of a woman, if she did say so herself. But to whom would she play.

To the east she learned of the struggle of the Welsh and the mighty Norman warrior, Brian of Penthievre. He was a cousin of the king and a leader of part of his army, but he was to young for her mature womanly wilds to be effective, and he was unfortunately married. Ribald, the next oldest of the Brit cousins of the King, was also married, and not aggressive enough to suit her taste. The titled brother of the men of the house of Brittany was Alan Rufus. Perhaps him!!!

Alan was also a cousin and a General in William's army and more importantly not married. This **could** be her answer. He was about her age, and if not, no more than a couple of years her junior, but that did not worry her. What did was his reputation as a loner. He had never been known to seek out women either for marriage or lust in his conquest. Her spies defined him as a perfect warrior, always drilling and practicing for war; a man without vices of wine or the flesh, his only confidant was the King himself. 'Twas rumored he was a haunted man who saw visions, a man who readily applied this clairvoyance to win his battles.

This would be her conquest then; a man without heirs or female ties. A man she could introduce to the joys of intimate behavior, if need be, more importantly though, a man who had the ear of the king.

She sent out messages to the king and to his major supporters to feel free to call upon her should they be near at hand and in need of assistance. To each she sent the same message, but to Alan she made it a more personal one lightly scented with the spores of the Pimpernel, a delicate native scarlet flower. The messages bade them welcome, should it mean medical assistance, supplies or a haven, if mattered not. She would answer the call of her sire and new king. Godiva was shrewd enough to know that sooner or later either Alan Rufus or the King himself would have to come through her lands to deal with the Lords of Northumbria. When they did she would be ready.

Soon enough her chance came, for the lords of the north finally rebelled, as she suspected they would. The two brother Earls as well as the lascivious Waldheof were making rumbles of war. To that end she knew the time had come. Alan Rufus de Richmond marched first to her lands and she bade him welcome.

It was time for a conquest of her own. She wined and dined him as his men rested and encamped in her fields. The campsite was well prepared, for the Saxon army had proved up on them only months before. Now this new army used her lands and found them comfortable, with fire pits and walled springs easy to hand. There even remained the raised frames from which to erect tents.

Godiva made Alan aware of her interest in him by sly glances and open smiles, as they dined alone in the great hall of her manor house. She used the ruse of slightly brushing against him whenever they were near each other, but never to overtly, for she needed him to feel that he was the initiator.

Godiva was wise enough to know that a woman who is openly aggressive, often would be bedded, but the man would usually considered his conquest less than a lady. Therefore the thought of amour must be his, and the courtship carefully protracted.

Alan rested and recuperated on the lands of Godiva for three days while he waited for a message from either William or their ghost advisor Judith. Each day he supped with the amorous Lady of the land at her insistence. However she need not push, for she intoxicated him. He knew not what to do though, for he had never been a lady's man. There had been no time for him to learn the intimacy of courtship, beside perhaps she was just being a gracious hostess and had no real interest in a warrior knight of a foreign land. Alan was aware that her fame was widely known, and none knew of her ever accepting the advances of her many renowned suitors. From all accounts every eligible man in England had pursued her at one time or another, but all were rejected. Perhaps it was true that the lady and her Abbess were haters of men, but Alan believed it not, for to him she was far to gracious and her charms were almost siren-ous in nature.

The day came far to soon when the message was given and Alan had to move his men northward to quell the uprising of the two Earls. He summoned his men and mounted his steed to lead them out. As he turned, he spied the Lady standing under a flowering dogwood tree near her manor house. In a rare moment of uncontrolled ardor, he spurred his horse forward and reached the Lady in a bound. She raised her hand to him. It held a delicate perfumed handkerchief of white lace, scented with the same Pimpernel fragrance, which had graced her letter. He reached for it and she held his hand. He turned it and kissed her palm, a nature act, and one he had seen others do, but had never performed himself.

She said quietly, *"Take care my handsome knight, least you take my heart. Be of care in body and soul that you may hurry back this way unharmed. And please plan to tarry next time, for I would know you better."*

Two months later, Alan rode triumphantly back along the trail south. His was a path to London, thence to William to report of the happenings at York and beyond, but the trail could also lead through the lands of the Lady Godiva, with only a small deviation. Her parting words had haunted him and gave rise to visions, which for the first time, his witch grandmother had not put in his mind. This thoughts guided him toward her manor house.

He arrived during the dark of the night. He should have rested with his men who had reestablished their camp upon the manor grounds, but he was not wishful of tarrying till morn. Perhaps he had misunderstood her innuendos, but he did not want to wait longer to find out. His mind had been a whirl of thought of her since their last meeting and if not for his diligent subordinate's ability and the constant vigilance of the witch, he might well not have return at all. His mind, for the first time, had not been in the battles that he fought, but upon a dogwood tree and a lady with a kerchief delicately scented with the Scarlet Pimpernel.

Alan dismounted and handed the reins of his charger to the stableman. He entered the garden of the manor and bade the house servant to alert the Lady of his arrival.

Mere moments later she appeared. She was dressed in her finest gown and her hair was down, hanging long and shining in the glow of the candles. She curtsied and smiled at Alan, then rose and took him by the hand saying, *"Our sup awaits my Lord."*

"How did you know I was coming my Lady." queried the now shy knight.

"I have my ways", she said. *"You are not the only one who has the knowledge of clairvoyance,"* she said with a laugh.

The meal passed in minutes it seemed to Alan. He was completely absorbed with the lady, enchanted by her style and grace. He knew not where the time went, for the servants had long since finished serving the meal. The lady finally told him that they should move to the garden, that the servants must clear the hall, and make ready for the morrow.

Alan realized he had stayed long into the night and asked her to forgive him his trespasses, for he had not noticed the time. She took him by the hand and told him that perhaps he had forgotten that he had promised to tarry on his next visit. Still holding his hand, she strolled into the gardens and out the manor gate.

Here, there was a small trail, which led down a hill and away from the manor house. The moon was full and it gave a soft light to the path ahead. Alan knew not were they were headed, but it mattered little, for the warmth of her hand and the very intoxicating scent of her had captured him, and he could not have escaped even had he wished.

They walked for perhaps a quarter mile, neither speaking, just enjoying their closeness and then Alan saw a flash of water. In the clearing ahead it was tumbling over a rocky streambed making a merry bubbling tune. Its ripples were reflected by the steady flow of the summer's moon. Suddenly Godiva released his hand and moved forward toward the water's edge. It gave a glow, which illuminated the Goddess that he beheld.

She ran quickly to the stream, turning to glance back but once at Alan. It was a look of coy promise mixed with a slight giggle of mischief. She removed her slippers and stepped timidly into the stream, testing its temperature, then whirled and looked at Alan again, before slipping from of her dress.

It was a quick movement and it caught him unprepared. He barely saw her beautiful body flash in the tree shrouded dissipated moonlight. She was there and then gone, immersed in the shining turbulent stream.

The look she had given was one of promise, and it aroused something in the mighty red haired Brit; something, which had lain dormant for a long time now. There had been no time for girls when he was younger. His was a life of study, and training; one of trials and battle. In his youth, the urges of vengeance displaced all, but with the death of Wacy he was made a leader of men who must fight for **Empire**. There had never been time in his life for women. The last twenty years there was time for nothing save battle and conquest.

Now this woman had brought fire to his loins and heart. She was a Celtic-Saxon, a titled Dane, a woman not of his people; a potential enemy to his quest of **Empire**. What was he to do?

Alan looked quickly around to see that the area was free of prying eyes and hidden enemies. It would not be the first time that a warrior had been lured to his death by a beautiful siren, though he hoped with all his heart that this was not the case.

The wet sands squeezed between his toes as he hurriedly removed his chain mail, tunic and leggings. His sword that had ever been his companion these last few months, he laid carefully atop his garb.

Godiva had quickly moved to the deeper, darker water, surprised and embarrassed by her own sudden urge for this man. She turned and watched as he disrobed in the soft glow of the moon's light.

Godiva's eyes took in the muscular body as it slid from the hidden folds of his attire. This was to have been her conquest, not his; but she now found stirrings within herself as she watched him disrobe, then move toward her. She knew that she had wanted him when first they had met. Not because she loved him, but to solidify her position and lands. Now she felt something different. It had been growing since their first meeting. He was paradox of men, strong and intimidating in public, yet shy and reserved when alone with her; and now, with his return, it was near to carrying her away.

Her smile of promise began to waver as she took in his physique and quiet assurance. It was replaced by one of yearning. She suddenly remembered that she had missed what the feel of a man's touch could do. Her husband, the older Leofric's touch had been a chore to her at first, but even with him she had found desire as they grew accustomed to each other. Now with maturity, came a deeper desire to be fulfilled, to be touched and caressed; to be wanted as only a woman could be, by a man she also desired. There had been no time to think of such things in the past, for she had to protect her lands and her people. The lecherous lords of the English had not stirred her, but now with the perceived need for a tryst, her emotions began to run wild. Her heart began to beat with anticipation and, yes even true desire.

She waited for him in neck deep water. He dove and swam effortlessly to her beneath the stilled waters of the sparkling stream. His hands came up to her and paused almost trembling there to explored her breast, then they came on up to caress her face. They embraced and kissed, their bodies molding to each other. Suddenly theirs was a heat that belied the cool of the stream and the time of day.

She pushed off from him with a smile and small giggle. Alan came for her and she dove under the water and swam for a rock shelf, which extended from the far shore.

Alan pursued her, and she gave up quickly as he again embraced her and pulled her to him. The water was shallower here and the moonlight glistened off her breast, as droplets ran down her slender body. He separated from her slightly, letting his eyes look long upon her glory. Never had he seen anything, which stirred him more. She was perfect in shape and form, a nymph or siren of legend. A woman such as Alan had never seen. He had to possess her.

Godiva blushed under the intensity of his gaze, and was glad for the half-light of the full moon. Its rays were sprinkled through the forest, which lined the stream, but reflected enough that each could get an ample eyeful of the other. She was no naive young girl and this was no teenage boy. She knew she was attractive; she counted on it to hold her lands in the world of men. But this was different. She felt the beginnings of something, which she had never known. A desire for a man, because he was a man, this man, this Brit/Norman, this glorious redheaded giant.

They came together, pressed hard against the outcropping of stone, to which she had swam. Her soft breast pressed hard against his powerful chest. He raised her up to sit slightly upon the smooth rocky outcropping. Her knees and legs reached out to him, pulling him to her. A wave of warmth spread across them as they coupled. They held each other tightly, each aware that they had finally found something which they had been seeking their entire life.

Spent, they clung together for a long time, neither speaking just holding on to one another. Alan released her and moved his hand to her face and ran his fingers along the smoothness of her skin. He bent and gently kissed her on the lips. Then she smiled, before nipping him on the ear. She then pushed quickly away, left the stone ledge and swam for the opposite shore.

Alan chased her to the embankment. Reaching her from behind, his arms encircled her and pulled her glistening body close to him. She laid her head back against his shoulder and gazed up at the stars.

"I wish we could stay like this forever," she sighed. *"Never to worry about the affairs of our fiefs or retainers.*

"Ours is not a single destiny, but that of a people." Alan answered.

"Yes, it has been that way for to long it seems. I had forgotten the pleasures of the touch of a man and the thrill of passion, I have been alone a long time now", she spoke.

Alan answered her with a kiss, and she responded with a renewed hunger, almost a desperate passion, turning in his arms to face him. A moment later, they lay entwined upon the sands of the stream. The starlight captured their gleaming bodies and seemed to join them together as one. For a while they found solace and pleasure in this simple joining. Forgotten were the dangers of the rebellions around them, and the intrigue that had brought them to this place. There was still the uncertainty of the future, but for the moment there was—**this**.

Days stretched into weeks and still the Knights of Alan Rufus camped on the lands of the Lady Godiva. It is said that when any two young fighting men get together for more than a day, a contest of abilities will ensue. It was so with the retainers of Alan Rufus. Wrestling, sword fights, joust, games of chance and skill were taking place on a daily basis and often as not, one or more of the Knights would be seriously injured. They swam, fought and played board games like, *Latrumeuli, Tesserae, Hnefatafland and Bocce.*

The competitions became a daily occurrence and the people of the shire often came to marvel at the skill and endurance of these men of France, especially the available maids of the surrounding Manor lands, and there were many. For the wars had depleted the land of its youthful males, and these were strong, handsome and virile young combatants. By the end of the first week a viewing stand had been erected and Alan Rufus along with his host, the beautiful Godiva made daily use of it, even to the point of granting the winner a kerchief of the Lady as a trophy.

Daily and mayhap even hourly the admiration of this Lady grew within the heart of the veteran warrior leader. Theirs was becoming an affair of the heart, which appeared to be taking on stately grace. Alan's men came to think of, and some openly spoke of her as Godiva, the Lady of Rychemonde.

Only one thing overshadowed their bliss. Each was of an age, which deterred the outlook for children, and Godiva had already had a miscarriage during her youthful days of marriage to the late Leofric. The mid-wife and Druid medics brought to her by the Abbess said that she would never have more children, news which had at first mortified her. How could she consider herself a woman when she could not, nor ever have birthed children? Godiva had barely survived the emotional upheaval of the miscarriage of her teen years, had it not been for her friend the Abbess, she was not sure she would have; and now she feared that she was either truly barren or too old.

In her early years, she had not easily gotten over the feeling that she had let her husband down. A man needed heirs to carry on his lineage and name, someone to whom he could pass his titles and lands. With Leofric, she had tried to perform her wifely duties in those areas, but to no avail. It was as if her loss of the first child left her forever barren, a punishment of the gods. Her only solace was her friend the Abbess, who continually plied her with herbs and teas, in an effort to heal her friend physically and emotionally. But, with the death of Leofric she experienced an easement of that desire and the need for the Abbess' herbs.

She pledged herself to the service of the Church, her serfs and their welfare. She tried to fulfill her own need for children, through the lives of those within her fief, and to them she was an Angelic benefactor loved by all.

Now her one burning desire was knowledge. Knowledge of how this news would affect her new love? How would he take it if she could not give him heirs? He himself was getting older, perhaps in his mid thirty's or even nearing forty. The chances of them having that kind of a family were remote.

True, Alan Rufus de Richmond had never had children of his own either. There just had never been time to get involved to the extent of getting married, and his cousin's distaste for bastard children, kept him from the occasional prostitutes who offered to have him sire one of their whelps.

His Spartan lifestyle did not lend itself well to the acquisition of a family of his own either, but now things were becoming different. The future was upon them, and he could at last see the end of his grandmother's vision quest and with it; the likelihood that he could at last settle down to a normal life. Children would have been a nice addition to the lands and titles he now would inherit from the conquest of this new land; but they were not essential. He still had his brothers and already they were producing sons to carry on the family line.

What worried Alan the most now, was what this most beautiful woman would want in life. During one of their love making sessions, he had mentioned the children of his brothers. Though he had not voiced a proposal or wish for children of their own; he had noticed a sadness or sorrow appear within her eyes. A most caring and giving person, this Lady Godiva, she would have made a splendid mother; and Alan's one regret in the whole tragic affair was that they might never have that opportunity.

Alan offered her wine and, when Godiva accepted, he poured two goblets from a decanter atop the bed table. Time was short, for he must soon again tend to the affairs of maintaining a strong military presence in his realm, if he intended to stop future rebellions. For now though, there was the joy of this most perfect Love, something that could last. An **Empire** and a woman to share it with, who could ask for more.

The wine and lovemaking had an effect on Alan, and he slumped into a restful sleep. His was a sleep without dreams, perhaps the first of his turbulent life. He awoke refreshed and happy. He was full of joy for this new life. His eyes fluttered open to find Godiva resting on her elbow looking at his face.

"What's the matter, can't you sleep?" he asked, as he reached for her.

"No, I was just watching you. We don't know how long we have and I did not want to miss any of it," spoke the sensuous lady.

"We have a life time left to us, if you wish it." Alan said.

"*Maybe, but with the King in Normandy, and you in charge here; how can we know? At any minute one of your Lieutenants may call you away, or your precious King might need help on the Continent and send for you.*"

"*You make it sound as if you hate or despise him. You neither know, nor understand him. His is a driven life.*"

"*Alan, what do you really think of him? I know he is your kinsman besides being our new King, but tell me what is he really like?*", she asked.

"*He is a great man. A born leader if ever there was one*", surmised Alan, after a moment's thought. "*He inspires loyalty in all who get to know him. There is an Aura of power around him that others seem to recognize, and are attracted to; much as the moth is attracted to the flame. It is an ill resistible force. I don't know how else to describe it.*"

"*You know, there is a saying, that a man's greatness can be measured by the number of his enemies, and his true worth by the loyalty of his friends. Our King William, it seems has many of both. That is, if you are any example*", said the lady Godiva.

"*He is a complicated man and ours is a complicated trust. Yes, we are cousins, as well as friends and companions in war*", offered Alan.

"*Made more complicated by his contradictions of nature, at least in his handling of his enemies, wouldn't you say?*, queried Godiva.

"*How do you mean?*" he asked.

"*Well he slaughters his enemies in the field without quarter. Yet he is willing to let those which openly oppose him orally, to live and even offers them land and titles; as he did the Welsh.*"

"*Ours is a shrew King, my dear. He will try to turn an enemy into a friend when he can. He will use bribery, flattery or even marriage of his female kin to accomplish his goals; but know this—he never forgets, and once you have betrayed him, he can call down the fires of hell upon your lands. His is a scorched earth policy to those whom he feels have belied his trust.*"

"Remind me to stay on his good side then, for I do not wish to lose either my lands or head!" laughed Godiva.

Alan ran his hand over her supple body, pausing to caress those special areas where he had learned she desired most, and then kissed her gently on the lips before saying, *"It is **I**, of which **you** need worry, my lovely nymph-ish winch! William will neither bother you nor your lands as long as I stay happy."*

"And are you happy my Lord?" she whispered, gently nipping his ear.

"At this moment, I am more so than at any time in my entire life."

Godiva beamed with joy, rolled on top of him and began to again fulfill his every desire. Her kisses made his heart flutter; it was almost more than he could bear.

How, he thought, had life allowed him to miss this sweet amour of abandonment of individuality for so long? This must be how the Gods had meant for man and woman to be; two coupled for life, one an extension of the other, a perfect blend, and the universal being. He knew that these feelings were something that he deeply desired to never again be sated of.

The wheel of time continue to turn and days moved to weeks as Alan found one reason or another to tarry at Godiva's side.

But as predicted by Godiva, the call was finally given and Alan was again rushing his knights outward toward the boundaries of his new lands; even as the noonday sun cleared the low clouds of the English countryside. Once again the flames of rebellion were upon the land and he must quell them quickly and ruthlessly. He must demonstrate that the Norman and English were now one people with one King; and this at least, would not change for the next millennium and beyond. The seeds had been planted for Judith, himself and William. They had only to wait and carefully trim the weeds of rebellion for the growth of their—
Empire.

On his last night before departure, Alan lay with Godiva in a gentle embrace, but in the small hours of the morn, he arose and dressed without a word. She eyed him pensively wondering what he would say.

Alan was not accustomed to speaking sweet verse to his love, but in his statements, he was oft profound and this was one of those occasions, for he wanted Godiva to know how he felt.

He knelt at her bedside and took her proffered hand. He then began—*"Each of us is born to a special purpose. It influences us, directs our footsteps, and is our link to God's greater objective. It radiates down upon us all the days of our lives, and to follow it is our destiny. That destiny is not a foe, but a friend. It is not to be worshipped as a god, but as a manifestation of him. In times of peril, it is his way of preparing us for that, which is still to come, for life, as death is always a struggle, of strength, of skill or of desire."*

"Tonight, my dear, my destiny is you, and I am at peace. Tomorrow it may be the sword and death, but never will it not also be you. I tell you this not to frighten or coerce you, but simply to prepare you. Until then my heart is gladdened that our souls have touched however briefly, for our destinies are now upon us."

Godiva threw her arms around him and said, *"If that be a question, then the answer is YES—if not then the answer is still YES!!!"*

Alan returned to his men to sleep in the wee hours of the morning, but to him came only troubled dreams, for the witch was not happy that he had allowed events to progress so far so quickly with Godiva. He still had work to do, for yet the land was not tamed. Judith had her King, and he had already produced heirs to build her **Empire**. Her grandchild, Alan, must now be the hammer, which drives the nail. He had no time for love and definitely not with a woman who might not sire him heirs. There was still work to do before Alan could settle down or rest. There were still the requirements of **Empire**.

Godiva arose before dawn to see Alan off. They had been together for nearly two months now and she could hardly bare to see him leave. His trips back to his men before dawn had fooled no one she feared, for already she had heard the servants whispers. But she cared not, for the first time in her long years as Mistress to these lands, she felt worried not for her people, but joy for herself.

She hurried to wash and dress that she may see Alan off. A soft tap at the door stilled her. She covered herself and bade them enter. It was her chambermaid with her breakfast, but followed closely on her heels was the Abbess.

Godiva started to speak to them, but the aroma of the morning meal hit her and her stomach began to churn. She barely had time to reach her chamber pot before she regurgitated her previous evenings meal.

The Abbess took the tray from the maid and pushed her quickly from the room. Godiva wiped her mouth then rinsed it with fresh water. She turned to the Abbess and said, *"excuse me, 'twas perhaps tainted supper meat."*

The Abbess looked at Godiva for a moment, turned to the window which faced the Norman army readying itself in the distance, before saying, *"Perhaps, but I have heard rumors of you and the Red-Headed Norman, who is now Earl of these lands."*

Godiva turned on her, and snappishly answered her—*"He is a Brit, not a Norman!!"*

"Small difference my Lady," answered the Abbess, *"but ill-regardless of whether he be Norman or Brit, let us deal into another problem. How long have you been bedding him?"*

Godiva was taken aback. She said, *"That would be my business, but if you must know, we are in love and have been since Summer's eve."*

The Abbess counted slowly in her mind. *"That would make it about six weeks now, would it not."*

"Yes," said Godiva, *"and the happiest six weeks of my life!"*

The Abbess looked disturbed and said, *"my dear, in these happiest six weeks of your life, have by chance your moon cycles appeared?"*

Suddenly Godiva understood what the Abbess meant. She looked at her bewildered, and then a smile crossed her face. *"But that would mean,—I am—with child. Oh Dear Abbess, let it be so. I have dreamed of it for years, but thought it impossible."*

"My child, we are as sisters, I have known you these long years since last you were with child. This is not a good thing. Back then you were married to an Earl. Now you are a widow. A child now would be a blight on your reputation. All your good works would be for naught. You would be seen as a common street wench. Don't you understand? You cannot have this child!!!"

"*I will!*" Godiva yelled. "*This is a gift from God, no one can take it from me. I will gladly give up all for this child. Besides, Alan **will** accept it! He **will** be its father!*"

"*My dear,*" said the Abbess, slowly shaking her head. "*He is a warrior. Look out your window. Those men you see assembled there will march off to fight, many of them will not return. You cannot depend on men,*" she said. "*Both of us had learned that lesson long ago.*"

Godiva, who was already a flush with emotions, fell on her bed weeping uncontrollably.

The Abbess smiled to herself and moved to comfort her. "*There, there my love,*" she said. "*I will go get you some herbs to settle your stomach. We will talk of this matter more on the morrow.*"

Alan fought through each battle in a fog. His training would not fail him and the witch Judith kept him moving forward, but his mind strayed constantly southward. It was ever a whirl of dogwood blossoms, sparkling streams and the scent of Scarlet Pimpernels.

When Northumbria finally came under control, Alan and his court guards hurried southward. As they approached home, they encountered a slow procession headed back from the distant Abby. At the lead were Godiva's court retainers, with the common folk of the nearby fiefs following closely in the sad procession.

A chill ran down Alan's spine as he watched the mournful troop. A few glanced their way, but quickly averted their eyes. Alan gave an order and one of his squires galloped forward to intercept the procession. Only a few minutes were wasted in discussion and then he wheeled his steed to return to Alan on the run.

"*My Lord,*" cried he. "*Tis dire news!!*"

"*Be quick with it then,*" commanded Alan.

"*'Tis the lady Godiva,*" he continued. *She is poisoned. 'Tis said the Abbess did it with herbs and foxglove, and then she slit her own wrist and bled to death in the Lady Godiva's dead arms. These you see on the road,*" he motioned with a sweeping arm, "*have just returned from her burial.*"

CHAPTER 16

▼

Brian Penthievre de Richmond and the Insurrection of the North

Again in 1069 a fleet supported an insurrection in the north and west from Denmark, but this too was ruthlessly put down. Harold's sons were back raiding the West Country again. Earl Brian of Penthievre, the brother of Alan Rufus de Richmond, met them with extreme prejudice and they fled back to Ireland.

In the Welsh lands, Edric the Wild, had taken Shrewsbury and then quickly moved on to Chester. It was an open field for them, for Alan Rufus de Richmond was dealing with another uprising in Northumbria. Mordoc and Edwin, supported by the Danish King Swien Esthrithson, had led a new revolt. Aided by the Earls of Waltheof and Gospatrick, together with the pretender Edgar the/Etheling, they had thought to break away from their Norman masters. There to build a new Kingdom in the lands of York, but Alan Rufus de Richmond now claimed those lands and he was not a man to take lightly.

He had let them live when last he had defeated them, but at those times each rebelled separately. Now it was a different story for they had all rebelled at once, a plan to divide and conquer the Norman and Brit forces.

William was still tending to events on the Continent, leaving a void of leadership to deal with Edric. It fell once again to his Brit cousins, but in the form of Alan's brother Brian this time, for Alan was still in mourning.

The events in the redheaded Brit giant's life had left him severely distraught and it did not serve one well to aggravate the testy Richmond. He had often fought ruthlessly, but now it was as if he was a rogue lion, fighting for the shear thrill of his bloodlust. Neither friend nor foe was safe and until he simmered down, William decided that Alan's brothers must take leadership of his army. Brian was available, so it was to him that the task fell.

Edric, it was said, was married to Gondul, of the fairy and elfish folk of lore. He could appear and disappear at will in the wilds of the Welsh Marcherlands or so the folk tales reported. Perhaps it was truly so, far neither William nor the Richmond brothers were ever able to bring him to the point of the sword.

Brian Penthievre de Richmond captured a squire of the man of the wilds in his first battle with him. Edric had slipped away into the wilds of Marcherlands, but his man could, if properly persuaded, shed some much-needed light on the expertise of this will-o-wisp. When questioned of the Welshman, Brian learned a peculiar tale. It went as this—

"In the lands of Weston-under-Redcastle in the south of the shire and into the forest of Clun, Edric is master of all. He is charmed above all men and yea will never catch him, for 'tis impossible to catch that which is magic and of the Wee Folk."

Alan was not amused and drew his sword to the man's throat for a civil answer.

"Pray harm me not sire, for I do not lie! He is enchanted. I saw it myself," supplied the squire.

Tell your tale then, and be quick for my temper and patience be short for those who would thwart the King.

"Once while on a hunt for boar", started the frightened squire, *"he and I became lost, for the wood seemed changed in the half light of late eve. We came at darkness upon a large manor house of which we knew not. Lord Edric said he had never*

noticed it within the wood before, and warned me to be careful, for it was surely the work of witchcraft. We were lost though, and tired and hungry; so we went nearer, just to see what kind of people lived there.

As we crept towards the lighted windows, we could hear music playing. Peering in Lord Edric said he saw a room of ladies in fine gowns dancing in a graceful circle. As they danced they sang most sweetly, for though I would not look, I could hear the music and the beauty of their voices. Their language was not discernable to me, for I had never heard this language before, to this I will take Oath."

"As lord Edric watched, he noticed one young women in particular, tall and slender but more beautiful than the rest, truthfully more beautiful than any he had ever seen. He fell instantly in Love."

"Come he ordered me! We must find a way in. 'Wait!' I yelled it might be a trick, witchcraft designed to ensnare us. But the music drew Lord Edric onward until he found a door. There he stealthily entered. I am sorry to say, I was afraid and waited by the door."

"He burst into the room and grabbed hold of the young beauty by one of her hands and managed to carry her off. I readied the horses and we rode swiftly away. Suddenly the wood became familiar and we made it to our own Castle in due time."

"Edric ordered the best food and wine be brought his prize. He professed his love to her tirelessly for three long days and nights without the Elfish beauty saying a word in return. Neither did she eat or drink. Finally at the end of his wits, he called his retainers and arranged for a troop to go into the forest in search of the manor. He must know more about her and her people. Perhaps he should speak to them of an arrangement for a formal betrothal. The young beauty heard these orders and chose that moment to speak for the first time."

"She said that she would remain and be Lord Edric's wife, for she was now sure of his love. She said she would bring him happiness and good fortune, but he must never say another word of her sisters or her home. For on the day you do, she told him, you will lose both your luck and me. On that day you will despair and die."

It was an impressive tale, but one in which Brian believed not. However the elusiveness of Edric could not be denied and gave Brian and the Normans pause for thought. After all, the story of a specter advisor coming to his brother Alan in his dreams was a wild tale also, though one not many knew about.

"What be this lady's name?" asked Brian de Richmond.

"She is known as Lady Fay to those at court, we hear that the Lord in private do call her, 'my pretty Fairy queen'. Though 'twas not meant as offense to his majesty William and the true Queen, his lady, Matilda. Of that, I am sure my Lord." said the squeamish squire.

Brian held the reins of the Welsh lands, though never truly conquering them. The Earl of the Wilds, Edric, remained at large; but in time he came to accept the Norman. He even assisted them to stop the raids of the Danes on his as well as their new lands of the Norman **Empire**.

CHAPTER 17

▼

Northumbria

News of uprisings continued in the lands, and with Alan temporarily distracted William returned from the Continent to help deal with them.

Thus Alan Rufus and King William were together again, and they chose the Northumbria area to battle first, for there the forces sacking it had slaughtered hundreds of loyal Normans in the city of York.

Earl Waldheof, King William's rebellious nephew-in-law had been said to have had the Normans run by him at the city gate in single file so he could have the pleasure of personally slaying a hundred of the Frenchmen, with but a stroke each. Somehow his hatred for his wife's uncle had welled up to the point where he had decided to kill all who considered themselves associated with the Norman King. He felt sure that at last events favored his revolt and his on ascension to the throne. William, he thought was detained in France and Alan distracted over the murder of his mistress, the Lady Godiva.

Alan though still in mourning was awakened from his lethargic mood by William's arrival and by the constant pressure of Judith. He summoned his retainers, many of which were now married and settled with Saxon wives throughout the Earl of Richmonds eleven estates. They assembled alongside William's army and made ready for yet another campaign of war.

But when word of William and Alan's approach reached the Danes, they fled to their waiting boats and commenced raiding the coast in a hurried departure, while still seeking assistance for their revolt from the Danelaw part of England.

Here the two Norman armies split. Alan moved to the Fens, while William moved to the Pennine hills to deal with the rebellious Welsh of Cheshire and Stafford shire.

'Tis said war is as life, a constant struggle. Since time immemorial, the hardest moments have not been in battle, but the waiting. It is a time for sharpening swords, lances and battleaxes, repairing armor and chain mail; but also a time for thinking. The thinking is perhaps the hardest.

In battle, a man fights and lives or dies, it is solely at the whims of the fates. He depends on strength of arms, keenness of steel and his skills and that of his companions. He may prepare for all contingencies, but in many cases it still comes down to the luck of the day.

Those thoughts, along with images of his loved ones, keep a man's blood a boil with a will to continue, to accomplish, to live, and to survive.

Since the dawn of time, man has fought against man. Sometimes he fights for land, sometimes for love, gold or vengeance; but always with this will for personal survival.

In the Christian histories, Cain slew Abel and then cried out to his God for mercy that he might himself survive. He was afraid that others would slay him. His God put a mark upon him then banished him unto himself, apart from his own kind. But still his will to survive was strong and he found a mate and in time sired a nation of men. When man loses that will to survive, indeed he loses all.

Alan it appeared had lost that primordial drive for survival. He still fought as a demon possessed, but no longer did he shield himself in times of peril. He at times used no shield at all and thrust himself into the thickest of the fray, slashing and hacking his foes as if daring them to hold and fight him personally. His ferocity often broke the line of men ahead of him of its own volition, as he wielded a sword in one hand and a battleaxe in the other. His own gallant men had to redouble their own efforts to stay abreast of their Lord as he smote his enemies. More than once he fought all the way through a line of his rebellious enemies and had to turn and reenter the fray from the rear to find someone left to fight.

Perhaps thought William, the fens would be safer for his closest confidant. Of late he had been riding into battle as a man possessed. He seemed to not care whether he lived or died, but that 'tis a dangerous way for a man in his position to live. William found no fault in his fighting ability though, for Alan could fend off any ten men without even trying, and often did. It was his leadership, which might fail him, for a man who cares not for his own life would not properly see to the lives of those entrusted to him.

The tie up of William's forces with that of Alan's brother, Brian of Penthievre, who had just come fresh from his victory over Harold's sons and the Irishmen, would prove to be to much for the Rebels. With the two Norman armies now acting as one, Edric the Wild took his men and fled to the hills leaving the Welsh and Englishmen of Cheshire and Staffordshire to fend for themselves. These were quickly defeated at Stafford and the Normans razed the countryside, burning and plundering all. This action quelled the rumbles of rebellions in the Welsh lands. Though Edric occasionally forayed out and caused mild trouble, he was now much subdued. He solemnly pledged to no longer be the cause of his people's misery.

Now William, and Brian Penthievre de Richmond, moved quickly to help their kinsman Alan with the old problem of the Fens and Northumbria. Here, Herward the Wake, a local landowner was stirring up trouble anew.

New Danes had migrated to the old Saxon held lands seeking lands and wives. The lands were much depleted of young men and these were generally welcomed. The problem was that they had never felt the bite of Norman steel and thus were fiercely independent and readily supported a new uprising.

Alan Rufus was meeting strong resistance from these newcomers and the locals were burning the bridges over the rivers and streams, which were swollen with rain. It was an attempt to hold him in check and save these new husbands and fathers. The reinforcements of Brian and William though were not to be deterred, they spread out and flanked the roadways used by Alan's army and the rebels and their resistance quickly fell.

William made his way to York, suffering heavy losses from ambush as he went, but succeeded in cleansing the countryside of troublemakers by killing any who appeared to oppose him. York, by now was in an atrocious condition with the buildings in ruins and the Castles destroyed. His Normans ranged afar and captured every living man who could have been possibly been old enough to have bore arms. These men he brought to York and forced them in the rebuilding of all of the Castles that the Anglo-Norsemen had destroyed. Next he re-garrisoned them and warned the populace that his patience was growing thin. Men would be welcomed into his Kingdom for husbands and workers, but rebellion must end or all would suffer.

Alan Rufus gladly took control of the subdued lands for it would keep him close to the tomb of Godiva. Though denied her love in this life, hers was an image never far from his thoughts. The Witch once had promised that when the land was no longer at risk and his brothers had sired sons to carry on their line, he could marry if he so wished. But, that dream was now over. Judith had tried to console him, but no specter could understand the flesh and blood desires of the living. Mayhap once she had known, but she must have forgotten. She could never understand his yearnings for Godiva's touch, her voice, her warmth. He could have lived his life in leisure with the style of an elder Earl and statesman in his home at Richmond, had she been with him. The castle Rychemonde was near complete now and waiting for him, but he knew now that it would never be a home, at least not for him.

All he could do was make sure that his brothers did not share his fate. They must know love; have children and lands to secure their Brittany line. Alan was at last awakened from his lethargic mood. He had a new purpose and a new plan. Yes, a subdued land for his brother's heirs it was a Noble Quest.

Now with an army ready and at hand, he turned his attention to Chester, a province that had refused to readily accept his Norman King. This would solve that problem, and offer access to the Norsemen based in Ireland. Should they decide to continue their raids into the Cumberland, he would move to eliminate them. Chestershire heard of his coming and knew fear. Dreading the fate of their neighbor shires, they opened their gates and welcomed the Normans without resistance.

It was now time to heal an Empire and William would try to do so with diplomacy and bribery rather than bloodshed. He knew that Alan tired of battle and if he could give his trusted confidant and cousin rest he would. The first truce he offered to Jarl Osbjorn, a Danish lord, brother to King Swein of Denmark, to whom he offered an Earldom or Danegeld. Thus the chances of revolt in the Fenlands, which Alan Rufus de Richmond had vowed to control next, was now greatly reduced by the bribe to Osbjorn.

The Norwegian King Swein had lost an ally in Osbjorn. Fearing the growing legend of the Red-haired Brit, he took to the seas and vowed to continue the fight. He decided he would protect the Isle of Ely with his ships, and from there, beef up the forces of Herward in support of his revolt. He also encouraged the sacking of Petersburg and its Cathedral, which was controlled by the Normans.

Here Swein made another fatal mistake for the rape of their holdings did not amuse the Church and the Vatican threatened to get involved. King Swein saw the complication of a Holy war and decided to accept a monetary bribe to sail for home and leave the Misty Isles to the Normans forever. The Norwegian King Harald Hardrada had given his life in pursuit of a Danish Empire. He, Swein of the Sweinlands would not also do so, at last gone forever was the Norsemen's final quest for a Danish **Empire**.

The sacking of the holy relics at Petersburg also caused the rebels of the Isle of Ely problems, for the outraged monks now showed the Normans the secret causeways through the Fens. Without the backing of Osbjorn or Swein, the Fenmen were left hanging out to dry. Alan led his men into the marsh with the stealth of a crocodile and the renewed strength of a lion. They came upon the Fen Isle without their foreknowledge and Ely fell in 1071, but Count Herward and a few of his men escaped. These were as always to cause further trouble later, but never again to the berserker Brit, Alan Rufus de Richmond.

For four years the trials and tribulations seemed to be at an end. At last, thought Alan, he could return to his solitude and the lands that he had grown to love. At Rychemonde, which most now called Richmond, he retired. He sometimes disappeared from public view for days at a time within the walls of his new fortress home, but he always reappeared in time to hold court on the fifth day of the week—Thor's day. This was the day on which Godiva had made her infamous ride. Remembering weekly her sacrifice for these people would give him a reason to have mercy unto them and to administer true justice. Thus, his new people came to see a different side of their feared Earl. He planned to use that new found acceptance to settle down to a quiet life.

While his enemies feared him, those who lived under his protection at last found justice and peace. Alan, through his constant studies of ways to benefit his people, had found the theory of the Danelaw practical and fair. He introduced it to his new lands and dealt out this new justice as fairly as he could. Godiva had been an example of a benevolent Lady; he would try to be so also, as their new Lord and protector.

Still as Alan's benevolence grew, his health failed proportionately. His brothers and fellow lords noted a change in his pallor, week by week. It seemed he was as a prisoner without the benefit of the sun. Something must be done, thought his brothers Brian and Stephen, but when they went to get him, he never seemed to be about. It was as if he would vanish into thin air.

Perhaps if the peace remained, they would have time to shore him up, to heal him and return him to his former vigorous self. But it was not to be, for the storm broke again in the spring of 1075, with 'the Revolt of the Earls.'

The two Earls were both half English and half Norman. Both had supported William in his claim for the throne in 1066. Ralf, Earl of East Anglia, was English on his father's side and had been born in Norfolk, but he had grown up with his mother's family in Brittany.

Roger, Earl of Hereford was English on his mother's side and born in Hereford, but of a Norman father. He was also Ralf's brother-in-law. The two plotted to bring in the Danes for support of a new coup. They also sought the assistance of Edric the Wild and Earl Waltheof. These were already harrowing the Normans and they thought them suitable allies. A successful uprising by the four would cut England in half and create a new Kingdom.

Edric the Wild maintained his promise of not being the catalyst for retribution upon his people, thus he rejected the plan outright. While the earl of Waltheof considered it, it was a distinct possibility.

Once again Judith's advice was the key. Through an ease, which belied his power, Alan Rufus de Richmond learned of the possibility of a pact between the four. He managed to send word to Waldheof to hold off or this time suffer the loss of all his lands. Then in a surprise move, Alan attacked Roger of Hereford, utterly destroying his troops and power base before moving to deal with Ralf. Roger was captured and imprisoned for the rest of his life as a criminal to the state, his lands and home disinherited, though his life spared.

Alan it appeared was once again his old self. Flying into battle unheedful of his own safety. A berserker of old Viking lore, who was never to be denied his final victory.

The onslaught was too much, for Ralf fled his lands, abandoning his people and sought out the Danes for aid. In the months of his absence, his wife Emma tried to hold the coastal Castle Norwich from siege. For three months the armies of the Normans held her bottled up inside, not wishing to make war on a woman, but determined that she must surrender.

She was not at fault, thought Alan. Maybe she was as Godiva, merely a woman wanting the best for her people. He gave orders that she was not to be touched, but the battle must continue.

In the dead of night on the fourth day of the fourth month of the siege, the Witch came again to Alan and foretold of Ralf. His pleas for help to the Danes had finally been successful and Alan must hurry in his destruction of fortress Norwich or the Lady Emma would surely be reinforced in less than a week.

A plan was immediately put into action. Alan ordered the siege machines to advance and stand at the ready, for the morrow would bring the final conflict. His brother, Brian de Pentheivre, was placed in temporary charge and Alan moved out alone to make a last minute try to save this Lady of the land's castle of Norwich.

The surface of the water gave way to darkness, but one with cool fresh air. Alan gulped it in, for his lungs had started to burn from the long swim. He could make nothing out from his surroundings, for the darkness was near total.

Alan reached out a hand and made contact with the cold, rough surface. It was of flagstone and carefully fitted to form a smooth textured and even floor. A set of steps led to a landing and Alan stepped up. He pulled the thong from his neck, which had secured his father's sword to his back, as he swam. He might have immediate need of it in this quest.

He was cold and wet, but at least he had made it this far. It was dark here, as dark as the inside of a tomb. That unpleasant thought and all its connotations came easily to Alan's mind, for his specter protector had spoken against this plan. He was hopeful that it was not a prophetic omen of what awaited him further into the lower passageway of the castle.

He climbed on to the stone floor and looked back at the underwater passage. Only a slight discernible light could be seen within its depths marking the open sunlit sea beyond. At another time of day the entrance could have been waded with air to breath, but now the tide had filled the tunnel and temporarily sealed it. Had Alan waited only a few hours, it would have been an easier task, but time was something he could not afford.

The darkness held no fear for Alan, for his grandmother had always been at hand whispering of any unknown danger whether day or night. She had often told him that no supernatural source held personal dangers for any man; only his mind could do that. Alan's only concern now was for a potential inability to cope with the real dangers the dark held, and these were always human, and of flesh and blood. Had he felt the presence of Judith, perhaps he would be better prepared, but she was busy elsewhere and had seemed to shun him for she had not wished this errand.

Judith had however made Alan aware of this entrance to the castle proper, a secret way that none other than the Thane, Ralf and his Lady Emma knew. The witch had intended it as a means to enter and subdue the Castle Norwich's retainers without undue lost to Alan and his own men. She had also foretold that no guard would be waiting during the times of high tide. She never meant for it to be a way for Alan himself to commit some insane skullduggery in trying to alleviate the need of killing the Castle's lady.

Judith's wishes and her power, as any that is wielded in a subliminal way, may be easily misread. It was a power that Alan had never understood. At times its messages were crystal clear, while at others murky and unfathomable. Alan surmised that there has never been a form of power that did not evoke multiple consequences, just as there has never been a sword that did not cut both ways.

Be careful, be not reckless was Judith's final word of warning to her independent minded heir. She still had need of this redheaded giant of a grandson General. He still had to direct her plans for **Empire** and recklessness now, might upset it all. Still within Alan there was some drive to save this lady from herself and Judith, try, as she might, could not deter it.

The subterranean path was to be a means to this end, but not a final end in itself for the new Earl of Richmond. However, Alan was strong willed and his lack of enthusiasm to destroy the lady had led Judith to reluctantly assist him though she would not do so overtly, for she still felt it was the errand of a foolish heart.

Alan's loss of his one true love, the lady Godiva, had wroth in him this change; as all who truly knew him could see. He was still the perfect warrior in style and leadership, and fought with a will of purpose; but there was a weakness now, a flaw, and a noticeable difference. He now thought too much for his on good of the affairs of others, especially women who were in leadership roles, such as had been the Lady of Coventry. These played heavily on his mind as he debated the future of Emma of Norwich.

Slowly Alan moved forward down the winding cavernous corridor. With each step, he would pause and listen intently for some sound of movement ahead, always alert and ready for ambush. For even though the common people of the area, whom he had interrogated, knew not of the lower caverns; there could still be sentinels on duty here even at high tide. But listen as he might, he heard nothing save the steady movement of the bay waters at the tunnels concealed entrance behind him, a soft slapping sound of water upon flagstone.

With his left hand on the wall itself, maintaining a steady contact with its rough-hewn texture and his right ever vigilantly gripping his father's honored sword, he moved forward. Suddenly he felt the shaft of a torch mounted in the wall. He ran his hand up it, groping it from one end to the other. He found the upper end still warm to the touch. His hand held a sooty resin, which smelled of fresh smoke. So, this tunnel had been used recently. At least since the siege had started and probably within the last twenty-four hours. A way for escape or a route for reinforcements, Alan knew not.

Perhaps the lady was not yet ready to die here in this place for the sins of her rebellious husband and was even now ready to flee, but Alan had to be sure. The small sloop that he had concealed adjacent to the tunnel's exit would carry but three or four persons and she had to be one of them or he would allow none to escape.

William's orders were plain enough; those in power who rebelled were to be put to the sword. Whether they be man or woman, it mattered not. Their retainers who fought for them would be given a second chance, as they had in the old days in France. They could join as loyal vassals of the King or die alongside their Thanes.

If it came down to it and the Lady was captured after this long siege, she would be put to death. Alan himself would so order it, for to not do so would be to set a precedent; and others might get the false impression that they too could revolt and expect leniency. Her only chance was to escape before the walls fell and Alan was determined to give her that chance, even if it must be at the point of a sword.

Here the floor of the pathway started to slope gently upward for perhaps a dozen yards, then Alan's foot encountered a raised platform. He reached out with his foot and felt along its surface and discovered it was a stone step followed by another and still another. At last he must be beneath the castle proper. Slowly he moved upward perhaps twenty-five feet or more. The dampness, which had ever been present around him, seemed less pronounced here. And then Alan saw a thin line of light ahead. It ran from the wall on his left and continued across in front of him to the other side of the corridor. It had to be a crack in the wall ahead, perhaps light from the bottom of a doorway. It appeared to be high over Alan's head, but as he ascended the stairs it came parallel to be eyes and then began to fall with each step he took upward. This was an indication that it was indeed a slither of light from a door at the apex of this staircase.

Suddenly Alan was there. He reached out and made contact not with stone, but with the smooth surface of Oak. His hand traced the outline of the door, but found no handle. To the right there was a small opening and into it he reached. Here was a latch of sorts built into the wall. It extended into the main body of the thick oaken door. Alan pulled outward on it's shaft. Silently there was movement of the door swinging inward slightly and a draft of warm air greeted him from within the hidden staircase.

Alan paused, for with the rush of warm air came the sounds of two men talking. He could not make out the words well, but there were definitely at least two and possibly more awaiting him should he continue through with his present course. Perhaps he should wait, but not to long for the attack would come at first light whether or not he returned. Brian, his brother, was at the head of his siege army in his absence and Alan knew that he would not fail to lead the attack at first light with or without Alan's input.

The five Brit brothers, now known as Richmond, were bred for leadership and all that it entailed. It would never have been a choice for Brian to wait. The plan for the attack was scheduled for the morrow, and he would not fail.

The time seemed to drag by, but still Alan waited. The sounds of conversation waned and were replaced by a soft snoring sound from the outer chamber. Alan eased the door to the lower staircase open and covertly stepped into the chamber. He then eased the door closed least some errant draft spoil his surprise for the sentries at hand. He heard a soft click as the locking mechanism reinstalled.

The room was merely an alcove off the main hallway with the door concealed behind a mural of some forgotten Lord. This was an effective way to hide its actual purpose. To the left was a recessed area, which held a candle, and if he was not mistaken, also a second lever to open the door from this side once it was swung shut.

Alan eased his head out the alcove opening and immediately saw the source of the snoring. A guard was stationed in the main hallway between the alcove and another substantial doorway, but he was propped up and sound asleep, an offense that would have had dire repercussions had he been a part of Alan's army. The door he was supposed to be guarding must hold someone of importance to the land. If Alan were not mistaken, it would be the Lady Emma herself.

But what of the second voice he had heard? There was on one else in sight at present, but for how long? Could the other guard be stationed within the chamber? Not likely, unless it was a close relative or lover!!

Alan moved closer, sword at the ready. He would try to eliminate the guard without alerting anyone else and then see what the room held. If fortune was with him, he could be in and out before anyone even noticed. The guard wore no helmet, so a quick blow to the head would neutralize him with little effort.

Alan moved forward, alert for any other movement within the halls. His foot caught the edge of the alcove wall as he made his move and he stumbled. There had been very little noise, but enough to awake the guard. The hall was darkened and in the half-light, the sleepy guard could not make out Alan's form as he fell upon him. He managed to cry, *"who goes…"* before Alan silenced him permanently with a strong stroke of his sword. Unfortunately the blade sliced through the upturned neck completely and clanged heavily upon the stone hallways' wall.

From within the chamber came a woman's voice—*"guard what happens there, are we under attack?"*

Alan made no sound, but pressed himself tight against the wall by the doorframe. Anything could happen now. He was sure the guards cry had gone unnoticed except from within the chamber he guarded, but should the lady start a ruckus the hallway might rapidly fill with armed men.

Again from inside, *"guard what is happening?"*

She had approached the door and started to ease it open, there she saw the headless body prone on the hall floor. She stared in horror, her hand to her face, then before she could scream, Alan rushed her, pushing the door in with his foot and forced her to retreat into the room. In a bound he was upon her as she tried to catch herself. His large left hand encircled her mouth, nearly covering her entire head and tilting it backwards. His right arm, which still held the sword, swung around her pulling her backside to his chest. He moved the sword in place, its blade under her chin. An easy pull would slit her throat or even decapitate her as it had her guard.

Her eyes were wide, but Alan had to give her credit she stopped struggling immediately and waited for his next move. Alan spoke softly into her ear to minimize the sound of his voice. *"Do not struggle, I mean you no harm. Had I have wanted you dead you would now be so. Listen carefully!! At sunrise your castle will fall and you with it, if you are still here. King William had ordered you and your Thanes death if you are captured. I will give you another option. I have a small sloop moored at the underground entrance to your castle. You are to board it without delay and sail for the protection of the outer islands. Your husband will arrive in two days and you may rendezvous with him. You and he must forever vacate these lands and their titles. I am the Earl of Richmond as well as of Brittany, Alan Rufus. Go to my old lands. Your husband has lands there that I will see that he keeps and there you may make a new life. This one is forever forfeit. Do you understand?"*

She nodded her head and Alan released the hold on her mouth, but kept the sword at her throat.

"What would you have me do? She said.

Two days after the walls fell, a fleet of two hundred Danish vessels filled the harbor, but it was to late. The Castle Norwich and its lands were gone. With a look upon the smoldering ruins, Ralf swung his ships to sail away, just to see a small sloop coming in fast. It was his wife Emma; she had managed to escape through the tunnels and had waited at sea for the return of her husband.

Alan, it was said, had known of her escape, as he had known of the approaching ships, for Judith still watched his back. However, his love of Godiva and the courage of this Lady, led him to allow the escape. Alan stood upon the remnants of the battlements and smiled as he watched the Danish ships sailing away. The Thane and his Lady sailed for their lands in Brittany, but these English lands were now forever forfeited. Another price paid for the quest for **Empire.**

Earl Waldheof, though not a true member of the conspiracy, was advised by William's confidant, Lanfranc, the Archbishop of Canterbury to come clean of his part in the conspiracy. Waldheof's wife was the kin of King William I, and should have been of help, but the hapless conspirator's future was not to be, for Judith had whispered to the King, "*remember my son of the tales of the slaughter at the Gates of York. A hundred Norman heads rolled that day. A snake cannot be handled least it bite you. Now it is time for the worm to turn."* This and the warnings previously given Alan by Godiva of his designs on the throne sealed his fate. No longer would William allow a thorn to fester in his side, even if Waldheof was married to his own blood kin. Without undue ceremony, Waldheof was quickly beheaded.

The lands of the traitor Earl and slaughterer of Normans, were given in trust to Alan Rufus de Richmond and his heirs, so long as they could hold them in this land of northern rebels. Adelaide and her children, through the benevolence of Alan Rufus de Richmond, could live there as long as they swore allegiance to King William.

The years of turmoil continued off and on with the Danes to the north, the Welsh to the west, and even in William's holdings in France, but to each the King and his Normans dealt with the situation with determination and immense energy. The Cousins always seemed to be one step ahead of the conspirators, ranging from one end of the country to the other, fighting the flames of resistance and stamping on the smoldering flames of resentment.

At each point of trouble a new castle was raised and a loyal Norman placed in charge of its garrison. William would not let these insurrections continue. Alan Rufus had already established his, named Rychemonde on the River Swale near York, now he set out to build another for his brother Ribald at Middleham. A gift of his own ceded lands through William I. His other brothers would also have theirs lands in time as promised by William for their invaluable service at Hasting and since.

Ribald had been but sixteen when he entered the field of the battle at Hastings, but his lineage and training proved him a knight worth the title and William was good to his word of honor. Wealth and plunder came to those who followed him loyally into battle. Ribald married Beatrix de Tallbois, the daughter of the Sheriff of Lincolnshire and Nottingham. These lands he would pass to his own son in time. Judith said a son named Ralph FitzRibald, a.k.a Ralph Tallebois would control those lands and eventually seed it thoroughly with heirs.

Through out the land the throngs of revolt were temporarily quelled. With Harold Godwinson dead, as were Tostig and King Hardrada of Norway, the remaining Earls of the lands controlled by William were to weak to form a formidable force. Edric the Wild, Herward the Wake, Swein, Godwinson and William's nephew-in-law the Earl of Waltheof had tried and each had met ultimate defeat. No Saxon or Anglish leader rose to retake the reins of revolt, with these at last under control. Now it was time for William and his loyal Vassals to solidify their Kingdom and rest.

With each battle the power and force of William's rule had become more entrenched. Judith continued to visit, but told both William and Alan that her time with them was about up. Soon her debt would have to be paid in full. She came to each of her chosen ones in turn and told them that the land could now heal. Soon the land would blend with their Normans; first as Norman-Saxons, then as Norman/Saxon/Angles and lastly as Englishmen all.

The last fifteen years of his life, William had spent more time in Normandy than England. To England he entrusted Alan Rufus de Richmond and his strong-hearted brothers, Brian of Pentheivre, Alan Niger, William, Robert, Richard, Ribald and Stephen also of Pentheivre. They must defend her against those who would follow the way of Harold, and try to usurp William's throne.

Normandy was William's problem, for there were danger spots in Maine and in Vexin on the Seine River. Here the Norman Empire bordered the French royal lands. William's neighbors, in his absence had tried to take his lands. They had dared to become more aggressive and hostile toward the Normans, as they heard of the continued struggles in England.

Fulk the Surly in Anjou, Robert the Frisian in Flanders and Philip I of France, each sought alliances with Canute the IV of Norway. They thought that such an alliance would allow them to siphon off lands from William's Empire and he would be powerless to stop them.

Fight or diplomacy, William was not sure. For either may cause a weakness in his status. His son Robert Curthose was given the Countship of Maine. Fulk the Surly received a compromise in the treaty of Blancheland for control of Anjou. It gave him concessions, but required an oath of allegiance and support to William.

Now for the problem of King Philip, who had annexed the county of Mantes and the eastern part of Vexin.

Judith's spirit continued to advise both William and Alan through these years of turmoil, but with each year they saw less of her until on Easter night of 1085, she came to bid them farewell. Her time at last was over. For she had roamed the land for three score and ten years, a life past her own nature lifetime. It had been a gift of the gods, so that she could fulfill her pact with Cernonnus. In her last dream visit to Alan, she begged forgiveness for not allowing him time to marry and sire children. Hers was the need for a General, a man without fear to fulfill her plans for **Empire**. "*Though your cousin William's line shall reign supreme, to you and yours shall come an equal legacy. William's **Empire** shall not be known as Normandy by the generations to come, but by the name of the land of those who held it secure for his heirs—**Britain.**"*

Judith faded from their lives that day, and with her their fortunes it seems. Alan returned to the solitude of Richmond Castle, where he was seen less and less, while his brothers were left to quell the rebellious countryside.

King William was at a total lost for her advice, but he still had the problem of King Philip and France to deal with. William demanded the towns of Chaumont, Mantes, and Pontoise returned to him immediately. The French King made no reply and William led his forces into Mantes in a surprise attack, but while the town burned, he met an unexpected accident. His faithful steed shied from the bloodied remains of a Frenchman and reared. The horse fell backwards and crushed the chest of the mighty Norman Emperor.

William was rushed to Rouen, where he lay dying for five weeks. He had the assistance of some of his bishops and doctors, but neither prayer nor medicine could repair the damage of a half-ton charger.

To his side came his half brother Robert the count of Mortain. His sons William Rufus and Henry were also in attendance. His son Robert Curthose was away in attendance with the French King and had apparently attempted to assist the King in his war with William, thus William was not sure of wayward child's loyalty. In a last minute compromise, just before he passed from his mortal realm, he bequeathed England to Rufus, Normandy and Maine to Robert and Henry received a great treasure with which he could bargain for lands of his own.

So it was that William the Conqueror followed Judith in 1087 at the age of sixty years. He finally had entered a battle unprepared and alone. Although he could still easily defeat his enemies, he no longer was prepared for unforeseen events. In the years pass, his specter protector would have forewarned him of the nervous steed. But she was long gone and he lay dead upon a cold slab, now to his sons came the reins to his **Empire**. That which no man could wroth had taken only a skittish horse to accomplish.

Alan Rufus de Richmond was at his home near York defending the Kingdom for William, when he heard of the King's death while quelling the rebellious French. Alan Rufus still was not physically well, and the affairs of the Northland were never totally settled, for the Scots were ever stirring up their Danish kin.

It seemed to his court that Alan shrank with each passing week. Perhaps the cold and wet tunnel at Castle Norwich was to blame, perhaps his own secretive nocturnal trips were, but Alan's health slowly declined.

Within a year Alan Rufus de Richmond followed William in death. In the year 1089, he went to his grave without heirs of his own. His only mistress had been his struggle for **Empire**, for although he had romanced the beautiful Lady Godiva and tasted love; they had never found time to marry. His body was committed to the holy Abbey of Easby-Bury less than a mile from his home in Richmond. The Castle Richmond and its lands with the title to eight lordships thus went to his brothers each in their turn, Alan Niger and then Stephen of Penthievre. Each was to carry the Richmond name onward in time and history.

Snuggled within Alan's papers and ledgers pertaining to his lands, was found a last will, if such it could be called.

<u>To my family</u>—Brothers—Geoffrey de Boteral, Brian de Penthievre, Alan Niger, William, Richard, Ribald de Middleham and Stephen de Penthievre.

Brothers, to you I bequeath all my lands and titles, these for you to hold each in turn until heirs are produced to control our lands. In return, I ask but one thing. When you lay me down to my final rest, I ask that you place me near to the hand of my Lady Godiva.

Beneath the bowels of Rychemonde Castle there is a hidden passage, which leads to Eastby Abby. There I had the mortal remains of the Lady secretly secured. 'Twas rumored by her maids that she was with child when she was so foully murdered, and that has added greatly to my misery, for I have long desired that which each of you have found in plenty, family and heirs.

I am not ashamed to say that these nine years last, I have used the aforementioned tunnel to carry me to her and there to sit and unburden my soul.

Know yea this; that to her I wish to be bound in death, as we should have been in life. Some might think it a weakness for a man such as I, feared and thought to be callus of nature, to care for a Celt such as she; for throughout my life I have tried to hold true to the acquisition of fortune for our family. The fate of that family's bonds, and unto that mission, I have faithfully tried to fulfill. My sole reward, in this life's world will be the continuance of our line through you.

I have always known that this life is not an end for ones soul, for almost daily throughout my life I have had a reminder. To that end, in the next life whether it be Heaven or Valhalla, I wish only Godiva's acceptance of me as a part of her otherworld existence, a joy that was deprived to me in this present.

Brothers, when my soul has been laid to its final rest, I ask that you close the tunnel and seal its airshafts that no other may desecrate that which I had built in my desire to be near her. Afterwards erase all references of her and my common bond, if need be, of my very existence, that no man shall ever defame her image. To those of her fief, she is seen as a Saint, while I am not; but of her, I would have no ill word spoken. This I bid you do, in my solemn memory.

—Alan, Earl of Richmond

With England at last secure, Judith, Alan Rufus de Richmond, and William I (the Conqueror) had each moved to the pages of history and legend. Theirs was the dream.

TO BUILD AN EMPIRE TO LAST A THOUSAND YEARS
-------------------**ALL HAIL BRITANNIA!** -------------------

Post Script

William I—aka the Bastard—aka the Conqueror was born in 1027, the illegitimate son of the Norman Duke Robert, a.k.a the Devil, a.k.a the Magnificent. Some had called him the Devil, and he did not marry Arletta the common daughter of a tanner of Falaise. Hence William was called the Tanner or the Devil or Bastard by his enemies, which were many. Despite the ill regularity of his birth, his succession as Duke was recognized by the Norman barons in 1035 A.D., while at the age of nine years.

Duke Robert the Devil was so named because his mother had made a pact with the Devil to ensure that she and her heirs would rise to greatest as King and Emperors of Europe, and they did.

Duke Robert the Devil of Normandy impregnated his mistress, Herleva of Falaise. Because of the Devil's curse upon him, rather than marrying her he persuaded her to marry his friend Herluin of Conterville. After William I's birth, she had two other boy children: Bishop Odo of Bayeaux and Robert de Mortain, both of which became famous and important in Norman history.

Duke Robert died in 1035 when his illegitimate son was 9 years old, but persuaded the Norman lords to accept him as heir to prevent internal war. Norman's friends and relatives of his father, including Gilbert of Brionne, Osbern the Seneschal and Alan of Brittany, became William's guardians.

By now William was 36 years old and an amazing strategist. He had learned how to lead an army and saw the advantages of pledges of loyalty by others as his vassals.

In 1064 Harold of Wessex, brother-in-law to Edward the Confessor-King of England was shipwrecked upon Norman lands. He was captured by Count Guy of Ponthieu and imprisoned at Beaurain.

William saw a chance for a coup. He had already established his blood ties to the aristocracy of England and now he asked for and got the release of Harold to his protection. Harold was given control of one branch of William's knights and assisted in his attack on Conan of Brittany. William defeated Conan at the Battle of Dinan and William exaggerated Harold part in the victory and knighted him. In return Harold pledge his allegiance to William and promised to aid him in his quest for the Crown of England should Edward die without heirs. Harold also was given promise to marry William's daughter Eadmer.

Harold returned to England and when Edward the Confessor became ill, Harold went to his bedside. Harold, alone at the bedside, said that Edward asked him to accept the throne for himself. Edward died 5 Jan. 1066. The next day the Witan (counsel of Saxon Lords) accepted Harold as King. They chose from Harold, William the Conqueror, Edgar Etheling and Harald Hardrada.

Edward the Confessor—King of England and his son in law Harold Godwinson promised William the lands of England if Edward died without heirs. But when it happened Harold broke his sacred oath and took control with the blessings of the Saxon aristocracy in 1066.

William appealed to the Pope and received his blessings to take the Crown by force if necessary. With twelve thousand men William landed at Pevensky and marched on Harold at Hastings or Senlac on Oct. 14, 1066. After defeating and killing Harold and most of his Saxon lords, William marched on London. The Saxons surrendered and offered William the Crown. He was Coroneted on Christmas Day in West-Minster Abby.

William died as he had lived in a constant battle for Empire. In Rouen on Sept. 9, 1087 while leading his men into battle, his horse reared and fell backwards crushing his chest. His son William II ripped the Ring of Power from his finger as he lay dying and proclaimed himself King of England. He gave Normandy to his elder brother Robert. But many of the people felt Robert should rule and the threat of it led to a tyrannical rule by William. A revolt in favor of Robert arose by the Norman barons. William II ruthlessly put it down, but in doing so created many enemies. He was killed with an arrow on a Royal Hunt by parties unknown on Aug. 2, 1100 A.D..

The rule of England fell to his heirs and that of his kin, but for the next thousand years each could trace their lineage back in time to the womb of the White Witch of Falaise Normandy—Judith.

The Descendency of English Royalty

Vortigern (425-450) British ruler during the late Roman Period. Known for inviting or at least allowing the Viking Saxons of Germany to settle in the area.

Hengist (450-488) First Saxon King of Kent. Claimed to have been invited to Angland as a mercenary soldier by Vortigen. There were from seven to ten independent areas established by Saxons during this time.

/ELLe (477-491) King of South Saxons. First overlord of all Anglish Rulers south of Umbria.

Cealwin (560-593) King of West Saxons. Second overlord of all Anglish.

/Ethelberht (590-616) King of the Judes or Kent. Third overlord of Angland now called England by some. First to convert to Christianity. Married Bertha a Franish princess, granddaughter of Clovis-the first Christian Frank King.

Raedwald (616-616) King of the East Angles. Fourth overlord of England. Killed Ethelberht to acquire the rule of the Anglish.

Edwin (616-633) King of Northumbria. Fifth overlord of England. Son of Aelle of Deira. Married the Princess of Kent and became a Christian.

Oswin (634-642) King of Northumbria. Sixth overlord of Angland. Son of King Ethelfrith. He lived in exile from 616-634 in Ireland.

Oswiu (642-670) King of Northumbria (now called Oswy). Seventh overlord of England. Also a son of King Ethelfrith.

Wulfher (670-674) King of Mercia

Ethelbald (674-756) King of Mercia

Offa (757-796) King of Mercia. Often called <u>Rex Angloram</u> King of England in his royal charters.

XXXXXX (796-802) period of unsettled heirs. Three dominant kingdoms emerged—Wessex, Mercia, and Northumbria.

Egbert (802-839) Merged the former kingdoms of Kent and Essex into his land of Wessex. The other lands had to pay homage to him although they were technically independent.

/Ethelwulf (839-855) son of Egbert

/Ethelbald (855-860) son of Ethelwulf

/Ethelbert (860-866) brother of Ethelbald and son of Ethelwulf

/Ethelred (866-871) brother of Ethelbert and Ethelbald, son of Ethelwulf

Alfred or Elfred (871-899) King of West Saxons, brother of Ethelred and Ethelbert and another son of Ethelwulf. He united the English kingdoms to face a Danish invasion of Danish Vikings. In the peace treaty, the Danes lay claim to all Northumbria or Scotland, hence called Danelaw.

Edward (899-925) the elder. Son of Alfred or Elfred.

Athelstan (925-939) son of Edward. His was probably illegitimate.

Edmund I (939-946) brother of Athelstan. Also illigitimate.

Eadred (946-955) another brother of Athelstan and Edmund—illegitimate

Eadwig (955-977) son of Edmund I

Edgar (957-975) the peaceable. Brother of Eadwig, also son of Edmund I became King of all England with the death of the last Northumbria Danish King. Included Wessex, Mercia, and Northumbria.

Edward (975-979) the Martyr. Son of Edgar. Murdered by his half-brother

/Ethelred at Corfe, four years after his Coronation.

/Ethelred (979-1013) the Unready. Son of Edgar. When he had his brother murdered, the Danish Vikings decided to reinvade. King Harold Bluetooth of Denmark invaded. The Danish King Harold was overthrown by his son Swein in 988, who continued the attack of England. To avoid a route by the Danes, Ethelred entered into a mutual defense treaty with the Normans of France./Ethelred later married Duke Richard's daughter Emma. This created a tie of the two royal houses—Norman and English.

Swein (1013-1016) King of Norway, Sweden, Denmark and all England, including the Danelaw or Scotland.

Cnut (1016-1035) King of England. Son of Swein married the widow of/ Ethelred whom he killed. His marriage to Emma put the titles of Normandy England, Danelaw and Norway in a common house.

Harold I (1035-1040) King of England and Northumbria. Illegitimate son of Cnut. An objection was issued by Queen Emma, who had legitimate sons by both Cnut and/Ethelred. She thought these should inherit first.

Harthacnut (1040-1042) King of England. Son of Cnut and Emma. His death ended the Danish Royal line.

Edward (1042-1066) the confessor. King of England. Son of/Ethelred and Emma. This returned the Wessex Saxon lineage to the throne. His older brother, Edmund II, Ironside, who was away at the time. Edward married Edith, the daughter of his main rival—The Earl of Godwin.

The assembly of Saxon Lords elected Edward's brother-in-law Harold II. This angered both the Normans and Danes, who set out to invade England.

Duke William I from Normandy and Harold Hardrada, Prince of Norway.

Tostig—Harold's exiled brother assisted Hardrada.

Harold Godwinson (1066-1066) Elected King by the Witan upon Edward's death. He died at the hands of William the Conqueror at the battle of Hastings.

William I (1066-1087) the Conqueror, King of England, Scotland, Ireland, and Normandy came at last. He was related by blood to the monarchy through his great grand Aunt Emma, Queen of England with both/Ethelred and Cnut.

The Chronology of the Earls and Dukes of Richmond

(The Richmond lands were taken from Edwin, Earl of Yorkshire—a Saxon after the Conquest of England by William the Conqueror)

Contrary to the thoughts of some people the lands and titles of the Richmond family stayed along bloodlines from the first Richmond to today. Although the strings of the lineage may at times follow through female lines, they still exist. This works shows a kinship from the original Richmond to the Lennox, and thus a continuation of the line.

1070	**Alan (Rufus) de Richmond** (*Count of Brittany*) *arrived with William the Conqueror and received the fief of Yorkshire including the area of Loxley and the lands of Lady Godiva.*
1146	**Alan (Niger) de Richmond** *(brother of Alan Rufus) took control of Richmond after Alan Rufus' death*
1093	**Stephen de Richmond** *(younger brother of Alan Rufus & Alan Niger de Richmonds) took control after Alan Niger.*
1136	**Alan III (Niger) Earl de Richmond,** *(son of Count Stephen de Richmond. He married William the Conqueror's daughter.)*
1146	**Constance, Countess de Richmond** *(daughter of Conan IV, Alan Rufus' Nephew)*
1186	**Geoffrey Plantaganet** *(1st husband of Constance, son of King Henry II.*

1190	**Ranulf de Blundervil** (*2nd husband of Constance, linked to the tribulations of Robert of Lockley aka Robin Hood.*
1195	**Guy** (*3rd husband of Constance & brother to Viscount of Thouars*)
1200	**Arthur** (*son of Constance and Geoffrey Plantaganet thus Grandson of King Henry II. Arthur was murdered by King John while King Richard the Lionhearted was at the Crusades, because of a push to place him on the throne.*)
1203	***King John*** (*maintained control of Richmond to usurp power of the title and stop further would be rivals.*
1219	**Peter de Braine—Duke of Brittany** (*husband and cousin of Alice the eldest daughter of Constance and Guy, Viscount of Thourars*)
1235	**King Henry III**—*Peter renounced his allegiance to England because of events in Normandy and France. So the Crown held it for 5 years.*
1240	**Peter Savoy**—*Uncle of Queen Eleanor, granted by Henry to keep it in the family of Richmond heirs.*
1268	**King Henry III**—*Peter willed the title to his niece, but she declined and returned it to the Crown.*
1268	**John, Duke of Brittany**—*son of Peter de Braine and Alice. The Title was returned to the original line of Alan Rufus through 1. Alice and Peter 2. Constance and Guy 3. Conan IV (Alan Rufus' nephew).*
1342	**John of Gaunt**—*son of King Edward III & also from the line of Maud de Richmond d/o Stephen I & her husband Walter de Gaunt (Remember Walter was the son of Gilbert de Montfort and Alice)*
1372	**John de Montfort, Duke of Brittany**—*the title was surrendered by John de Gaunt to his cousin John de Montfort when Gaunt married Constanza, Queen of Castile..*
1399	***King Henry IV** seized the title and lands after Montfort's death and used as a Dukedom for sons then grandsons. King Henry IV was the son of John of Gaunt and Queen Constanza of Castile.*
1414	**John Plantagenet, Duke of Bedford & Richmond**—*third child of King Henry IV and Mary de Bohun.*
1452	**Edmund Tudor**—*brother of King Henry VI—Richmond kin shown above.*

1485   **Henry VII**—*Son of Edmund Tudor . He later became the new King of England after the death of his Uncle Henry VI—who died after his only son Edward was killed at the Battle of Tewksbury, leaving no direct heir. Henry VII's mother was Margaret Beaufort the seventh child of King Henry VI's brother John Beaufort. His parents were thus first cousins.*

1525   **Henry FitzRoy**—*son of King Henry VIII and Elizabeth Blount*

1536   *The honour of the title to Richmond reverted to the Crown when Fitzroy died without heirs.*

1613   **Ludovic Stuart**—*aka 2nd Duke of Lennox, Earl of Richmond and later Duke of Richmond—grandson of Henry VII through his oldest daughter who married to James IV, King of Scotland..*

1624   **Crown**—*the title revert to the English King when Ludovic Stuart died without heirs*

1641   **James 4th Duke of Lennox**—*nephew of Ludovic Stuart and also of the line of Princess Margaret and King James IV of Scotland.*

1655   **Charles 6th Duke of Lennox**—*nephew of James and of the same Royal bloodline.*

1672   **Crown**—*the title of Earl or Duke of Richmond became extinct after King Charles I's death by execution. Oliver Cromwell took control of the Govt. as Lord Protector.*

1675   **Charles Lennox**—*illegitimate son of Charles II—Lennox was given the title when Parliament asked Charles II to return as the King of England after Cromwell's death.*

Royal Roots—Pre-Charlemagne to Alan Rufus de Richmond

Charlemagne was the King of the Franks from 768 to 814 and Emperor of the Romans from 800 to 814. His empire contained all of present day France, Germany, and Italy.

The following is his lineage to the first of our line and includes Charlemagne's father and grandfather.

*—Direct lineage

*Charles Martel (the hammer)
*Pepin the Short
*Charlemagne 747-813 + Hildegarde 758-783
*Louis I the Fair or the Pious 778-840 + Ermengarde
*Lothair 795-855 + Ermengarde of Tours ?-851
    1. Lathair II 827-869
        a. Boso 885-936
            A. Willa + King Berengarius II of Italy ?-966
                1. Rosela (Susanne) 952-1003 + Count Arnoul II
                    a. Count Baudouin IV + Ogive de Luxemburg
                        A. Maud + William the Conqueror
*Ermengarde II a.k.a Helletrude + Count Gieselbert
*Regnier 850-915 + Alberade of Mous ?-916
*Adelaide + Robert 920-967
*Adelaide II de Vermandois 950-975 + Count Geoffrey I Grisgonelle of Anjou ?-987
*Ermengard de Anjou + Count Conan I of Rennes 960-992 m. 980
    1. Geoffrey, Duke of Brittany 980-1008 + Hawise

    2. Judith of Brittany 982-1017 + Duke Richard II the Good of Normandy
*Geoffrey of Brittany 980-1008 + Hawise ?-1034 (aunt of William the Conqueror)
    1. Alan III of Brittany 1000-1040 + Bertha ?-1084
      a. Hawise 1029-1072 + Hoel, Count of Cornoville ?-1084
        1. Hoel II, Count of Coronville
          A. Alan IV "Fergent" Duke of Brittany ?-1148 + Maud
          Maud was daughter of William I aka the Conqueror.
            1. Bertha?-1167 + Alan, Earl of Richmond
    2. Adele of Rennes
    3. Eudon aka Eudes, Duke of Brittany
*Eudes, Duke of Brittany & Penthievre 999-1079 + Agnes
    1. Geoffrey I Boterel
    2. Brian of Brittany
    3. <u>Alan Rufus de Richmond</u>
    4. Alan Niger de Richmond
    5. William
    6. Robert
    7. Richard
    8. Stephen I, Count of Peathievre, Earl of Richmond + Hawise
      a. Eleanor de Penthievre 1040-1138 + Alan de Dinan
        1. Alan de Dinan
      b. Geoffrey II Boterel
      c. Alan Niger III, Earl of Richmond 1098-? + Bertha of Brittany d/o
      Alan IV "Fergent" and Maud
        1. Conan IV "le Petite" of Brittany ?-1171 + Margaret of
        Huntington d/o Earl Henry de Warren & Ada
          A. Constance, Countess of Brittany and Richmond
          + Gui de Tourars Count of Brittany & Richmond
        2. Constance
        3. Enoguen of Rennes
        4. Brian de Bedale FitzAlan
      c. Henry 1100-1183 + Maud
        1. Henry 1152-1152
        2. Alan 1154-1212
        3. Conan ?-1210
        4. Geslin ?-1225

    5. Stephen
    d. Maud + Walter de Gaunt s/o Gilbert de Monfort & Alice
    e. Theophania
    f. Olive ?-1200 + Henry de Fougeres ?-1154
  9. Beatrix of Normandy
  10.Godfrey of Brionne & Eu 953-1015

An unknown Drummer Boy led soldiers

There is a legend that Richmond Castle and Easby Abbey are connected by an underground passage. Many years ago when soldiers where stationed at Richmond Castle they found the passage in the Castle cellar.

The soldiers persuaded a young drummer boy to march down the passage beating his drum. The soldiers above ground could hear the beat of his drum and followed it along the riverbank and through the streets of the Borough of Richmond. The sound became faint and eventually stopped not far from Easby Abbey.

The drummer boy was never seen again and no one knows what became of him. The people of Richmond were saddened by what had happened and erected a monument to his memory above the spot where his last drumbeat was heard. In time the entrance was again sealed to keep others from the same fate.

Please read others Novels presently available in the continuing Saga of the Historical Richmond Family.

1. Empire----------------The Richmond Saga 1066

2. Robert's Quest-------The Richmond Saga 1821

3. Andrew's Way--------The Richmond Saga 1821

4. Harm to Others------The Richmond Saga 1862

5. Jesse's War------------The Richmond Saga 1863

6. Jim's Push----Utah Beach to Prague–The Richmond Saga 1944

I am currently seeking information and have plans for stories dealing with the Richmond family in these areas.

1. The English Civil War
2. The American Revolution
3. The Creek Indian uprising
4. The Battle of New Orleans
5. The Great Depression
6. Word War II in the Pacific
7. Korean War
8. Vietnam War
9. The Gulf War

Be Patient!!!!

0-595-27841-8

Breinigsville, PA USA
08 December 2010

250904BV00002B/24/A

9 780595 278411